Purge of Flame and Song

Darkness of the Living Forest
Book Three

Eldarkin Publishing Limited
United Kingdom
© 2021 Meg Cowley
www.megcowley.com

Cover design © Meg Cowley 2021

ISBN: 9798471899629

All characters, places and events are fictional. Any resemblance to real persons, places or events is purely coincidental.

The moral rights of the author have been asserted.

All rights reserved. No part of this publication may be reproduced, copied, stored or distributed in any form, without prior written permission of the publisher.

BOOKS BY MEG COWLEY

All of Meg's books are available on Amazon in eBook, print, and audio formats.

World of Altarea novels

Books of Caledan

A fast-paced fantasy filled with magic, dragons, and intrigue, that epic fantasy fans will love.

The Tainted Crown

The Brooding Crown

The Shattered Crown

Pelenor Chronicles: Rise of Saradon

A sprawling epic fantasy quartet of intrigue, betrayal, peril and romance.

Heart of Dragons

Court of Shadows

Order of Valxiron

Mark of Fate

Tales of Tir na Alathea: Darkness of the Living Forest

A fast-paced epic adventure of unlikely allies facing darkness together.

Flight of Sorcery and Shadow

Ascent of Darkness and Ruin

Purge of Flame and Song

Other fantasy series

Morgana Chronicles

Discover Arthurian legend as you've never heard it before in this original and gripping high fantasy tale of a young Morgana Le Fay.

Magic Awakened

Relic Guardians

Tomb Raider meets Indiana Jones plus magic in this fast-paced magical urban adventure fantasy, co-written with Victoria DeLuis.

Ancient Magic

Hidden Magic

Cursed Magic

Gathered Magic

CHAPTER 1

Morrigan Lilika Bellatrix of House Mallory lay limp in the palanquin. Her raven hair fanned around her, washed and neatly combed. She still wore her scarred, black fighting leathers, though the worst of the dirt and gore upon them had also been scourged. Moved by the jolting of the horses on the rough road, her limp hand emerged from the folds of the scarlet cloak that covered her in soft woollen warmth. That and the magic that protected her from the biting cold.

Even so, Vasili Dariel Drakar of House Ellarian leaned in to tuck her pale, slender wrist and hand back under her makeshift cover. He was glad for the leather gloves that prevented true contact between them. Did he revile it or desire it?

His insides shuddered with the liberty he took, protective and well-intentioned though it was. She would flay him for it if she were in possession of her full and terrible powers. To know that he had dared to touch her was even worse than the scarlet cloak of her enemy keeping her warm.

Before them, Tournai, the capital city of the realm of Pelenor, loomed. Soon, Morrigan would be awakened from her enforced slumber. Vasili had no idea what would come to pass then, but he knew it would be disastrous for them all. And especially for her.

Once she realised fully that she was in the captivity of the Winged Kingsguard, her mortal foe, once she realised her citadel had fallen, and her people were fled, dead, or taken, her cause in disarray...Vasili was no fool. Magic stripped or not, he feared her ire. He did not know if General Elyvia comprehended what the young woman was truly capable of. The general would underestimate Morrigan to her own downfall.

Elyvia was sensible enough not to wake her, at least. Morrigan had been unconscious for days now, only taking on the small dribbles of water that Vasili could feed between her parched lips. The slowing of her mind and body meant she would not starve or wither, but even so... Once more, the revulsion against every fibre of her being warred within him for the empathy her vulnerability elicited.

They had briefly stopped at the Dragon's Nest, the outpost on the route from the hidden valley where the Dragon Riders of the Winged Kingsguard had found the secret fortification of the Order of Valxiron.

It had been enough to provision them for the rest of the journey, heal the wounded, and tend to their most prized prisoner – Morrigan herself. She alone was accompanied by a full guard and General Elyvia to Pelenor's capital, Tournai

– alongside Vasili, who had begged his commanding officer, Captain Tristan, to allow him to travel with her.

Vasili still bore the scars of her cruelty, but when he looked upon Morrigan's waxen visage, her face frowning even in ensorcelled slumber, and those twin crescent scars slashed upon her cheeks a reminder of her danger, he could not help but feel a stirring within him. A determination he could not dismiss.

The young woman, so close in age to him, so close in status, but a world apart in their life experiences, was an abomination to all who looked upon her. He alone had seen inside her world and the darkness with which she had been raised. It was all she had known. How could she have become anything other than a fearsome and powerful warrior of her people and advocate of their cause?

And so it was that Vasili trusted no one else to advocate for her welfare. Why should they? Morrigan was their sworn enemy. She would die before she renounced that. Skies above, he knew he was an imbecile for thinking she was not beyond salvation, beyond redemption. Vasili gritted his teeth against that self-deprecating thought. He shivered and drew his cloak tighter as an ill-placed winter breeze fingered down the back of his neck.

Morrigan had been hard to transport, even unconscious upon dragon back. The dead weight of her threw off Vasili's dragon Icarus' balance, and even Icarus baulked at seeing her strung and bound to the dragon like so much chattel. Besides which, midwinter imminently approached, and the snows gripped the north of Pelenor once more for a long season of it. Charms and sorcery aside, Vasili did not want to risk harm to her from hours and days of flying in the frigid air.

Now, Icarus circled above them, ever watchful, with the rest of the guard, and Vasili and several other knights of the Winged Kingsguard escorted the horse-drawn palanquin on foot. It was a summer palanquin, commandeered in haste and entirely unsuitable without their elven magic to protect her from the harsh elements that battered it. Pale, diaphanous fabric wreathed it, so insubstantial the winter winds simply blew through. Leaving Vasili an ample view of their charge within.

Looking vulnerable and yet made of dragon-steel at the same time, deadly even in her suppressed state, Morrigan ensnared his attention. Vasili could not tear his gaze away, so filled was he with a constant churn of nausea and sickly swooping worry. He was terrified that she would wake and further petrified that she would *not*.

He wondered if she perceived anything around them. Whether she could taste the city smoke on the air that heralded their imminent arrival. Whether she had any sense of time or space. Whether she had heard any of them talking of her and the Order of Valxiron, of the battle they had faced, and what was to come in not-so-hushed tones on their journey.

Before them, a mountain range loomed. Isolated in the centre of Pelenor and far from the peaks they had travelled from, it was a cradle of life for the realm and the dragons that guarded it. A single peak jutted before the others, and upon its slopes, Tournai nestled. Grey as the mountain it sat upon and crowned in white from the falling snow, it was devoid of life and colour that day, washed out by the wreathing clouds that teased the mountains into and out of view above the tallest tower.

There sat the former royal palace, where once a king had ruled and which was now their destination. The chambers of the High Council of Pelenor – who would no doubt be aware of their coming. And the prisoner they brought.

Vasili shivered again, but not from the cold. Did he dare stand before the High Council and advocate for their enemy's welfare?

CHAPTER 2

Their booted footsteps clattered on the cobbles as Vasili and his peers wound up the tangle of streets, escorting the palanquin bearing Morrigan to the citadel. The sound was lost within the hubbub of the city. It was an assault to Vasili's ears after almost a year of the still silence, creaking trees, and whistling winds of the Dragon's Nest outpost deep in the mountains east of Pelenor. With every step, his pulsing headache swelled.

They had collectively strengthened the wards upon the palanquin and Morrigan within to protect her. The heart of Pelenor was as safe as anywhere could be; however, Elyvia trusted no one with the enormity of the treasure they returned with to Tournai.

He could feel the tug of his soul bond with Icarus, his dragon, as the dragon drew away, and the swell of contentment as the dragon entered the dragonhold. There, they had dwelled and trained before moving to the outpost under Captain Tristan. No doubt their old bunk – a cave deep inside the mountain – would have been long taken by another, but there was ample room for them to take up residence once more. Vasili knew Icarus would find them a suitable place to rest there whilst they were in the capital.

He wondered how long that would be. What was Elyvia's mission? To break Morrigan? To take from her all the information on the Order of Valxiron she had? To rehabilitate her? Vasili clamped down on the darker thought that followed.

To destroy her.

Elyvia had every right.

Morrigan was the fiercest supporter of Valxiron anyone could find, after all. Probably responsible for taking lives in the battle they had fought so bitterly in. And culpable for goodness knew what else. He did not want to imagine.

Out there remained the greatest perpetrators, somewhere on the wind. The grandmasters of the Order of Valxiron. Morrigan's own mother, their oracle. Every league Vasili had travelled with Morrigan thus far, he had expected them to fold from shadow and wind to smite the Winged Kingsguard down. There had been nothing. No sign. The Order's highest, it seemed, had gone to ground, but it would not be forever. It was a discord against the surrounding city, where peace, life, and happiness reigned.

Unbothered by the falling snow, curious onlookers stopped on the crowded street, slowing their passage even further, as they stopped to gape at the strange assortment of Winged Kingsguard escorting a covered palanquin on foot through the city in the middle of winter.

Around them, the Tournai residents had adorned the city for the midwinter festivities. Evergreen boughs, berries, cones, and ribbons adorned the houses, shops, and buildings. Huge, decorated trees, hung heavy with decorations and twinkling with faelights, were bulging centrepieces in every square they passed. Market stalls crowded around them, the stallholders hawking giftware and food. The smell of spiced wines and fresh pastries and meats soaked into the air – inviting at any time.

Ordinarily, it would have lifted Vasili's spirit. Midwinter – a time of celebration, of feasting, of family, cheer, and camaraderie. But Vasili's heart felt heavier than it ought to have done.

It had been nearly a year since he had seen his family – his parents and his twin sister, Venya – at the previous year's midwinter festival. It had not been long since he had thought, deep in the bowels of the mountains and at the hands of Morrigan's torture, that he would never see such things again. His family. Midwinter celebrations. The sun upon his face and the caress of a breeze upon his cheek.

However, it did not lighten his heart to walk the streets of the capital once more. It left him feeling bittersweet. The suffering was far from over yet. Skies above forbid that the suffering he had seen in the battle in the mountains would come here to these gentle people.

He longed to see his parents and his sister, but, as members of the High Council themselves...his parents might be forced to pass judgement on his misconduct. After all, it had been by great fortune that he had uncovered the citadel of the Order of Valxiron and, together with Icarus, ensured Pelenor was not caught unaware by an enemy nestled in the heart of its realm. However, it had been Icarus and Vasili's disobedience that had led to it all, and

Icarus' loss of control that had allowed their capture, compromise, and perhaps led to more bloodshed than was necessary.

Trepidation wormed through Vasili at that thought. He set his face sternly, letting not one flicker of his emotions break through, and closed ranks around the palanquin. Between the striding Kingsguard, no one could see Morrigan within. It was for the best. The folk of Pelenor would do better not to know the monster that Vasili and his fellow knights had brought into their midst.

At last, they ascended into the citadel, passing through the highest gate of the city and into the former Royal Palace. At its heart, it had once been a true fortification, but generations and centuries of elven royalty had turned it into a sprawling, genteel palace for pleasure, not war.

No king had ruled there since before Vasili's birth. The mad king, Toroth, was a spectre of fairy-tale now amongst the children of the city. The legacy of his accursed rule had been a nobler democracy born of great suffering and hardship from the last time Valxiron had been vanquished from Pelenor's shores.

But now, General Elyvia, and Vasili with her, brought the impossible and painful news that Valxiron had not been truly defeated. Vasili had seen that darkness with his own eyes. Felt its poison seeping into his bones.

A flurry of activity greeted them as guards filed out to ensure no crowd followed them under the arch and into the courtyard, where the horses halted and Elyvia strode forward to greet the High Council members who flooded out, having clearly been waiting for them.

All bore the same grim expression as they beheld the

palanquin and the hidden charge within. He hardly knew any of them, but then, a flash.

His father.

Vasili's heart soared and crashed at once as his father, pale-faced and drawn at the news they had brought, stepped from within the swirling ranks. They bore the same raven hair, the same olive skin, the same violet eyes. The same height, now Vasili was grown, the same build, the same little physical quirks, like the way Dimitrius' mouth pulled to one side in the ghost of a frown as he searched the crowd of Winged Kingsguard for his son.

Until their eyes met. It was improper for them to acknowledge each other, and to have stepped out from his rank to embrace and greet his father would have been unforgivable. Even so, Vasili felt the very moment his father Dimitrius' attention locked onto him.

Unbidden, Vasili's lips tugged in a smile, grim though the moment was, and his father's eyes softened. Vasili inclined his head to his father ever so slightly. Dimitri replied in kind, unseen to those around them in the flurry.

His father's gaze searched him, and Vasili could see the worry in the faint crinkle in his father's brow. Now was not the moment, but later, they would have the time to reunite.

Where is Mother? Vasili's attention passed across the High Council, who were busy surrounding Elyvia and the palanquin, plying the general with questions, and making arrangements for the prisoner to be transferred inside. Harper was nowhere to be seen.

No matter. He would see them all later. Harper, Dimitrius, his sister, Venya. A dull ache stirred in Vasili's heart, made keener by the fact they were all now so close after such a long time apart. Vasili could wait a few more hours. His attention dropped to the palanquin. To the too-small figure inside who seemed nothing more than skin and bone, shrouded in that scarlet cloak.

Vasili was not sure whether the courtyard was unsafe for her – or for them. She would rend them flesh from bone if she awoke in her full power at that moment. The High Council clearly recognised the threat. Vasili followed Morrigan as she was bodily carried into the bowels of the castle, through corridors too narrow for the palanquin to go. To where she could be secured for her own safety and those around her.

Something in his chest tugged at the sight of her being carried like a sack of grain, and with as little dignity. She lolled between the two soldiers, one of whom had her legs and the other her bound arms. In her scarred, black fighting leathers, she looked just like the prisoner of war that she was. Not a young woman, the product of a cruel and merciless life, but a weapon and a warrior.

As they walked, Vasili could feel the ancient magic of the castle's wards closing around them like the air growing stuffy and charged before a storm. In the oldest parts of the castle, where they now marched, were the remnants of the original fortress. Giant, worn stones moved by magic and the strength of dragons. Scarred with their claw marks. The facade of the modern palace above had been built for pleasure. Down there in the dark, it had been made for war in an age long past.

At last, they reached a cell, and it was hastily prepared whilst they awaited, breathing in the stench of sweat and excrement and fear. Supplies were fetched. A bucket to piss in. Some rushes for the floor. A basic wooden pallet filled with compacted straw and topped with a paltry, tattered blanket.

There was no window, the only light being outside the cell in a brazier burning faintly red and throwing off warmth that was instantly swallowed by the winter chill. With them, they brought faelights to guide the way, but when they departed, Vasili wondered how much it would feel like that dark mountain he had been imprisoned within, as though one had been swallowed by the very rock itself.

It was no better or worse than where he had found himself in the hidden city in the mountains and at Morrigan's mercy, Vasili knew. Still, he pitied Morrigan for a fleeting moment as compassion spiked within him. No one deserved that. Yet she was the most unforgivably despicable. And so, did she?

CHAPTER 3

They carried Morrigan in, and Vasili caught a brief glimpse of her as they set her down. Her leathers were dark, scuffed, and worn, and her hair tangled, wrapping around her shoulders and neck like tendrils of seaweed. The twin scars gleamed on her pale cheeks in the faelight.

"She truly is the oracle's heir," Lord Halkian, one of the High Council, remarked, with an almost awe-like hush in his voice. He stepped into the cell, shadowed by Vasili's father. Together, they blocked Vasili's view of her. "I can sense her power, dormant though she be."

"Think of what she will know," said Dimitrius.

She will never tell you, Vasili wanted to say. *She will die before she betrays her people.*

Surely, they knew that? Maybe they didn't care. Maybe, just like the Order of Valxiron, they would stoop to such levels of violations, and what she would not freely give, they would take anyway for their ends.

That was what he feared most for her, that perhaps his

people were no better than hers. That they would break her and their own morals to claim victory at any cost.

The sensation of falling greeted Morrigan first – a sickly swooping deep in her belly that ignited instinctive panic demanding her to right herself.

Morrigan fought against it all – the invisible constraints that seemed to bind every inch of her mind and body into nothingness and the awakening that tore her from that warm, safe, thoughtless cocoon.

Her sense of touch returned first. She was not falling – not at all. She lay upon a hard, flat, and cold slab. That coldness seeped through her leathers – which were rough upon her skin from...*battle*! It came rushing back. The assault upon the stronghold. The Winged Kingsguard, curse them, raining fire and death down from upon high.

Vasili. The fight between them, as she realised the depths of his betrayal, and how deeply that cut, for she had shown him things he had never deserved. Had she known, deep down, that he was a traitor? Or had she truly begun to believe that she had saved his soul from such damnations?

Hah. Imbecilic girl, she berated herself. Of course, she had never believed in him. She had known all along, never trusted him. It had been the grandmasters' protection – those cowardly knaves – that had forced her to accommodate him. For she had been satisfied, momentarily, when he had revealed his true colours after all – and proven her right.

They had clashed so bitterly until his blasted dragon had appeared. She had taken a moment to wonder at it – the deep green hue of its scales, the sleek, shiny muscles, so different from the malformed, dulled beasts the Order bred in the valley. How much, in that moment, she had coveted the fine specimen.

She remembered how then, the thing had floored her with its tail – then, nothing.

Strangely, Morrigan did not hurt. Mentally running through her entire body, she had sustained nicks and grazes in the battle, jarred more than a few bones, and would have welts and bruises, yet none of it could she feel.

What have they drugged me with?

Yet she did not feel addled. It was only then that she considered that she was healed – had *been* healed, by either time or other hands. That thought was alien. Unwelcome.

It was warm too, and even though her skin crawled, as if some animalistic part of her recognised it was unnatural, for the first time, she was *warm*. There was no relentless draught. No incessant seeping cold that chilled her to the bone.

Where am I?

Breath whooshed into her chest, the sound deafening her as she realised she could hear, and then see, as light, muted and warm, permeated her closed eyelids, and incoherent murmurs rumbled around her.

She tried to sit up but could not move – her limbs would not obey her, her arms and legs splayed upon the surface.

"Nnnggmmmrrrr…" Morrigan managed to growl out, the sound rolling clumsily around her mouth as though she were inebriated.

She heard the incoherent murmurs around her in

response. And the tightening of her limbs, chest, neck – as she was forced flatter still.

Wards, then. Not a failing of my body.

Morrigan managed to crack an eye open.

Walls. Made with giant bricks of grey stone. Old. Light. A lantern she had never seen before – its faelight warm and golden, its wrought design unnecessarily ornamental – not like the functional, spartan equipment in the stronghold.

Her gaze focused, sharpening on the shadows around her. Not shadows. *Elves.* Like her. Slim faces, angled features. But one familiar face stood out in sharp focus.

Vasili.

He wore a frown, an air of concern lacing him. Surprise flashed through her as she realised that he was there – and what had happened. Rage and fear ignited her, and despite the bonds upon her, she flexed against them as a scream wrenched up her throat and tore out in a wordless howl of molten fury.

Their roles had been reversed in a sick twist of fate. Now it was she who found herself the prisoner, and he the captor. She contorted and writhed, but the wards held her firm, and it was with the impact of a punch that her breath faltered as she understood the depths of what they had done. Scoured and scraped and smothered her magic beyond her reach so she could not kill them all with her hands or sorcery or disappear into nothingness and spirit herself away.

It winded her with its loss, so hollow did she feel having that taken from her, that sense that was as second nature as breathing or seeing. And the howl erupted anew as Vasili staggered back, paling, at the force of her rage.

"I will kill you all!" she screamed, tearing her throat with the ferocity of her hatred for him, for them all, even as terror set her alight. Terror that she was utterly powerless against any of them. She would do whatever it took to get back to the Order – and to cripple Pelenor.

And most of all, she would relish breaking Vasili Dariel Drakar of House Ellarian and everything he stood for, one sinew at a time.

"*You!*" she screeched, turning the full force of her ire upon Vasili. "I will destroy you, traitor!"

A moment later, Morrigan slumped, unconscious by the power of Dimitrius' hand.

Vasili watched his father with apprehension. Here, Dimitrius Vaeri Mortris of House Ellarian was not just his father, but the Lord and head of his House and member of the High Council of Pelenor.

For a moment, the council chamber fell silent.

"What a deeply unpleasant young woman," Dimitrius remarked acerbically, his narrowed eyes fixed upon her, his expression inscrutable.

"If we are forced to this extreme every time she awakens, we shall reach nowhere quickly," Elyvia muttered.

What do you expect!? Vasili longed to rage at them. Would they have reacted any differently, to wake up unaware of their surroundings or state, to discover they were a prisoner of their sworn enemy? He supposed he was to be included in that tally as well. He was perhaps even more heinous, since he had betrayed her utterly.

Unease curled within Vasili. Surely he and Morrigan had

had no trust between them, nothing based on any solid foundation, but perhaps he had deluded himself into believing he had any kind of understanding of her – that they had any kind of understanding of each other. Whatever they had grown to, it was irreparably shattered now. To her, he was no better, and probably worse, than the rest of them.

Vasili supposed he ought to laugh at the irony of that. That he alone had been the one to try to save her, and for it, she would despise him all the more.

"What should we do with her?" Lord Halkian spoke up. The older elf was a steady, guiding hand in the High Council, a voice of reason – but decisive also, not above swift action to keep the peace and security of Pelenor guaranteed. He would not hesitate, Vasili knew, to neutralise Morrigan if she posed too great a threat.

"Please give her a chance," Vasili said, the pleading words out of his lips– trying, without meaning to, to second guess and subvert the older elf's thoughts.

Lord Halkian looked at him thoughtfully. "What is your relationship to this traitor?"

Vasili stilled. He knew what the undertone of that sentiment implied. *Are you compromised?* Lord Halkian really asked.

Vasili straightened.

"None to speak of, Lord Halkian, but I beseech you on the moral grounds of compassion. She has led a most cruel life, and I refuse to believe she ought to be damned because of that. I have hope that she may yet be redeemable."

Lord Halkian's expression remained unreadable. "Your compassion is admirable, but do not let it cloud your judgement. By all accounts – by your general's own accounts of *your* reports – she is a highly dangerous and volatile individual who, without due care, would wilfully cause death and destruction if possible."

His statement attracted nods and assenting murmurs from the council members around the room. General Elyvia, watching, said nothing, but her attention fixed upon Vasili.

Vasili swallowed. He could not refute that. She would. Her ire, should they let her regain consciousness, would be legendary – and terrifying – to behold.

"You are correct," he acknowledged, hoping it would not damn her, "yet...that life is all she knows. She is a young woman, but her entire childhood was spent in that dark void. She is a hateful creature, but she cannot be beyond salvation, and more than that, she is the key to understanding the Order. Their ranks, how they operate, where they hide...she was close enough to the inner sanctum of the grandmasters and the oracle to know *all* of that, if we can unlock what she knows."

"There is one way we can unlock all she knows," Lord Halkian replied dryly.

"That is *illegal*," Dimitrius countered swiftly, to assenting and dissenting mutters.

"They used such mind-breaking tactics upon your own son without such concern."

Dimitrius gritted his teeth. "I have experienced it myself. Deeply invasive and painful. However, their use of such abhorrent tactics does not excuse us to do the same."

Lord Halkian let out a little huff of laughter, entirely dry of humour. "You are right, of course. However, would you see us all doomed for standing upon our morals?"

Vasili felt nauseated by his words – the casual ease with

which he spoke of breaking the young woman's mind and the law. Worse still, heads nodded at his words. *How could they agree?* Horror filled Vasili.

"It is not so black and white," Dimitrius said.

Halkian's reply was derisive. "The Order will see it so. If we fail to act decisively, and they swoop upon us, our downfall shall be of our own doing. Does this woman's life matter to you more than that?"

CHAPTER 4

*L*ike a blade of grass before the maelstrom of a hurricane, Aedon folded before Solanaceae, Queen of the wood elves and their realm of Tir-na-Alathea, the living forest itself. No matter how much he tried to imprint the weight of Her presence in his mind, the memory never did Her justice. She took his breath away, struck fear into his very bones, swamped him with the aura of Her sheer power every single time.

Beside him, El'hari, commander of the Emuir guard, and Sirvardi, captain of the *centime* of warriors who had journeyed to Lune with Aedon and Lief to scourge the blight from the land, gracefully rose, and Aedon followed them. He was a head taller than them, but no more imposing. They belonged in this wood. Despite his long tenure there, he was still an outsider – and forever would he be. Worse, he remained their prisoner.

Aedon had come to change that. He hoped.

A gentle breeze caressed him with warmth, but inside,

Aedon felt chilled to the core. He had not been able to find comfort since before the terrible battle at Lune. What they had witnessed... He suppressed a shudder, keeping his expression impassive and his gaze upon the Queen, who demanded the attention of all in Her presence. It was not hard to give it. She was a living embodiment of a goddess, worthy of such wonder.

The sun behind Her crowned Her in a glowing aura that magnified the terracotta of Her skin. The rich depth of Her mahogany hair that tumbled down to Her thighs. Her lithe, muscled limbs, brimming with strength. Flowers adorned Her, a dress of glittering green gossamer hugging the curves of Her figure with dawn pink blossoms trailing from Her navel up Her torso, across Her breasts and one shoulder. Their petals pulsed open and closed in time with the rise and fall of Her chest, and from moss-lined hips fell drapes of fabric as fickle as the errant summer breeze that caught them, tugging and teasing the fabric into a gentle dance that belied the power of the female who wore them.

The sweetness of it caressed Aedon. The sweetness of nectar, the fresh, wet aroma of earth and life, almost tasted upon his tongue. Lulling him into succumbing to the powerful charm of the forest in the same way it tempted most outsiders into their doom. Aedon was under no false pretences. He had witnessed Her power, and the forest's, too many times to forget that again. He had borne the brunt of it more than once before. Long ago.

She remained as mighty as ever. Even now, the pure energy brimming from Her, connecting her life-thread to the forest around them which She sustained and which sustained Her, was incandescent.

Against that, Aedon felt insignificant and sullied. She was glorious against his tainted self, and he fought the instinct to shrink away in Her presence, unworthy as he found himself, such was Her intoxicating influence. A part of Aedon felt as though he would never be clean again after what he and Lief had suffered at Lune. The battle they had endured. The darkness. The devastation. The death.

The flat, mirror-like water before them of the seeing pool in the centre of the dozen vacant thrones reflected that horror still, playing endlessly over. The memories that they had given to Solanaceae of the terrible things they had seen and endured – and almost not survived to bring Her news of.

In the dark of night, the dead of Lune had come. Those elves who had garrisoned with Lief and who had succumbed to the darkness of the blight which had speared straight into the living forest after its awakening. Darkness of Valxiron's, lain dormant for millennia in an anchor of his power, rising from its hibernation in the fabled group of stone tors known as the Silent Sisters. How fitting that at the seat of a story of deception lurked another great duplicity. Hiding. Biding its time.

Not a single one of those elves in Lune had escaped. The darkness had taken them all. They had risen from the dead to fight against the living, reanimated by Valxiron's dark sorcery to infect the surrounding forest and life with darkness and death.

The living *centime*, the hundred warriors, plus Aedon and Lief, sent by Solanaceae to investigate what had passed and find the truth of the strange curse that had taken hold of the remote corner of Tir-na-Alathea, had not expected it. Not that they had known what to find.

After all, Lief and Aedon had had the briefest tastes of it before they had joined and fled, mere weeks before, but what seemed like years. It had been far worse than any of them could have anticipated. Not least of all Lief.

They had not expected to find the whole garrison dead by the hands of Valxiron's darkness, nor that Valxiron possessed an anchor – and probably many more besides – which had awakened his age-old darkness. One that made Aedon's toes curl with fear. A fear he could not bear to acknowledge, because it ripped open a lifetime of trauma and darkness and the possibility of being devoured by it all in the face of such hopelessness.

That was a power they still needed to deal with. For though they had defeated the blight in the forest, that anchor still endured, beyond the borders of Tir-na-Alathea at the place called the Silent Sisters. To face the blight in the forest had been far enough beyond the bounds of possibility. That they still needed to face the source of it, a greater power still, one that Aedon knew well, drenched him in despair.

That night, they had already faced death and certain doom. He half-wondered if it were a dream at all that he still lived. How had they survived? It had been a damned miracle. Aedon braced physically, threatening to fall even though nothing rushed him in that peaceful glade of the Queen's Forest. Such was the visceral feeling that swept at him with the memory of that dark night, sending his senses tumbling.

The tide of the dead had crashed against them, and it had nearly taken them all. At the moment of their last stand, the dead had risen anew, the *centime's* own dead infected with that blight and still warm from recent life, reanimated to fight against them. Skies above, he had thought for sure that they would not live to see the dawn.

That dread, so powerful, surged through him anew as though he were there once more, under those dark trees, hidden from the skies and the moon, choked by the stench of death upon the air, deafened by the screams of the elves he stood side by side with as, one by one, they were dragged to their brutal deaths by the hands of the dead.

He focused on thoughts of Lief to bring himself back from that brink – for she had not come to the Queen's audience and was resting after their ordeal. He thought of the curve of her mouth and the indent into her cheek as she smiled. That challenging twinkle in her amber eyes. The way her deft fingers constantly slipped the same loosening strand of hair behind her ears time and again. Those were memories for him now. It had been painful for her too, though in a very different way, and she had smiled rarely since, the light gone from her eyes.

The dead of Lune had been elves Lief had served with. Spent her daily life with. In one ill-fated case, loved. In the end, she had had to kill the elf whom she had once shared the most special bond with. Granted, that elf had betrayed her. Crushed her heart and threatened to break her spirit. But nonetheless, in the face of being ended by him herself, she had had to strike the fateful, merciful blow that ended him – or at least the dark spirit that had inhabited his body.

Aedon considered, with a sudden bolt of realisation, that it had been pure chance she had not died amongst their number to start with. Pure chance that Lief and Aedon had even met at all, let alone escaped. A strange tug roiled through Aedon at that, nauseating him. How close they had come to disaster. How close he had come to *never* knowing the vivacious, fiery elf he had fallen in love with.

Love.

It beat through him again, no matter that the Queen of Lief's people, great and terrible, stood before him. Solanaceae would surely kill him for the sheer pleasure of denying him the fulfilment of that love.

He was desperate to return to Lief. He needed her, more than he cared to admit to himself, to her, to anyone – and never would he admit it to Solanaceae. He loved Lief, and he had come so close to losing her. He did not wish to be parted from her again. Not least because of his own fear that somehow, he could, would, still lose her, but also the pain and fear he still saw flickering in her gaze as she remembered what had passed.

She needed him as much. Even as they had arrived in the safety of Emuir, he had seen the desperation in her eyes for him not to leave her. But the wishes of a queen could not be denied. They had to deliver the news they had brought, so catastrophic was it.

The Queen's flicker of movement before him pulled him from his reverie – as She tore herself away from the devastating memories presented to Her at the scrying pool. Her usually dark lips were pale, Her expression tight – with fury or fear or something else, Aedon did not know. She looked up from the dark water, regarding each one of them in equal measure.

"I shall call the full might of this realm," She declared, eyes glittering with ferocity. Defiance. Solanaceae would never cede willingly. Especially not to a darkness like Valxiron's. Aedon realised what She meant to do – to summon the lords and ladies of the realm. Powerful elves like Her. To formulate a battle plan. "You may leave." She turned away.

Aedon's heart sputtered. *No.* He did not want to lose what might be his only chance. He stepped forward and dropped to a knee. "I beg of you, my Queen, but a moment."

All stilled, as though the forest paused with outrageous surprise at his insolence. Perhaps Aedon imagined it, for a moment later, the breeze blew, the trees rustled, and life moved through the forest around them.

The Queen froze.

Sirvardi shifted beside him, and Aedon could practically feel the older elf's glare on the back of his neck. Aedon lifted his chin nonetheless. He still needed his freedom, now more than ever. It seemed that she had forgotten, or perhaps did not care – either was as likely – that she had promised him his freedom on the condition he would return from their mission to Lune to the very spot upon which he now stood.

He would not leave without asking for it, though he was smart enough to know that he ought not to demand it from her. He needed it to have any chance of being with Lief, if she would have him. He clamped down on the dreadful thought that stole his breath – of spending the rest of his life rotting in a prison once more, knowing that she was out there, wild and free, moving on, living without him.

"My Queen, I ask you." Aedon's voice shook. "You promised me that upon my return to Lune, I would have my liberty."

She watched him. A slight flicker of a smile curled Her lip, and a familiar triumphant dominance glinted in Her molten eyes.

He bowed lower still and dropped his gaze. He could feel

the shift in the energy around him. It became watchful. Focused upon him. He had piqued Her curiosity. She was unused to such a show of humility from him, after all. The weight of Her attention upon him had his very breath stilled, and he took a huge gulp of air.

Solanaceae stirred, shifting Her weight from one leg to another and sliding forward a pace. Aedon peered up at Her.

"And why should I do that? You committed a crime. You were punished for it – and your indefinite sentence is, by definition, not yet complete."

Sweat beaded on Aedon's brow, and his chest threatened to constrict upon what little breath he had left. *No!*

"I have remained at your pleasure for decades now. In these recent weeks, I have proven over and again my commitment to Tir-na-Alathea. I nearly spent my life for you and it, and I would gladly do so again. Despite all, I have come to love your realm and its people, and I would serve it – as a free elf. I stole from you in bad faith, my Queen, but to do good deeds."

That was true. He had stolen, decades before, a prized bottle of *aleilah*, a substance with miraculous healing power. "Lives were saved by that, and I do not regret it, nor the price exacted from me. You *promised* if I returned that I would have my freedom."

He knew She probably did not even care. Why should She spare a thought that nameless strangers – and mortals at that – had been saved by the grace of her land's magic? Panic sputtered to life in him. Was She about to renege on Her word? He thought they had struck a bargain – an unbreakable one by the traditions of their race.

Aedon steeled himself and spoke again, though it was

against his better judgement, and instinct warned him not to push too far with the capricious Queen. "I believe I have served ample punishment and repaid your realm for my crime with so many years of my life and my deeds in these recent weeks. I beg you to release me."

For a long moment, once more the forest around them held its breath. He could feel Her scrutiny upon him. Toying. Deliberating. His entire future hung upon the balance of Her whim. In the next moment, he could be free or imprisoned anew for an extended and miserable life, her promise be damned.

What would She decide?

CHAPTER 5

Listening to the back-and-forth filled Vasili with anxious energy. He shifted his weight from one foot to the other, biting his tongue. It was not his place to speak at council, except when spoken to, and he would not shame his father with a hot-headed outburst.

General Elyvia stirred. "Perhaps there is another way." She glanced meaningfully at Vasili, who stilled. "I hear both sides of this. We cannot compromise our own laws, and especially not the values and morals that uphold our society – else, we are little better than them.

"We may not have the luxury of time if the Order is impelled into moving sooner than anticipated. Taking their oracle's heir and destroying their stronghold is quite obviously an act of aggression – of war. We do not want a repeat of the dark times we all endured to bring peace all those years ago."

Elyvia glanced sternly around at the dozen gathered there in a loose circle around Morrigan's limp form upon the stone platform. Waiting for their silent agreement. One incline of a head at a time.

"I would like to propose another course. We have a little time – and no more. We ought to treat our enemy as we wish to be treated – with compassion, understanding, empathy. With a branch of peace extended as a gesture of our goodwill. How else are we to truly defeat our enemy? We cannot break them and call it victory, nor exterminate them. We must convince, persuade, *show* them the truth of our world. It is a better place than they believe. We must offer a merciful hand to them and draw them with us from the darkness and into the light. We owe it to our souls as much as theirs."

Dimitrius swept into a bow before her. "I could not have said that any more beautifully myself. 'Tis true, every word. But how can we ensure the success of such an important task?"

"I will do it," said Vasili, stepping forward before he had truly considered it.

The council members turned as one to regard him with gapes of astonishment, as though they had forgotten he was there.

"Son?" Dimitrius frowned.

"I have already spent weeks with her. I know her thoughts, what compels her, how she operates. Let me convince her she can trust me, and I will persuade her to open to us." Vasili raised his chin. "I know what I'm doing," he said, more confidently than he felt.

"You think so highly of yourself, young Vasili of House *Ellarian*?" remarked Lord Halkian sardonically, raising an eyebrow. There it was – the age-old judgement of his young age, tinged with the stain of his family name, still soiled after so long.

Dimitrius silently glared at the older lord. Vasili knew his father had always hated being so poorly judged without being known, on the basis of his name.

Vasili's cheeks warmed. "No, sir. But I believe in my general's vision, and I believe this woman can be turned from her path." In truth, he had no idea how he would achieve it, such was the vehemence of her violent vitriol, but he would trust it to no one else if he had the choice. Why else had he come so far with her, if not to safeguard her? And clearly, it was needed, if Lord Halkian considered shattering one of the most sacred laws of Pelenor.

Vasili dropped his eyes to where Morrigan lay, frowning even in ensorcelled slumber. "She is a hateful creature with a miserable existence, but I do not believe her beyond reaching yet."

Elyvia cleared her throat. "Agreed. She is young enough to still have a chance of turning. What a weapon she could be if she does so willingly."

Lord Halkian gave the general a measured stare. "All right. So be it. If we are amenable?" He cast his gaze around those gathered there, each one giving a nod of support. "It shall be so. You have a week whilst we attend the more pressing matter of the grandmasters' and oracle's whereabouts. Then we shall reconsider our course. We do not want to force it from her, but if there is no other way, it shall be done. For the greater good." Halkian glared around at them all. It sounded like a warning. Then he swept out.

A week? It was nowhere near enough, but he would

receive no more. Vasili's stomach churned with the impossibility of the task.

"We may as well begin immediately," said Elyvia as she watched Halkian go, with obvious dislike marring her otherwise pleasant face.

Dimitrius hung back until the others had filed out. "Are you all right, son?"

"Aye." *No.*

Dimitrius huffed, seeing through Vasili's lie. "Welcome to politics. You think you're on the side of good and right, and yet sometimes what we must do for 'the greater good' muddies the water. We do not always walk in the light." Dimitrius clapped Vasili on the shoulder. "I shall hold them off for as long as I can to give you a fair chance."

"Thank you, Father."

Dimitrius departed, leaving the large, silent council chamber empty aside from Vasili and Elyvia, with Morrigan's prone form between them, and two guards discreetly at the door.

"She is safe in this state," said Elyvia, dropping her gaze to Morrigan and clasping her hands behind her back. As she moved, her armoured shoulder plates gleamed in the warm faelight hanging above them.

Vasili bit back a reply. He doubted Morrigan was safe in any state. "Shall we wake her?"

Elyvia sighed. "Yes. Let's get this over and done with. It will become easier, I hope. Brace yourself."

CHAPTER 6

Morrigan floated in a viscous pit of tar-like nothingness. With every breath, it filled her lungs, choking and smothering her. It coated her skin and saturated her clothes, weighing her down with every saturated rag it dragged. Her chest was frozen, unable to take a breath. Panic or death taking her, she could not tell which.

Around her, a dirge-like drone wailed, through which she could barely sense the familiarity of the prayers she had sung a thousand times over in service to her lord. It gave her comfort in this strange, cold place that clung onto her, folded her inside, under, winking her out into nothingness.

She could not move. Could not resist.

Then a light burned through that darkness overhead. Steady and inexorable. Dim at first. Hopelessly so. A pinprick against a vast universe of onyx. It singed the edge of that black, sending tangy, ashy embers into the nothingness as it grew, feeding on the darkness before it.

The tar roiled around her, repelling that light, trying to shed it like water off oil. But still, that light burned, a sole candle against the onslaught of a storm. One ember at a time. Ashes drifted past her, flecks that stung, hot and angry, on her cheek, her arm, her thigh. Naked. Why was she naked? Morrigan's clouded, sluggish thoughts could hardly keep up.

The hole in the darkness grew, and with it, that light. It was too bright now. She could not see, but still, it burned her eyes with its purity. The faintest hint of air reached her, gently brushing away the acrid stench from her nose, one tendril at a time.

Awaken.

It was a command she could not refuse. She was a puppet, and another, her master.

Morrigan surged upwards, shedding that heavy, smothering viscosity, towards that light. As she approached the burning, fraying, tattered edges of darkness, the heat intensified, jarring at her; she was as cold as stone, and it sizzled her skin to be near. With each distance she ascended, limp and delightfully, liberatingly weightless, her breath returned. The pressure upon her chest lifted, and she took a deep, gulping, grateful breath of air scented with woodsmoke, musk, and citrus.

Morrigan's eyes flickered open.

Every muscle in her body strained as though reflexively. She was bound by some invisible bond – magic, then – but fabric stirred over her skin. Not naked? The thought confused her for a moment, still half in the strange dream. A stone ceiling above her. Cold, hard, flat surface at her back.

"Morrigan." The voice was guarded, cautious – familiar.

She turned her head to glare at Vasili. "I ought to have gutted you."

He smiled faintly. "I'm glad you did not get the chance."

She hated it, the ease with which he defied her. He had been utterly in her power, and now, in a sickly reversal of fortunes, she found herself in his. "Pah! If not for your beast, you would be dead by my hand." Morrigan bared her teeth viciously.

Vasili's lips thinned, but he did not remark on that. "You need to eat."

How long had it been? Morrigan had no idea. Her stomach felt hollow, though, with lack of sustenance, and now he had mentioned it...her tongue darted out to wet her lip. She was thirsty – but she would not ask for a drink. No doubt it would be poisoned anyway, and if not, well, she would not give him the satisfaction of knowing her vulnerable.

Vasili's glance flicked to someone behind her. Morrigan could not crane her neck enough to see them. But, a moment later, footsteps sounded, hard boots upon stone, she thought, retreating.

"I don't want anything," she said venomously.

"You will eat." His tone was level, even.

She snorted. If he thought he could force her to do anything...she was made of far stronger stuff than he, and he would underestimate her to his detriment.

His gaze locked with hers. His expression unreadable – yet not filled with the mutual hate she expected to see. "You need to eat, Lady Morrigan. You must keep up your strength."

"What do you care about my strength?" she shot at him, once more testing the bonds against her. They did not give. Frustrated, she reached down into herself. Nothing. No magic. Not a whisper of her power. It was sickening, as though she had been emptied into a husk, weakened to a babe. It enraged her – and terrified her. She shoved the latter away.

His lips slid into a lazy, lopsided smile, faint, and then gone after a moment. "Unlike your people, we are considerate to those in our care."

"You cannot get me to let down my guard, or whatever inane and utterly transparent strategy you have."

"Basic decency isn't a strategy."

"Then give me back my magic. I don't know how you've done it, drugged me, or ensorcelled me, but if you're so *decent*, allow me my full strength, and then we shall see how fair this arrangement is."

"Now who's inane?" He stared at her – but perhaps for his good sense, he did not smirk to rub salt in the wound. Did he take pleasure in their role reversal? She could not tell. "We're not that decent – or stupid."

The footsteps returned. With them, Morrigan felt herself pushed and pulled into a seated position by the magic binding her. Her stomach roiled with the strangeness of the sensation, and then rumbled loudly. Her cheeks warmed, and she gritted her teeth. So what if the physical needs of her body betrayed her? Her mind was strong. Strong enough to withstand whatever this whelp would throw at her.

"Thank you," he said to the older, female elf who brought a dish of something that smelled so divine that, for a moment, Morrigan nearly crumbled.

Poisoned, most likely. Don't fall for it. Morrigan sat rigid, suspended by the magic that bound her. And clamped her lips shut.

Vasili sighed as he pondered the obvious problem she had already considered – if she were entirely bound, how could she feed herself? He took the dish from the older elf. "I'll do it."

He loaded the spoon with a lumpy broth that smelled heartier and was thicker than any of the poor fare she had had in the mountains, where pickings were sparser and rations had to stretch further.

"Come on. I know you would rather I not treat you like a babe, but you understand we can hardly release you."

It was a fair comment. Still, Morrigan glared at him, her mouth sealed.

He hovered the spoon closer.

She did not budge.

"Come on," he said, exasperated. "You need to eat."

Stony-faced silence was her reply.

"Skies above, would you rather die than eat?" he burst out, the air of calm upon him shattered. He subsided at once, but the damage was done.

He shared a glance with the silent, older elf. One imploring for help. He received no response.

"I don't want to force you, Lady Morrigan," he said quietly, turning back to her. The spoon *clinked* as he rested it in the bowl once more. "I will not stoop so low, no matter how hateful you are, no matter how much you anger me."

She stilled – taken aback that he would say it out loud. "You're weak." The word oozed out of her.

But, contrary to her expectations, Vasili lifted his chin

and met her gaze. "No, I'm not," he said simply. "I'm decent – and there is a difference. I know you would probably rather die than break under any pressure I, or anybody else, could place upon you, but I do not wish to stoop so low. I will not break you. I choose a different path – I *fought* for a different path, because others were not so benevole—"

"I do not need your protection." Morrigan scowled.

"I'm well aware. You need kindness, though," Vasili said softly, and Morrigan thought she hated that more than his imperturbable calm. "Has anyone ever shown you kindness?"

Her eyes narrowed. *What fresh trick is this?*

"I'll take that as a no. I imagined as much, knowing you've grown up in that valley, at the hands of your mother and the Order." He shuddered, his lip curling. "Cruelty and scarcity are no way to raise anyone. I don't hate you for that, you know. I know you are only what they made you."

"No, I'm not," she shot back immediately. "I-I..." She scowled at him, a tremor turning her stomach at the uncomfortable feeling his words elicited. Kindness was a weakness, no? It was what she had always been taught. To be kind was to be weak, and weakness needed rooting out. Exterminating. Lord Valxiron deserved the finest followers. Strong ones. Unbreakable ones.

"There's a different way," he murmured. "A better one. I promise you – if you'll let me show you."

"I will never trust you." She glared at him and at the silent female who remained nearby, arms crossed, standing tall and alert – a warrior too, Morrigan reckoned – and impassive.

Vasili tilted his head. "Perhaps. Perhaps not. Will you at

least eat? You only spite yourself by starving." At her silence, he sighed. "Here. Look." He took a mouthful of the stew, chewed, swallowed. Looked at her expectantly, a brow raised. "See? Not poisoned. We have no interest in harming you." He held out a spoonful to her.

"And what then?" she said, turning her head aside so he could not place it in her mouth. "I shall be a prisoner forever? Tamed and captive? I think not."

Vasili shrugged. "The future holds a great many possibilities. For now, one day at a time. First of all, eat." He held the spoon out expectantly.

Her stomach rumbled mutinously again. Her body railed against her strength of mind, as weak as she was. Her stomach yawned, cavernously empty and wanting, for that hearty meal. Morrigan set her jaw and kept her head turned away.

"Fine. Have it your way. Waste of a good stew."

The female at last spoke. "I'll have them return her to her cell." Her quiet voice passed out of Morrigan's hearing as she bent close to Vasili to keep their conversation private, though her gaze lingered on Morrigan.

Morrigan stared defiantly back.

A dozen guards arrived – an amount that flattered Morrigan into a devilish smile as she beheld them – for they revealed how much they concerned themselves with her 'welfare'.

They do fear me. As they should.

She was the oracle's daughter and heir, after all, a position of covetous high standing within the Order of Valxiron and one that came with great and terrible power. Power that, unfortunately, despite the strength of her own magic, she had not inherited yet, or she would have annihilated them all upon the spot. But even so, that mere thought reminded her of who she was and what she represented.

Kindness. Pah. Weak, foolish, cowardly traitor.

CHAPTER 7

The grimoire strained against its bounds, cursing her in tongues she had not yet heard – but the meaning of its vicious words was clear. It stank of sulphur and bitter smoke, and had it not been such a fascinating tome, it would have been entirely repulsive – from the scaly hide oozing dark, staining pus to the carved bone that made a macabre embellishment promising wrack and ruin to any who dared read from it.

Venya Rowena Bettany of House Ravakian glared at the monstrous tome of magic, blood, and parchment and pursed her lips. "Oh, do be quiet. You're giving me the most heinous headache."

Knowing it would most certainly not heed her request – the opposite, more like – she flicked a slender finger.

Instantly, the snarling tirade ceased as her magic wrapped around the grimoire.

Ah. Blessed silence.

Venya shifted in the hard, wooden chair. She rolled her shoulders against the ache that threatened them, but her hand did not stop, nor the scratching of the quill as she penned notes into the grimoire's record.

The report was far less interesting than the grimoire itself that rested, restrained, upon the desk before her. A condition report, during which she had noted that there was some wear in need of repair on the scaly spine and that the binding spells had begun to erode in one corner. That would be the job of a qualified librarian to fix.

The grimoire itself, however... Venya set down the quill carefully and blotted the ink dry upon the parchment. She slipped on the thin, grey, leather gloves beside her. They were an essential of the job she had been tasked with. They appeared entirely insubstantial to face the magical and detestable grimoire before her, but their appearance was deceiving.

The magic imbued within the supple, skin-tight, dragonhide gloves was enough to protect anyone who should wear them from the ill effects of any grimoire. It meant that Venya could handle those that oozed poison, or spat fire, or leaked curses – any number of dangerous skills that would otherwise most likely incapacitate her, or worse.

As a newer trainee librarian, fresh into the sun-yellow-trimmed robes of the rank, Venya's usual gloves were brown leather and given the most basic of protections for the low-level grimoires she usually worked with. To serve her punishment – to handle more dangerous tomes – those gloves had been traded upwards.

At first, Venya had begrudged the duties that took her

away from her training to ascend to full librarian status in the Athenaeum. Now, it was the part of her punishment which felt rather like a reward. When else would a lowly trainee librarian like her get to handle such interesting grimoires as this one, *The Curses of Nosserillium*? Not that Venya would tell the First Librarian Nieve that.

No, at least this meant she got to indulge her passion for the beastly grimoires. That it was beyond her ken only made her hungrier to know more. One day, would she be able to read or speak that tongue? Perhaps then she could devour its secrets. For now, she had to be content with handling it. And listening to its no doubt colourful language.

Click. The sound echoed through the vault as the door unlocked. Venya worked alone in the administration vault, a safe, windowless box under the mountain, fortified with locks both physical and magical to keep whatever it held inside.

In years gone by, that had been necessary. Being a librarian was not considered a *safe* career by any stretch. Not when the books had teeth, claws, and magic more malevolent than half the Athenaeum's applicants. The administration vault was secure for a reason – no one would come to save her if this tome went on a rampage.

"Drat," Venya muttered to herself. There would be no extra time to spend looking over this hideous beauty if someone was breathing down her neck. She would have to bind it and return it to its designated vault at once, deep in the heart of the Athenaeum, Pelenor's archive of books, grimoires, curiosities, and more, set into the very mountain that the city of Tournai was built upon.

There were three doors in total – one of iron to ward magic, one of steel to ward claws, and one of magic to ward most anything else. The clunk of the second door sounded – then the quiet sigh of the third.

Beatrix, librarian and Venya's dear friend, appeared through the shimmering doorway. "Hi, Venya, morning Nyx! Oof, it stinks in here," she said, wrinkling her nose, the stench stopping her dead in her tracks. "And it's cold."

Venya was warm enough, truth be told. The magic heating the place was not entirely terrible, and she had remembered to bring a fur-lined cloak with her that day. Though, she had to admit, she could not feel her toes.

"At least it's warmer than your working quarters," Venya replied, hiding a small smile behind her hand. Beatrix currently worked in one of the magically cooled vaults, where grimoires who needed arctic temperatures lived. It sparkled with a permanent hoarfrost, and the air was so cold, one had to be careful not to lose the tip of one's nose to it, let alone the grimoires.

Bea pulled a face. "Yes, well. I've had enough of numb fingers for the morning. Are you coming for lunch? Even the canteen will be warmer than down there."

"Gladly." Her daily reprieve from the dark, stale vault was lunch in the canteen upstairs. She wasn't permitted to leave the Athenaeum at present. Not for the duration of her punishment. Venya stood, made sure the grimoire was securely bound with chain and spell, and followed Beatrix outside.

Venya wrapped her dark cloak around her. Her hands were pale as snow against it after months of not enough natural daylight in the winter months. There would be a *lot* of making up to do when spring came. How she longed to sit in a sunlit field, soaking up the natural warmth of the day, drink in the heady perfume of a flower-filled meadow, and lose herself in a good book. However, she no longer begrudged her duties. Mundane though the task was, at least she was permitted to work with grimoires too interesting for her paygrade.

It had almost been a *month*.

Venya took a deep, grateful breath of the fresh, cold air in the tall halls. The two wound their way upstairs to the outside world. There was the canteen that serviced the hundreds of librarians living and working at the Athenaeum.

Almost a month of being stripped of her usual duties and consigned to punishment after her infraction. Soon she would return to this world. How busy it would feel after near isolation, with just Beatrix's forbidden occasional visits for company and motivation. And Nyx.

Truth be told, she was happy enough with that. The only thing she truly missed was the variety of the vaults she usually worked in and the grimoires she already had a rapport with – plus those new ones she encountered on a daily basis that kept her hunger for learning well stoked.

Venya had never been particularly sociable, nor did she get along with many of her cohort. Not as the daughter of the Houses of Ellarian and Ravakian. Those names, her very blood, had cursed her before she had even set foot inside the Athenaeum. Beatrix and Nyx were the only ones who did not care about any of it – or judge her.

Nyx was sleeping today. Venya patted her pocket softly.

The innocuous brown mouse inside did not move. It turned out that the *Book of Beasts*, Nyxastriatamun, or, more fondly and commonly called by her, 'Nyx', was not a fan of the cold. That day, he had been particularly lethargic.

He had been the saving grace in her early days of punishment when she had bemoaned the loss of her liberty. It had been through her own poor decisions, he had reminded her without much sympathy, but he had also borne her complaints with patience and steady compassion.

"Psst. Nyx," she said. "It's lunchtime."

That got the little brown mouse roused. Her pocket squeaked.

Beatrix burst into a fit of giggles as they walked past a gaggle of apprentice librarians, who turned at the strange sound.

"Winter vegetable pie today, Nyx," Beatrix whispered loudly.

"Shhh," Venya said, nudging Bea in the ribs with an elbow.

Beatrix grinned and shrugged. Nyx was their little secret. Not even Nieve, First Librarian, knew about the little escaped grimoire that Venya was inadvertently keeping as a pet. Nor would she, if Venya had anything to do with it. She had gotten in enough trouble already – that might see her cast out of the Athenaeum for good.

"I'm trying to repair my career, not end it," growled Venya.

"Never mind that," Nyx said, running up from her pocket to crouch on her shoulder, nestled beneath a long curtain of Venya's raven hair. "I'm starving."

Venya rolled her eyes. She still did not understand how a book, never mind one that could turn into a variety of monstrous and adorable beasts, needed to eat, but Nyx did not pass up any chance for food. "You're going to get too fat for my pocket," she warned. "And then, where will you go?"

"Perhaps I'll be a cat. You can have a pet cat, can't you?"

"Not until I'm a full librarian." And that was years away still. Venya sighed. Besides which, she rather liked Nyx in his canine form as a rather sweet, large puppy with huge paws, floppy ears, and curling fur of golden brown. The only otherworldly sign Nyx presented was the feature uniform across any shape he took – his eyes. Golden rimmed and slitted. She still did not know enough about him. To her constant infuriation, he was ever mysterious on his past and his making.

"Come on. Some food will cheer you up."

It definitely would, Venya decided, not least because there were just a few more days left in the stuffy vault until she was *free* again.

Free to explore all the possibilities of the interesting notes she had managed to squirrel away, of making grimoires, blood sorcery, and all manner of interesting titbits she would otherwise not have managed to discover.

"You're going to have to stop pilfering those," Nyx said.

That evening, once more alone in the private confines of her room – save for Nyx's ever-present company, of course – Venya thumbed through the grimoire she had *borrowed* from the vault.

Venya shot the innocuous puppy a stinging glare. He lounged at the bottom of her bed without a care in the world. "I didn't steal them. We're still in the Athenaeum, in case you hadn't noticed. Technically." *Sort of.* They were still within the confines of the building. That counted, she reasoned.

The puppy winked. "Tetchy tonight, aren't we?"

"You would be too if you'd had to spend the day doing what I've been doing," Venya muttered. "I'm not lucky enough to be able to nap the whole time." Although she found interesting curiosities in her temporary duties, she was growing tired of the long hours spent in that stuffy place.

Nyx chuckled and curled up, closing his eyes.

Venya shot her eyes skyward. *The Book of Beasts* was a curious grimoire indeed, one about which she still did not know half as much as she wanted to. Nyxastriatamun was enigmatic when it came to revealing much of himself.

"Did you finish translating the Tir-na-Alathean poem yet?"

"No." She had lost track of that one – a job that ought to have taken her a couple of weeks in her spare time. Now, all her spare time was taken up by the more pressing issue of exploiting whatever grimoires her temporary position allowed her unprecedented access to. "I'll get back to it when I'm done with this one."

"You said that with the last book," Nyx reminded her.

Venya winced. "They're all so interesting, I can't help it."

"You were definitely made to be a librarian. 'Just one more book', indeed…"

"Can't you translate it for me? To save time? You know all sorts of things, right?"

"I'm a grimoire, not an encyclopaedia. Besides, I speak the tongues of beasts, not men and elves and fae."

"Beasts, you say?" Venya cocked her head, intrigued. Nyx was such an enigma, continually surprising her but being rather economic with disclosing anything much of himself. And so anything he relinquished, she grasped hold of. "*All* beasts?"

"Hmm," Nyx said noncommittally.

If she micro-analysed it, maybe it was an affirmative. She groaned. "Oh, come on. You must give me something more to go on than that. You can speak to all creatures?"

Nyx simply sighed, closed his eyes, and pretended to be thoroughly asleep.

Venya muttered a choice curse under her breath. She would draw no more from him – or *it*. She still wasn't sure what gender Nyx possessed, if any, only that he spoke with a distinctly male timbre. Maybe that meant something – or nothing, just like the rest of Nyx's cryptic clues.

Knowing she could expect nothing further from Nyx, she turned back to the grimoire in her lap, unconsciously stroking her gloved fingers down the edge of its leather cover. Beneath her supple touch, it shivered, silent and pliant, upon the cloth across her lap – another necessary protection, like the gloves, against grimoires' powers and arsenals of hostile weapons.

Beside her lay a quill and an open notepad, in which she jotted down intoxicating snippets as she found them in the tomes she secretly raided. Learning was a hunger that never subsided within Venya. This grimoire was especially juicy, diving into some of the aspects of grimoire creation itself.

She had only dared to bring this one up to her room as it wasn't one of the grimoires that described blood magic formation. They were dark tomes indeed. One had even spit literal brimstone at her as she had attempted to open it to peek inside at the contents. It had been agonising to return that to the shelf. Ever since her fleeting conversation prior to her punishment with Nieve, the First Librarian, about grimoires and their formation, it had been a topic that burned at her.

Some grimoires were made with forbidden blood sorcery, Nieve had told her. *Others with light. Not all grimoires are evil –* a common misconception.

After the peril Venya had endured, almost releasing a terrifying grimoire upon the Athenaeum and accidentally unleashing a beast that injured another librarian thanks to her error, Venya had no desire to revisit the danger of that time. Nor the punishment upon her that it had resulted in. She had been lucky not to lose her position and career at the Athenaeum. That mistake had almost wiped away a lifetime of aspirations.

Still, though, that insidious desire to know more tugged at her. It was a dangerous path to follow as she strayed along its borders – that of right and what she knew to be beyond the scope of her work and Nieve's permission. If she was caught, her career *would* be over.

And so she had smuggled them back to her room, one at a time, her heart thundering in her chest with each illicit action, knowing she would be punished beyond her worst nightmares if she were caught. All the same, the rush of it thrilled her. Perhaps the daring escapades she had already ventured on had emboldened the timid librarian whom Nyx had once called "Mouse" in all good faith.

Because, in addition to being shy, Venya was also realising her own growing stream of impatience. That impatience would not be sated until she had answers, much faster than the First Librarian was willing to cede them to her.

CHAPTER 8

*A*edon knew that Solanaceae deliberated before him not out of the goodness of Her own heart and moral compass but on an entirely dispassionate basis. How could he best serve Her – and, crucially for him, was he of any further use?

That she had not immediately released him as per their bargain told him that she had no intention of honouring it in such simple terms. Aedon cursed himself. He ought to have been more specific – he knew as well as anyone that a vague bargain could further damn if not careful. Vague bargains led to unexpected outcomes, and usually unpleasant ones.

Freedom is freedom though, right? She cannot manipulate that...can she?

He dared to glance up. Her brow furrowed in a strangely mortal semblance of confusion. As though She had not expected him to ask or to make such an impassioned plea, devoid of any of his usual ego and fire.

He could see as well as She. The moment when She realised he truly was broken. Not the exciting plaything She had sometimes tortured for fun over the years with this anguish or that. But truly defeated.

And with that realisation came a curl of Her lip.

Distaste. Good. Disdain me. Be disgusted. Set me free.

"You play a clever game, my thief," She allowed.

'Tis no game, he longed to protest, but he knew that would be folly. He could see Her calculating how She could turn him to serve Herself, to still control, to win. Never would She, the great woodland Queen, child of fae and elemental, be seen to yield to a mere Pelenor elf, base creature that he was in comparison to Her demi-god-like status.

"I will concede that we made a bargain for your freedom."

Aedon's heart dared to soar.

She crushed it with Her next words.

"However, I rather value you and your *talents* too much."

Aedon hollowed. *No, please. Please don't keep me.*

Solanaceae took a deep breath and let out a lazy exhale. In time with Her rhythm, the blossoms adorning Her slowed their dancing petals. "I shall give you your liberty, Aedon Lindhir Riel."

As She spoke his name, a jolt rushed through him. Magic. Hers. The power of Her word as Her bond.

"You shall have the freedom of my realm and all others. However..."

Aedon stilled.

"...You still belong to *me*. You will serve whenever I desire."

It took a second for it to sink in. The gravity of what She had said. The gift and the curse. He would be free, but ever at Her beck and call? Half a freedom. A shadow of liberty. Indentured to Her, always.

The soaring relief that had erupted at her initial words, at that one word – freedom – crumbled and plummeted into a dark depth with the gravity of her condition. Frustration warred with fury. It was no freedom, merely a semblance. He would be a beast upon a chain. His freedom would be tenuous at best.

Skies above, what did She want from him? Even in the rush of thoughts, he knew. Control. She always wanted the upper hand. Always wanted the victory – whether it was first or last blood.

"Thank you, my Queen," Aedon murmured after half a moment. He would get no further. If he pushed it, She could as easily rescind what little she had given. And he knew She would, out of pure spite.

She did not answer. Their conversation was done. His welcome would be outstayed if he tarried any longer.

He wanted to rage. Surely, she was not so made of spite as to be so dogged with it? Their old enemy rose, a peril as grave as they would ever face, and she was more concerned with making sure that she pulled the strings of Aedon's fate.

Bitterness soured within him. They had had a *deal*. A simple and straightforward promise. She had reneged upon it, finding a loophole. Aedon was furious at himself more than Her. He knew Her nature well enough. *I ought to have safeguarded against this.*

Aedon stood and bowed deeply once more before the

impassive Queen, who already called forth Her magic to summon the powerful beings of Her realm.

El'hari and Sirvardi hovered on the edge of the circle of chairs, under the ivy and plant-choked stone arches. Waiting for him. The expression on Sirvardi's face – grim verging on anger at his insolence – and that on El'hari's – thinly veiled concern – told him they had waited because they feared what their Queen would do to him for his disrespect.

"Come." El'hari chivvied him away and lengthened her stride. Sirvardi soon peeled off in the direction the *centime* had halted.

"You don't half push it, my friend," El'hari said when they were out of hearing from the *centime* commander, and she levelled an amused stare at Aedon.

"Wouldn't you if you were in my position?" Aedon snapped, not in the mood to hear it. "I was in that hole in the ground for a long time. I'm done."

"You've changed," El'hari remarked thoughtfully. "I remember when you arrived. I had scarcely expected to see you again, and yet there you were. Defeated and broken in more ways than one. You welcomed your punishment back then. You would have gladly never seen the light of day."

Aedon did not respond. Shoulder to shoulder, they strode up the inclining, winding path between deciduous trees as tall as castles, with trunks as thick as houses. Far above them, branches crisscrossed the sky, casting the forest floor into heavily dappled shade under the bounty of ever-present leaves. Bridges snaked between the giant specimens, for the wood elves' realm was as much in the canopy and the decks and dwellings there as on the forest floor.

El'hari led him to a staircase winding around one of the

giant boles. "I can see you've changed, anyway. I wonder what, or perhaps *who*, is responsible for that, hmm?" She shot him a sly but not unkind smile and nudged him with her elbow.

"I..." He could not even deny it. He did not want to. It was not like it was shameful, only that he was so terrified it still might all disappear, but perhaps not, if he was *free*, even not in entirety. He could not begin to imagine what it meant. Exhausted, still battle-weary and reeling from that, it was too much to contemplate in that moment what the rest of his life might look like – and whether it would contain Lief.

"Where is she?" he asked quietly, turning a pleading gaze upon El'hari. His anger at Solanaceae drained away. Lief was more important at that moment. He would find a solution to the Queen's manipulation another time. Somehow. "I must go to her."

"Where do you think I'm taking you?" El'hari's face softened. "I could see the state she was in. I had her brought here, since she is neither a member of Sirvardi's *centime* nor my own. Truth be told, she is the last of the Lune garrison. I thought it best to treat her like a guest for now, until such time as I figure out what to do with her. You'll have adjoining quarters as the Queen's guest too. I'll have them made up at once in light of your new, ah, liberty."

By the way she said it, she had some unshared thoughts on the terms and conditions that came along with his newfound freedom. Aedon pushed the thought out of his head. Damned be it all, but he was still *alive*, and Lief, and they were both *safe*. Above all else, he was grateful for that. He would sift through the wreckage of the rest later.

El'hari climbed steadily beside him, following the curve

of the stairs around the tree. Most Pelenori elves did not have a head for heights, but as a former dragon rider of the Winged Kingsguard, though that felt like a lifetime ago, Aedon relished the chance to lift into the heavens, limited as he was on his elven feet far more than by the wing of a dragon. Part of him longed for that. To break free of the canopy, which still felt oppressive above him, containing him, and fly truly free in the boundless skies above, with no boundary but the stars.

He paused when she did as the stairs ended and a balcony began. El'hari rested a hand on the vine-and-orchid-covered wooden railing. It flowed with the same shapely ease as all else in the forest, Sung from the living trees themselves.

Behind El'hari, inside the very trunk itself and wound around the branches, was a dwelling also Sung from the trees. Flowing wooden branches wove what looked like a gigantic cocoon around the space within, which Aedon knew from previous visits long ago to Emuir – as a guest, not a prisoner – would contain enough room for a snug, cosy bed and little else. A curtain of leaves shielded the door, and spells wreathed it, providing privacy and solitude for those within. The balcony held a couple of chairs and a small, wicker table for dining. The forest surrounding offered the rest of the bounty anyone needed – fresh springs and pools to wash, food to eat, and more.

"I shall not disturb her – this is where I leave you for now, my friend. I'm glad you made it back." The sombre tone of her voice betrayed her sadness that so many had not. He wondered if El'hari had known many of them personally. She probably had.

"I'm sorry." He had faced the same loss of friends in arms before.

"There is nothing for you to be sorry for. By all accounts, it is thanks to you that the blight is now scourged from Lune and that some more lived to see the next sunrise. Even if She will not thank you, I shall be grateful."

Aedon inclined his head, touched that she would regard him so highly, especially in light of their fractious first meeting long ago. How much they had both changed.

El'hari glanced over the forest sprawling before them and sighed. "I have much to do. I shall see you soon, perhaps in a day or perhaps in a few. Until then, rest, recuperate, and heal, my friend." She pointed. "Over the brow, there is a wonderful and private guest spring you can both bathe in. It will be empty."

Aedon needed it. Desperately. He longed to scrub and scour the blackness from his spirit and the travel dirt from his skin.

"Food will be brought to you morning, noon, and night. If you have any other needs, return to the gate – down that path there – and ask for me."

"Thank you."

El'hari turned to him and, after grasping both forearms in as close to a hug as the enigmatic warrior would ever likely exhibit, left, padding down the stairs with practised silence.

Aedon watched her go. He took a deep breath as he turned back to the cocoon. Lief. He rushed forward and swept aside the leafy curtain. Muted sunlight filtered in from above, where the branches wove together less solidly than the walls, allowing tiny shafts of light to filter into the inner space.

He paused abruptly, thrown for a second by the empty space. A round bed, more of a nest, almost filled it, neatly made, with soft pillows and woven throws – all thin and light with the forever-warmth of Tir-na-Alathea, the forest of eternal summer.

There. Beside the bed. Huddled in the corner, with her knees drawn to her chest and her face buried in her arms.

Her auburn hair glimmered in the shafts of light as motes lazily curled through the air in the small space. It was dirty after the days of hard travel, and no doubt, like him, she had remnants of battle upon her. She looked small. Frail. Hopeless.

Damn it, he regretted leaving her. Queen's wishes be damned. She had needed him, and he had known it, and he had left her anyway, to float, alone and bleak, for however many hours as he placated Queen Solanaceae.

"Lief." He rushed across to her and sank beside her in what little space remained between her, the bed, and the wall and wrapped her in a wordless embrace.

She moved slightly to reach out and grasp his arm, to nuzzle her face into him, and to shudder as sobs wracked her. He caught a glimpse of eyes with dark shadows under them, hauntingly blank.

He held her until the light began to fade outside. At last, stiff-limbed, and with a growling stomach, he stirred. "Come. We need to eat. You'll feel better."

She shook her head into his chest.

"Then we need to rest." They could wash the next morning. Or whenever she was ready. It would wait. Much as he longed to cleanse, she needed him more, and he would not leave her again – not unless the Queen gave him no other choice.

He could feel the anguish leaking from her, colouring the space between them, seeping into the very magic of the forest air. His magic reached out protectively, for he longed to shroud her in warmth and comfort, but he knew he alone could not fix the well of grief open within her, pouring out in a torrent that would wash them both away if he tried to sever its flow.

He had never seen her so before, and it unnerved him deeply. Ever, she had been fiery and vivacious. Fearful, yes, in the face of foes greater than they. Filled with dread when they had met what had passed in Lune – understandably so, for all they had had a taste of in that dark night was hulking shapes prowling through the black brush of the forest and the stench of wicked sorcery upon the air.

He had seen her brimming with joy, magic, life, and love. He had seen her incandescent, with molten eyes as she Sang the border whole with the *centime*. A wood elf in her full ascent, swaying to a power that was not of this world.

He had seen her angry, balls of red on her cheek, hands fisted – mainly at him, he had to admit. That thought brought a little warmth to his heart. The snark-filled hate-love they had nurtured unwittingly over that journey together. Gods, he had infuriated her, much the same way that she had incensed him with her pig-headed, stubborn refusal to believe he could be anything other than a knave.

He had seen her in the throes of passion as they writhed together that first night under a watching blanket of stars with fireflies dancing in the canopy above them. He had felt her entire body light up, as his had done, riding that wave.

It felt like he embraced a hollow stranger, one who had lost all of that vivaciousness, like a cracked vessel which had spilled its contents. She had not watched at Finarvon's end. He had made sure of it. He had ensured that she had not seen or sensed anything that came in that terrible final moment as the *dhiran* tore apart the reanimated corpse of her former lover.

But still. She had known what had passed, and he knew she would be filling in the cracks herself. Looping it over and over in her head, a nightmare vision that would never cease.

Aedon pressed a tender kiss to her forehead, imbuing it with healing magics, ones that would ease her into slumber and wash away the terrible spectres that would haunt her until morning otherwise, as they had haunted her into sleeplessness in the days since leaving Lune.

He stood, the movement awkward in the confined corner, lifting her and cradling her in his arms, where she nestled, unmoving. Unresisting. Uncaring, he knew, if his past grief were anything to go by. He had suffered such painful losses in the deep past. She moved in an inner world for now, and he could not reach her there. Not yet. Not until the hurt had calmed enough for her to venture out once more.

Pushing back the thin blankets with a gust of magic, he lowered her gently onto one side of the bed, untangling her hands from his tunic. Aedon kicked off his boots and, fully clothed, slipped into the bed beside her, wrapping her in a great embrace. Once more, her hands twined into the fabric of his shirt. A needless plea for that comfort and companionship.

"Sleep," he breathed over her, tucking her head under his chin. He did not bother with the blankets, mild as the night was, and simply lay there, feeling the rise of her chest against his, listening as her shuddering sobs subsided into the deep, calm breaths of slumber.

Please be whole again.

CHAPTER 9

*E*ventually, Aedon slept, though it felt like an age before his eyes at last slipped shut and all too soon that they cracked open, bleary and gritty, with the dawn light of the next day.

She stirred soon after, the natural rhythm of her body calling her to wakefulness probably sooner than she needed or wanted. Waking meant walking with that grief anew.

"Morning," he murmured into her hair.

"Aedon," she said, her voice cracked.

Aedon extricated himself slowly from her, their bodies having moulded and tangled together overnight. "I'm not going anywhere," he said quickly. "Just seeing if there's a drink outside." He was starving and parched, his stomach aching and hollow.

He slipped outside. Sure enough, on the table lay a tray carrying two wooden beakers and an arrangement of fruits and small cake-like things on a serving platter. He took a grateful sip of the cool, refreshing liquid, groaning with delight as it flowed down his throat. He picked it up and took it inside, backing into the curtain of leaves to sweep it aside.

"Here." Aedon placed the tray upon the foot of the bed. "We need to break fast."

"I'm not hungry," she whispered. As she spoke, he heard the growl of her belly betraying her words.

"Eat," he commanded, offering her one of the sweet cake-breads.

It was sticky. He took one and placed it in his own mouth. Sweetness burst over his tongue with a tart aftertaste. Some citrus-like drizzle on the top. Raisins injected more flavour within the floury, heavy crumb.

Lief regarded it but did not move. He stretched closer.

She obediently took the tiniest bite. Chewing and swallowing. She had a sip of the water under his ministrations, and he made her finish the small thing, barely more than a snack. It was a start, at least.

"Are you game for washing? I think it would do us both good."

Lief swallowed. After a long pause, she nodded. Perhaps she too felt the need to cleanse, even if she would rather sit in the pit of grief she carried.

Aedon slipped on his boots and fitted Lief's for her as she dangled her legs from the end of the bed. A part of him wondered at the oddity of it. The first time they had ever shared a proper bed. How often he had thought about doing precisely that. How he had imagined what they would do there. He did not resent a moment of it, but never had he envisaged they would spend their first night in any bed fully clothed and as celibate as a dwarven monk.

Hoping they would meet no one else, Aedon led them

both in silence down the great staircase and towards the brow of the hill that El'hari had highlighted. Over it, a cleft split the earth, and a small gulley with a stream in the bottom wound away. He followed it, stepping from stone to stone as a small outcrop rose to either side of them, forcing them to tread almost in the very water and balance from grassy hummock to stone and back again.

Up they followed the stream until they had to clamber up the side of a small waterfall. The stone faces around them opened out into a deceptive space, and trees, bushes, and vines overhung the place, crowning it in verdant green. Wet mosses clung to the vertical rock in a glistening emerald veil. Above, through a small circle, the pink of the fresh dawn sky brightened.

And they were alone. Beautifully alone. Blessedly alone.

Aedon breathed a grateful breath in the stillness and solitude of that space as he reached a hand to Lief to help her up behind him.

They were liberated at last from the oppressive company of the *centime*. It had not allowed them to speak or grieve freely for days, and the pent-up emotion pooled behind a dam that threatened to break.

Lief stood immobile, gazing around the space. Before them, a spring burbled from the earth, feeding an azure pool and the stream that they had followed. They stood upon green grass that the water lapped gently against. Aedon felt the urge to take off his boots and did so, sighing with delight at the soft caress of the grass blades beneath his feet.

Aedon turned.

Lief had not moved. He crossed the few paces to her and

took her hand in his. It was unnaturally cold. "Lief?" he asked.

She turned to him. Her eyes brimmed with tears. "Why me?" she whispered, her voice scratchy and hoarse.

He knew what she was asking. Why did she feel so damned guilty for still walking upon the earth of Altarea? For still breathing. For still daring to exist when so many others had been lost – and when it was by arbitrary chance that she had survived.

"I don't know," Aedon said honestly. If he thought about it too much, it would probably have broken him over the years. It nearly had when it came to the loss of his dragon, Valyria, who had sacrificed herself to save him. That had shattered him for a good long while.

"We cannot know why," he said, sighing and taking her other hand, clasping them between his own. "But we are here, and I am grateful for it. This is hard now, I know, what you have endured, but it will get easier with time, I promise. I am here with you."

He drew closer and wiped a falling tear from her cheek with a gentle thumb.

"Come. Let us wash. It will help, I promise."

Aedon slowly stripped off his tunic and leggings, standing before her naked. Her fingers fumbled with her buttons, and he stepped in to help. Once more gentle and unhurried. Ready to stop if she insisted. He pulled the tunic over her head, and knelt before her to unlace her trousers, sliding them down her thighs and allowing her to brace her weight on his shoulders as he slipped one calf free, then the other.

Aedon stood and led her towards the pool, gathering a

handful of moss from the cliff wall as they entered at one edge.

He hissed as the cool water slid over his skin. Refreshing and a shock all at once. A blast of magic soon fixed that, heating the pool to a comfortable temperature so that when Lief drew waist-deep alongside him at the deepest point, she was no longer shivering.

He could see that she had no inclination, once more lost in that inner world of bleak darkness. And so he washed them both, carefully and tenderly, with the hunk of moss, scouring away the physical remnants of the battle until their skin was bright and fresh. But still, the blight upon their souls remained.

Would it ever leave if the threat of Valxiron and his darkness remained?

Aedon dared not imagine.

※

It felt a blasphemy to don their travel-worn clothes once more, but upon return to the treehouse, Lief and Aedon found a fresh change and more refreshments awaiting them – and El'hari.

Aedon changed swiftly into a smart, matching tunic and trousers set. He pressed a kiss to Lief's forehead before he slipped out. Lief squeezed his hand in return.

Lief gratefully sipped at the fruit-infused spring water before she slipped into a long, flowing dress of lichen-green. With thin straps, and flaring from the bust, the light material floated around her with ease, far from the weighting of her usual attire. When was the last time she had worn a dress? Lief frowned. She could not remember.

She swayed on the spot, admiring how the fabric rustled and shifted around her, light as leaves dancing upon the air – for once, distracted from all that haunted her. As she swished, the scent of honeysuckle and amber, delicate and floral, teased her.

"Mmm," she sighed softly. Her heart lighter for a moment, she padded outside to join El'hari and Aedon but remained silent, staring pensively into the forest canopy around them as El'hari spoke.

It was beautiful, a bright day – but that shadow upon her had returned already. The phantom of the blight with it. Everywhere Lief looked, she expected the vibrant green life to curl and decay into dark, fetid, toxic death. She suppressed a shudder.

El'hari said, "You're both officially dismissed from your service to the *centime*. I thought you'd be pleased to know."

Aedon huffed a mirthless chuckle. "Very."

Lief shifted beside him. What did that mean for her? Did it mean her services were no longer required at all? Was she still a ranger of Lune? More than that, there was something that had been darkening her steps for weeks.

Aedon slid his gaze to her. "What is it?"

"The mouse," she murmured.

"Mouse?" El'hari raised an eyebrow.

She doesn't know.

Lief had been teaching Aedon the basics of glamouring, and foolishly he had attempted to glamour a mouse from nothing whilst on their journey from Emuir to Lune. Without a moment's thought, Lief had stepped in to save that mouse's life, glamouring it herself from Aedon's unintentionally poor attempt. It had meant the creature lived to thrive, instead of dying excruciatingly and slowly before them. She had no regrets about that.

However, she had Sung before a stranger. It was strictly forbidden to reveal the wood elves' most powerful magical power. The ability to infuse song with magic and the power to create life from that.

Lief steeled herself. She had to face that, much as she did not want to. She explained what had passed in a quiet voice, but she met El'hari's eyes and did not drop her gaze – to the point of defiance – unwilling to apologise still for it. Ready to accept whatever punishment the commander deemed fitting.

"I see. You Sang before an outsider, hmm?" El'hari glanced between Aedon and Lief. "What do you expect me to do about it?"

Lief frowned. "Well, Sirvardi said I would be punished for it." Her hands wound together. It was coming. What would it be? Dishonourable dismissal from her position? Imprisonment? Exile? Her thoughts spiralled, and she clamped her jaws together to stop a groan from escaping.

El'hari laughed darkly. "I think Sirvardi has more pressing matters on his mind than your minor misdemeanour."

"*Minor?*"

El'hari suppressed a smile. "Comparatively, yes. There are far worse things you could do. And, frankly, with what has passed, I do not wish to trouble the Queen with such infractions."

"So?" *What happens now?* For a moment, Lief hovered in

an uncomfortable purgatory. Was she to be punished? How severely? She straightened. "I understand that I did wrong, and I make no excuses or apologies for that. I will take whatever punishment you see fit."

"I won't be disciplining you, Lief."

"I don't understand." Lief frowned.

"Whether Sirvardi forgot or has purposefully omitted it from his reports to the Queen is his own business. I have no interest in your conduct under his command." El'hari gave Lief a pointed look.

Lief swallowed. *She will not punish me.*

"Given what's happened – what you've endured, your service to our people and Tir-na-Alathea itself – I should think you have redeemed yourself."

Lief bowed. "Thank you."

"There's nothing to thank me for." El'hari's gaze slid to Aedon, and the hint of a smirk danced across her thin lips. "Besides which, I rather think that Aedon seeing a Singing is of the least concern, being that he is of no threat to our people."

Aedon huffed, but he did not retort. "Not anymore," he murmured, shifting closer to Lief.

She stilled at the glaring statement of that subtle yet obvious movement.

El'hari's smile widened as she glanced between them. "I'm happy for you, my friend. We have a while yet before we may tend to peace, I suspect, but perhaps one day you will choose to place your roots here." She winked at him. "I must away. The Queen calls, and I must see what is afoot."

Aedon stepped forward. "Will you tell us?"

El'hari huffed mirthlessly. "If you remain indentured to

Her, I have no doubt you will be involved in one way or another, Aedon. Why do you think I came? You are summoned too. Our Queen plans for war."

Chills crawled down Lief's spine at that. She wanted nothing more than to find some way back to peace. If they had to fight again, if darkness came to them, or if they sought it out... She shuddered at the thought.

El'hari disappeared down the steps. Aedon wrapped an arm around her, rubbing up and down. "Are you cold?" he said, mistaking her visceral reaction for something more innocuous.

"No. Go. I'll be fine." Each word was a lie. Lief most certainly would not.

Aedon's hand twined through hers. "You're coming with me. I won't leave you again."

And, grim-faced, he tugged her down the stairs after El'hari. With every step, the bottom of Lief's stomach dropped more. A yawning chasm threatening to engulf her.

War. Tir-na-Alathea was going to war.

CHAPTER 10

Icarus the dragon had been an ever-present, silent spectator in a corner of Vasili's mind as he had tried to face Morrigan properly awake for the first time since he had compelled Icarus not to end her – and to save her instead.

Vasili could still feel the dragon's oozing distaste towards the lady. He could not blame his companion for that. She was ghastly in every way. He knew she would rather die than break under pressure, hence why he had devoted himself to a different path.

As he trudged down to the cells behind Morrigan, who now walked of her own volition – her magic still shackled, and her physical form surrounded by soldiers bristling with weapons all trained on her – he felt the weight of it all. His parents, and the council, had trusted him to deliver. He felt the bite of urgency nipping at his heels. They had not given him much time, and when it had elapsed...he did not want to think what would happen then.

I will reach her first, he vowed. Even though he had no idea how he would even begin to break down the impenetrable walls she had built around and within herself. *No one is beyond redemption or salvation.*

"Be careful what you wish for," Icarus cautioned him along the tendril linking their minds. "*You cannot make her choices for her.*"

Vasili's back rose against that. "It's not like that," he defended.

"*Hmm.*"

He shut out the dragon's reproach and continued to follow the group of soldiers and Morrigan, led by Elyvia, into the bowels of the castle. Into the lightless prison they descended, where the stale air hovered, thick and heavy with sweat, smoke, and worse. Vasili's eyes stung with it.

Skies above, they are keeping her worse than a beast.

His heart sank. The royal horses had better quarters. It would not do at all if he were truly trying to convince her they meant her no harm and that they were worthy of her trust. Not if they kept her in squalor. He would have to try to convince Elyvia, but it would not happen that day. Vasili suspected he had already pushed it far enough.

Elyvia warded the cell and left the guards outside it. She departed, stern faced, with Vasili in tow.

"You picked a potentially impossible task," the general commented. "She is strong-willed to say the least."

"Yes, ma'am, but it will be worth it if we can gain her trust."

Elyvia barked out a mirthless laugh. "I think we should have better luck drawing blood from a stone, but you have your chance. Use it well. Go now, sleep. It's been a long few days, and you will need all your energy to face her once more come the morrow."

Vasili followed Elyvia's instructions and retreated to the dragonhold, a mighty, vast cavern inside the mountain that served to house the huge dragons of the Winged Kingsguard. It seemed an age since Vasili had last set foot there. Cold air blasted him as he stepped from the tunnel into the hollowed mountain, exposed to the elements far above from the open summit and the network of caves lining the rocky chasm that wormed their way through the mountainside.

A tendril of thought tugged him up. So Vasili climbed up one of the four staircases that ascended that inner cavern, linking the caves and holes and nooks inside it with precarious platforms. Icarus' growing presence loomed. Vasili found him in a crevice out of the way.

The green dragon lay curled up in a ball upon a straw nest. Vasili slipped into the cave – which was warm thanks to Icarus' huge bulk. The dragon opened one eye. "Well met." He uncurled his head and snaked his long neck to meet Vasili, exuding a relief matched by Vasili's own.

Vasili rested his cheek against the rough scales on Icarus' nose, his hands stroking the dragon's snout. "You know, I still think every time we part, you will be beyond my reach."

Icarus huffed softly, pleasantly warm air brushing over Vasili, banishing the cold fingers of the winter chill around him that seeped insipidly around the edges of his cloak and down his neck. "I'm not going anywhere again," Icarus said quietly.

Vasili could still feel the dragon's burning regret – Icarus blamed himself entirely for it all. It had been the young dragon's headstrong rage that had led to Vasili's capture, torture, and attempted indoctrination into the Order of Valxiron in the despicable hidden fortress in the mountains.

Because of Icarus, yes, they had more intelligence now than they had possessed in the past two decades on the Order of Valxiron. And yet because of that, rider and dragon had been separated – an excruciatingly painful torment – and Vasili had been subjected to yet more torture at the hands of, most particularly, one Lady Morrigan Lilika Bellatrix of House Mallory.

Vasili shivered at the unwelcome thoughts that brought, and his eyes slipped shut. He still had nightmares every night. Every time he closed his eyes, he found himself back under that dark mountain with her, with his uncles, and with the dark power of the Order poisoning his very bloodstream.

It was a strange dichotomy to open his eyes once more and feel the old familiarity of the dragon roost around him. That old stone, worn smooth from thousands of years of dragons' passage and gouged in places with claw marks from dragons long passed...the very stone, he always felt, had a spirit of its own. Slow and sonorous, a whisper and no more, like some faded imprint of each dragon and rider who had stepped there had left behind them some kind of indelible impression.

After the time they had spent there – years in training – it felt like home, with all the familiar spiritual comfort that brought. He was there with Icarus, and a part of him still wondered if that was a dream, a wishful figment.

He still half expected the dark mountain to appear every time he awoke. Like his current reality was just a desperate dream. It seemed not. He was *home*. They both were. It was a welcome reprieve after the sickening fraught peril of the mountain fortress. It was a simpler place, a world away from the politics and darkness he now found himself embroiled in.

Icarus did not move and did not speak. He did not need to. So much of their essence – thoughts, emotions, wordless and spoken – seeped through the porous mental bridge between them. He simply remained frozen, offering his own wordless comfort as a balm for the distress and confusion of his rider.

Darkness had long fallen outside, and the cave was warm and dark, lit from without by the faint, golden glow of the network of faelights that dotted inside the mountain. Now he had finally stopped, Vasili felt bone-achingly tired. Gods, it had been a never-ending day. He longed to sleep, and for the first time, he felt safe to do so there. The cave feeling as protective as a womb.

However...Vasili sighed. He straightened, and Icarus cocked his head. Vasili said nothing, kicked off his boots, and slumped on the straw beside Icarus, leaning against his warm, rough, scaled flank. He closed his eyes, but sleep did not come. No matter how much he shifted and turned or wormed into Icarus' side to get comfortable – to the point that the dragon huffed with disgust at the constant interruptions to his own much needed rest – Vasili could not settle.

Vasili moved again, and Icarus growled quietly as Vasili accidentally elbowed him.

"If you do not stop fidgeting, I shall lay on you to keep you still," Icarus threatened.

Vasili grinned tiredly. "I'm sorry, friend."

"If you're not going to settle, go. You can be a nuisance there."

"Where?" said Vasili.

Icarus huffed. "You pretend I cannot see your every thought. I know you think of the wicked female – that despite everything she did to you, you still care of her fate. Go on. If you will not rest here, go to her. Do what you must."

Vasili swallowed. Something in his midriff swooped unpleasantly. "Are you sure?" *Is it a good idea for any of us?*

"I am. Mostly because I will be rid of you and your incessant wriggling. I know what you're like. You want to do the right thing, and you trust no one else to accomplish it. Go."

Vasili patted Icarus' flank and departed without another word. He trailed alone like a forgotten wraith in the night to take up a silent, lonely vigil outside Morrigan's cell, not really sure what he was trying to prove to anyone, even himself.

CHAPTER 11

Vasili's eyes ached, crusty with a sleepless night. He shifted his aching body, his numb buttocks, ruined back, and stiff legs complaining with every fractional adjustment. He had spent the night sat on the cold, hard stone with his back against the wall next to the door of her cell.

It was silent within – had been silent all night – and he wondered if she had slept, or whether, like him, she had lulled to and fro between exhausted waking and fitful napping as her body and its needs warred with her mind and its suspicion. Only the stirring of his own circadian rhythm told him it was time to rouse, for otherwise, it was a timeless, dark void down in the dungeons without daylight to guide him.

A faint tendril of thought reached him from Icarus – a question. He sent back an answer. *All fine.* He did not know what he had worried for – that she would be safe from others, or that they would be safe from her, but it had been an entirely uneventful night.

An entirely miserable one too, though for different reasons. The cold, hard stone was the least of it. The place *reeked*. Urine, faeces, vomit, sweat, blood, and scents Vasili did not want to think about, each fouler than the last. The sound too, from behind the cell doors – moans, and crying, wailing and shouting, swearing so colourful it made him wince. It was frigidly cold, and even his cloak did little to protect him. And the dark. Seeping. The faelight was a tiny pinprick against its all-consuming encroach.

It was hellish, perhaps even more so than the subterranean prison he had found himself isolated in with Morrigan...and he could not help but think of the hypocrisy of it all. *I'll lock you up until you trust me.* Vasili scoffed at the thought. He might as well cut off his own nose to spite his face if that was to be done. He might as well not bother. They would get nowhere.

On a whim, Vasili lurched to his feet, gritting his teeth and suppressing the groan that tried to escape. He stumbled back along the passage, past the line of cells, until feeling returned to his legs, and then he jogged up the levels of the castle and out into the half-light of a fresh winter's day. It was still better than the oppressive darkness of the castle's underbelly.

It felt so strange to follow the streets of the upper levels of Tournai to his parents' townhouse. A full turn of the year since he had last set foot there.

The door still opened to his touch, spelled to yield before the blood of their Houses, Ravakian and Ellarian. He chuckled.

Evidently his mother's threat that once he had left, he would be gone for good, was an empty one, and he had known he would be able to call her bluff. She would never shut out her baby boy. A small bell tinkled as he closed the door, and a shadow tumbled down the stairs, a figure haloed in light from behind.

"Darling!" His mother rushed down the stairs, and he couldn't breathe a moment later in her crushing embrace. How was it that even now, when he returned home in leather with the stink of battle still clinging to him, her embrace made him feel a young boy again?

"Mother..."

Ordinarily, he would have endured it for but a fleeting moment before pulling away, but instead, he folded her into his arms, so damned grateful that he had survived to see her again. The familiar perfume, floral and sweet, with a hint of sharpness, cloyed in his nose, no longer a figment of a half-forgotten memory but as real as them both.

She pulled away, wrinkling her nose. "Oh, my dear, you do smell a little. Do you need to bathe?"

Vasili grinned tiredly. "Definitely, but I think it'll have to wait. Is Father here?"

"My boy." The answer came before Harper could open her mouth. Dimitrius strode along the hallway from the kitchen with a dusting of flour across the chest of his smart robe. Now Vasili had pulled away from his mother, he could smell something inviting cooking for breakfast. His stomach rumbled.

"Come for breakfast, hmm? I should have known." His father smiled, clapping him on the shoulder. "It's good to see you, Vasili." Without the trappings of their working roles, he meant. Now, they could speak freely, outside the obligations of Kingsguard or High Council.

"And you. Both of you." Vasili's answering smile drooped with exhaustion, like the rest of him. "I need your advice." He looked between them.

They shared a glance.

"Breakfast it is, then," his father said, beckoning him through to the dining room.

When Vasili had wolfed down a stack of freshly toasted slices of bread smeared with sticky blackberry jam, sweet honey, and oozing, melted, golden butter, he sat back, groaning with relief. The Dragon's Nest did not have such fine fresh fare. Vasili had survived at the outpost on tack and dried meat, with the occasional hard roll, bit of cheese, and fresh game. It was too deep in the mountains to fare any better.

The High Council had heard his full account, but his mother leaned forward, her grey eyes shadowed with worry. "Truly...how are you, Vasili?"

Vasili met her eyes. "I did not think I would see you again," he said truthfully.

"Do you have to go back?" Harper turned a baleful glare on his father. "He doesn't, does he, Dimi? We can stop it."

Dimitrius cast her a sympathetic but slightly exasperated look. "Harper..."

"You cannot admonish me for worrying about our son." Her eyes glistened.

Normally it annoyed Vasili, her protectiveness, but he could start to understand it now that he had gone into true peril. Her pain at losing him had been one of the torments in that dark place, after all. He had regretted the hurt it would cause them if he died there.

"I'm fine, Mother. Honestly." It was a bald lie. And she did not fall for it, tutting at him.

"He's a grown male now," Dimitrius said. "He gets to choose his own path, and as much as we *both* wish to intervene at every turn, we must let him walk it, whatever happens."

"I need your advice still though," said Vasili. He was not above that, not all-knowing or arrogant enough to believe he could weather all storms. Particularly the one sat far beneath Tournai citadel at that very moment.

He had already shared his idea with Icarus on the way up. Icarus had called him an idiot for it.

"I have an idea, but I don't think you'll like it. Hear me out."

CHAPTER 12

Morrigan had hardly slept, jolted awake upon instinct every time her exhausted mind and body tugged her desperately to slumber. Disorientated in the constant dark, the only light a faint crack under the warped, aged, wooden door, she had no idea how long had passed. It seemed an eternity.

It was a different kind of denied existence to penitence, that was certain. Often, she chose to go without sleep, water, sustenance in the name of pious devotion to her master, but this...having it all wrestled from her control sent her helplessly tumbling into uncertainty like a leaf upon a gale. Her nerves were more fraught by the next morning, after a night enduring the cold and the stink of the accursed place and listening to the haunting suffering of other faceless prisoners there.

Those, and the rat. She was not sure whether she pitied or loathed the damned thing. Scratching and scuttling around all night, trying to burrow into her pallet, skittering around her cell. It too was a prisoner of that labyrinth; it must have been, for Morrigan could not see how it would be there by choice.

The place was a cesspit, and when the revolution came, when her people came to liberate her, rise up, ascend into their true place, she would start by torching it. She would raze every stone herself if that was what it took to see it annihilated, this place of her oppression, this citadel of their strength.

A scrape on the stone outside.

A clank of keys in an aged lock.

The screech of rusted hinges.

Morrigan threw up her hands against the light. One single faelight outside, and yet it was the brand of a thousand suns to her after so long in such darkness, and she hid her eyes behind her palms, cursing the lack of her magic to aid her in adjusting or casting out to protect her.

"Lady Morrigan. I brought you some breakfast." Vasili. That hateful, traitorous smear.

Morrigan's hands fell, and she glared at him under thunderously slanted brows.

He dared to step over the threshold, extending a platter to her.

Valxiron take her, was that *bread*? In the hidden mountain fortress, flour was so rare they could not make it. They had half-starved in that valley, as her stick-thin figure could attest to, more bone and bare, wiry muscle than anything else, but this...

Her own despicable stomach betrayed her with a monstrous growl as the scent of fresh, still warm bread wafted over to her. And an *apple* on the side of the plate.

There had been no fruit all year in the hidden city. And what they did receive before that year had been puckered, stunted, and half-withered and rotten anyway. They had still eaten it. It was better than starvation, after all, and they had come close many a time.

Morrigan had always been raised to welcome that suffering. Repentance, her mother had called it. Necessary for martyrdom. Necessary for their lord.

Morrigan had to force herself into stillness, lest she leap up and snatch it from him, devour it all like a caged and starved beast before him. That would be to her eternal shame.

"Lady Morrigan," Vasili said, a note of irritated despair in his tone. "You ought not starve yourself."

She spat at his feet – though she was so thirsty that nothing came out. Only the sentiment.

Vasili muttered under his breath, no doubt cursing her. His hands fell from offering the plate to her to holding it before him.

It gave her some strength to know she could still, stripped of her power and strength, get under his skin. He could not control her spirit, at least. Dark satisfaction curled in her – and then surprise at his next words.

"You're not to remain here," Vasili said, his tone carefully neutral, stiltedly so, as he kept any emotion from it.

Her head jerked up.

"Eat, and we can leave." He held the plate out again.

Damned be him, it smelt *good*, carving through the sickness of that place. "Where?" She slapped down that softening part of her that wanted to break and eat.

"A place more befitting of your rank and my intentions."

She narrowed her eyes.

"You will be permitted to reside under house arrest at Lord Dimitrius of House Ellarian and Lady Harper of House Ravakian's abode," he said stiffly.

She stilled. Ellarian. Ravakian. Both names of her *own* people, the people of her lord, and yet...

"They are my parents. I will remain there with you, to ensure your good conduct."

Interest gleamed within her. She was to be invited into the house of traitors? The opportunity was irresistible in itself, and to boot, she would leave this hateful dark hole behind. "What's the catch?"

"I beg your pardon?"

"What's the price? Do not think that by agreeing, I agree to sing for you. I will not betray my people or my master. Nay, I shall not utter a single word to you," she started vehemently.

Vasili held up his free hand. "I do not ask you to. It comes with no conditions attached. Merely that I wish to see you in greater comfort than this squalor, as a gesture of our good intentions."

Morrigan frowned at him. There was definitely a price. She just did not see it yet. There was *always* a price. It was what she would have done, after all – made it worth her while to as much disadvantage of the other party as possible. "All right," she said slowly and uncurled from the corner where she sat huddled on the paltry pallet, her legs tucked to her chest to conserve what warmth she could. Her arms shook as she propped herself on the edge.

He stepped forward and checked himself at her venomous glare. She did not need or want his help.

"Do you want to eat first?" *To give you the strength.* It was implied.

Morrigan contemplated for a second. *Yes, I do.* She did. But she warred with herself – she did not want to eat from *his* hand, damned be them all. However, if she were to starve herself, she would be weakened. Less prepared when the time came for revenge and escape.

Morrigan gritted her teeth. *I am proud, but I am no fool.*

Wordlessly and without looking, she reached up. The cool plate slid into her grasp.

Inside, she still fumed. *If he dares think me weak...* She had already promised a thousand times over to herself to rend him sinew from bone. He would pay. One day, he would pay.

She tugged the plate to her waiting lap. The hunk of bread was an inch thick. Soft and creamy crumbs. A hard, freshly baked crust gleaming against the light spilling in from outside, which at last she had become accustomed to. She sniffed it suspiciously, trying to feel, blindly without her magic, for any hint of poison or duplicity. Nothing. Nothing but the painful watering of her tongue.

Not caring whatever she looked like to him, Morrigan rammed it into her mouth and tore a huge chunk out. The softness of it made her gag for a second, the golden richness of the butter such an explosion upon her tongue – which was so used to nothingness, and ash, and grit – that it took her aback.

Valxiron take her, she hated him even more at that moment. That he got to eat *this*, whilst she and hers scratched a living from the harshness of the mountains.

She ate it all but for the toughest corner of the base. Her mouth was so dry, the moisture of the butter quickly gone. She tore into the apple instead. A sugary burst of juice crashed upon her tongue. She suppressed a groan of pleasure at it, despising herself for feeling anything other than hatred.

In silence, Vasili remained, watching her or not, she did not look. Told herself she did not care.

She ate the apple right down to the core. Her stomach hurt – but with the pressure of being full, not empty, now. It both energised her and made her lethargic. The last crust and the apple core remained on her plate. She tipped them off into the corner between her pallet and the wall.

"Hey!" said Vasili, stepping forward. He was close. Too close.

She retreated instinctively, baring her teeth.

He frowned at her but did not come closer. "Keep it on the plate. It'll go rotten down there. I can dispose of it elsewhere."

"They're for the rat," she said defensively, regretting the words as soon as they passed her lips. The little wraith of a creature deserved food – and her pity. But she did not want his.

His lips parted. And then, "It's for the what?"

"Rat," she ground out. Meeting his eyes with a fierce glare. Daring him to say a damned word more.

"Right," he said, ever so faintly. A pause. As if he were deliberating whether to ask further. He did not. "Well. If you're ready. We'll go."

She laughed and shoved to her feet, steeling her whole body so that he could not see how much she longed to tremble with exhaustion, malnutrition, and tamped-down fear.

"I've made sure there's fresh clothes for you, and a bath drawn up," Vasili said, eyeing her with more shrewd suspicion than his pleasant words gave clue to.

She did not answer and marched past him. Straight into the arms of the gaoler, who shackled her at wrist and ankle. The chains burned and buzzed with foreign magic that blanketed her senses, dizzying her once more.

Morrigan gritted her teeth. "I'm still a prisoner."

Vasili gave her a stare.

He was weak, but perhaps he was no fool either, damned be it.

For the first time, Morrigan wished she had womanly wiles. She had devoted her entire life to following Lord Valxiron's teachings, and her mother's, the oracle's, footsteps. Love was not for any of them, and lust was forbidden to her. She was as pure as she would be the day she was served up to the master's purpose in divine will.

At worst, at best, whichever it came to, she might be married off to a male of the cause's choosing to further their cause. As the last Mallory, it was something she expected – after all, she had to bear an heir to carry the family bloodline one day – but she had given no thought to it. To being a brood mare, sold off to the most advantageous party. Her attention had ever been in service to her master.

Yet she knew how men worked. Had seen it. Valxiron take her, she had seen how Grandmaster Ellarian the younger coveted her. A lip curled in disgust at the mere thought of him. Thank goodness her mother had better ideas than that. And yet it left her woefully, inadequately prepared to manipulate them all with the advantages of her sex.

She had watched, nonplussed, the affairs of men and women, as little as she had seen of them in the Order's hidden citadel over the years. She knew nothing of that. Not that she intended to whore herself out to anybody, for anything, to defile the vessel of the future oracle. No – but her body was a weapon, however she could wield it. Her attention bored into Vasili for so long, he shifted on his feet, his cheeks growing ruddy, and he looked away.

The tiniest smile curled upon her lips. One way or another, she would best him and be free. Who needed womanly wiles anyway? If she had no sorcery, all she needed was a blade.

CHAPTER 13

Wood elves crowded the forest now. As Lief and Aedon followed El'hari closer to the heart of the Queen's council, the numbers swelled, and the commander had to forge her way through. Everyone had heard. The wood-elves of Tir-na-Alathea, for the second time in a century – and already the first had been unprecedented – were going to war.

Lief had been immune from that, at the time stationed far to the northwest, away from Lune and the Pelenori border. There had not been the time to summon the whole realm to Pelenor's aid at Valxiron's rising several decades before. She was a young elf by any standards, but she had heard the tales. Absorbed them with sickly fascination, hanging onto every word. And been glad that it had seemed a world away from her painful inexperience and blessedly peaceful existence. It was someone else's life.

Now, would it be hers? That darkness teased her again. She did not want to face it anew, Queen's army or not.

El'hari forged into the heart of the stone arches. Aedon and Lief fell back and hovered in their shadows, neither keen to be seen by the formidable Queen who waited before Her throne. The other thrones were now occupied by a dozen lords and ladies of the forest realm, so still they could have been statues.

Waiting for their Queen's orders.

The last lord arrived, a tall elf with a cloak of ivy flowing down his back and a crown of oak sitting between two antlers. He inclined low before the Queen and then took his place.

At last, She stirred.

"Is your task complete?" She asked imperiously of the lords and ladies seated around Her.

"Aye, my Queen," they answered one by one.

"And did any of you find anything untoward in our realm that I must know of?" She glared around them, hawklike in Her scrutiny.

"Nay," came the answer, one by one, save for two. As Lief and Aedon listened, they understood. The Queen had sent them to hunt through their lands. Hunt they had. Those two had discovered minor aberrations of darkness in their lands – and dealt with them.

The Queen's nostrils flared, Her lips thinned with rage, as the two recounted in swift order the discovery of isolated pockets of dark sorcery in their lands close to Lune.

The seeing pool in the centre of the circle of thrones roiled and thrashed with the violence of their visions. Lief's stomach roiled and thrashed too. She was glad not to be able to see it from where they lurked, not quite sure whether they were welcome to listen.

The Queen said, "It is spreading."

No one dared answer Her.

"We must cut the head from the serpent," Solanaceae said, Her head turning slowly, those glittering amber eyes surveying those before Her. Today the flowers woven in Her cascade of hair were red orchids, gleaming and crimson, as though She wore a headdress of blood.

"Our lands are free from this blight, but this will not ever be so if we do not see it exterminated in entirety beyond our borders. It will return, time and again, picking at us like a predator hounding prey, growing stronger even as it weakens us. I will not see it."

Her last words rang across them all like a command, and the very air around them, filled with magic as it was, contracted with Her feeling. Skies and roots forbid that ire ever turned upon her, Lief thought. The air crackled with Her power, as though with the pressure of a building storm, ready to be unleashed to devastating effect.

"I will leave nothing unturned. This time, we shall be sure of Valxiron's doom and the obliteration of his ilk, and I shall see it done myself. We shall depart Tir-na-Alathea for the Silent Sisters after a Singing at our full strength."

A Singing! A thrill rushed through Lief, dangerous and alluring. The Queen meant to invoke the legendary magic of their race and the land to strengthen Her people for what was to come. A bold measure indeed.

"There, we will destroy the anchor that Valxiron placed there and the darkness that dared enter our lands from it. Onwards we will go to Tournai, and I will see that they aid us."

Lief shared a glance with Aedon. Solanaceae was determined to end the scourge of Valxiron, though they had no truly known way to do so. By the way the Queen spoke, She did not intend to leave the Pelenori much choice in the matter – and woe betide anyone who stepped in Her way.

CHAPTER 14

A part of Aedon wanted nothing more than to remain in the now cleansed forest with Lief, in that haven away from the darkness that battered the outside world. But he knew that, Queen's will aside, he could not do so in good conscience.

"We must go too," he said unhappily to Lief as they returned to the treehouse, breaking the stunned silence between them. He had felt her tumultuous emotions at the summit, leaking from her, telling him, without a word spoken between them, her mixed feelings of the Singing and the call to war for a nation famed for its lack of intervention in most worldly matters.

"Yes. Back to the Silent Sisters and then to Tournai?"

Aedon's mood lifted slightly. "Aye. My old home." The word was strange upon his tongue. It had been so very long since he had called any place home, really. Even the woodland realm had been nothing more than a prison.

As they climbed to the treetops, each step now felt

dogged by the watchful wait of the change to come. Gone was any sense of rest and healing.

Back into the fray we charge.

Later that day, El'hari caught them once more. They had spent the afternoon idling upon the deck, lapping up the warm sunshine and birdsong of the forest around them. Taking what rest they could before it all changed once more.

"Twice in our lifetimes," she said, halting beside them without further greeting. "*Twice* in our lifetimes, and ordinarily unheard of. I cannot believe She will muster us all."

"You do not think it necessary?" Aedon glanced up at her. Of all the wood elves, they two knew well enough what they faced. He did not think the Queen had set upon a disproportionate response.

El'hari huffed. "Of course I do. I wish it were not, though."

"I wish to come. I have to see this done."

El'hari raised an eyebrow. "You may not be one of us – not truly, Aedon – but you are coming regardless of what you will. Do you not realise? Until we have the full might of the Winged Kingsguard and their dragon fire, you may be our best defence – and offense, I might add – against the darkness ahead. The Queen will have you with us. She does not truly know how to defeat this darkness, but your fire aided in Lune, and so it will aid Her now, if She calls for it."

Aedon sighed. "I had hoped to accompany you of my free will. I suppose what is the difference, if I had planned to do so anyway. Free or not."

"There is a large difference, as you well know," Lief said hotly, scowling, though she did not direct her anger at El'hari. They were all pawns of the Queen, after all.

El'hari glanced at her, expression impassive, for a moment, before she spoke to Aedon. "You're to travel with Her personal guard, such is your value to Her. It is a great honour. I am sure you are aware. Lief, you will be with Kinear's *cinq* once more, since you have no fixed company at present."

Lief's warm skin paled, and Aedon could practically imagine how her stomach would flip at that news.

"We must travel together."

El'hari snorted reflexively. "I beg your pardon?"

"She is my guard. My translator. My—"

"The Queen's word is final, and my decision on Lief's place. Be grateful that she comes at all. I did not have to include her. I respect you enough for that, Aedon, but do not push it. I am my Queen's commander before I am your friend."

Aedon met El'hari's eyes. Firm. Unwavering. He inclined his head. "Thank you." She had not needed to include Lief at all. They would find a way, somehow. At least, as El'hari said, they would not be entirely separated if Lief were to travel too.

"The Queen has sent an envoy to Tournai to warn them of our coming and our stop along the way. I suggest you make yourself ready, though I suspect that will not be difficult." After all, they had nothing. "The Singing will commence tomorrow evening and continue until dawn. After that, I suspect the Queen will be away early. She does not wish to tarry where *He* is concerned. Be ready. I may come for you sooner than planned."

Apprehension hooked itself in under Aedon's skin. Entirely banishing whatever was left of the restful feeling that had been tenuously building.

"I'll take my leave." El'hari tapped a hand on the railing, her own agitation clear. "There is much to do. Seeing as our people's talent is no great secret from you anymore, Aedon, I'll no doubt see you *both* at the Singing." She left.

Aedon met Lief's eyes. For a long moment, they said nothing.

"Never a moment's peace, eh?" Aedon said quietly, but even he could not bring himself to smile, nor feel any mirth at the sentiment.

Lief reached across the table between them. Aedon slipped his hand into hers. Her silent warmth was comforting, at least.

"I had hoped to choose my own path henceforth, but it seems the Queen still has first say in my movements and my freedom." It left him despondent. Had it been a gift, or merely a trick of the Queen?

"Still, though. You get to leave Tir-na-Alathea, truly, for the first time in so long. That is a good thing, no?" Lief replied.

He smiled at her, though it was weak and did not reach his eyes. She always found a way, through anything that faced her. Of course, she would try to find a way through this.

"I suppose so." That was a significant moment. He shifted in his seat.

Lief waited.

"It scares me, if I'm honest." It thrilled him, too, to a small degree – a carefully tended flame that he neither dared to stoke nor extinguish. He would leave this realm – be freer than he had yet been – and still, he feared it.

"Why?" Lief said softly.

Aedon swallowed past a lump in his throat. It was something he did not want to put into words, if he were honest. And so, he spoke into her mind instead.

"What will the world outside be like? Will it be as I remember, or will it have left me behind – changed beyond recognition? What about the people I knew and cared for? What of them?"

He did not dare to put any voice to his darkest fears. *Will they remember me? Are they still amongst the living?*

There were so few left whom he cared for, and they had existed as fully fleshed spectres in his mind, fading slowly over the years into shades of their living selves, but still, he could not bear to lose whatever might be left of them. Sometimes, it was best to remember people as they had been, after all. Sometimes, the reality was too painful.

"Oh," Lief sighed. She reached her other hand across the table to clasp his. "I do not know what to say. Look how well that turned out for me; look what remains of Lune now, and all those I knew and cared for," she said, a keen note of hurt betraying her own pain. "I do not think the same will be true for you. I will be there for you as you were for me. Together, we shall see the truth of the present – whatever that is."

"Thank you," Aedon murmured. "I do not know what I did to deserve you."

Lief glanced down, her cheeks flushing.

"What of you, in any case? Are you happy with El'hari's

decision? You do not have to come. If you would rather not face any of it, I support you remaining he—"

"No," Lief said quickly, her head snapping up once more to fix him in a burning stare. "No. I will not be left behind whilst my people need me. Whilst *you* need me."

Aedon stood, their hands falling apart, and he moved around the table to kneel before her instead, where he recaptured her hands in his. "Are you certain?"

"Yes," Lief said softly. She furrowed her brows. "Do you remember what you said? About obligation, and doing things because they were expected of us, or habit, or duty, rather than following what was in our hearts? It remained with me. I have scarcely been able to dismiss it, and what passed at Lune makes me all the more certain.

"We are free, but always within the confines of something. Perhaps the only freedom we have is some choice, but I will take that. I wish to choose my own path. I would follow you to Tournai, and wherever beyond, El'hari or not."

There. That fire in her gaze had returned. Some of the colour of her spirit, knocked and shaken by what had passed at Lune, starting to breathe once more.

"I want to see more of Altarea than Tir-na-Alathea. Pelenor, and whatever lies beyond. I know that now. I cannot do that from within the forest, can I?"

Aedon smiled. "No. I suppose not. I think you can't bear to part with me."

Lief smiled. The first time he had seen a true twinkle in her eye for weeks. "I can hardly admit to that. You would be incorrigible, thief." What had once been a slur against him, she now used with affectionate, flirtatious warmth.

Aedon stood, drawing her up with him and circling his

arms around her waist. "Who says I want to put up with you and your stubbornness, wood elf?"

Lief grinned wickedly at him, and it made his heart soar to see after how much of a shell of her former vivacious self she had been. "You keep returning."

Aedon chuckled throatily and pressed his lips to her, softly, tenderly, waiting for permission.

She gave it, tipping her head back and twining her hand into the fabric of his tunic. "You're the worst."

"You cannot resist."

Neither of them could. He had kept a respectful distance from her, not pressing any intimacy between them, knowing she needed time to heal, though he had craved it. Perhaps she had craved it too, by the way she tugged him to that treetop nest. He let her. Feeling lighter for knowing that, at least for a while, war and strife and Queen's commands be damned, they would not be parted.

They would leave the living forest – together, he hoped.

CHAPTER 15

You catch more flies with honey than vinegar, Vasili's mother had once told him as a young boy when he had fallen out with a childhood friend. Vasili had punched him in explosive frustration, not possessing yet the emotional tools to choose a different – better – path.

Vasili wondered if the same would be true for Morrigan. She bucked all other rules, after all.

He led her up through the levels of the castle straight into a waiting carriage. It was a small mercy, he figured. Morrigan was filthy and battle stained, pungently ripe after a night in the cells following their travels, and, shackled as she was, he had no desire to further humiliate and punish her by walking her through the streets in that state for all to see.

Inside the small carriage, the atmosphere could be carved with a knife, thick and brittle that it was. Morrigan sat perfectly rigid upon the wooden board seat, her shackled ankles together, their knees almost bumping. Her bound hands rested upon her lap, her fingers lost into clenching fists that made her knuckles yet paler upon her already alabaster skin.

She did not speak, her lips a thin line pressed together. She refused to meet his open, searching gaze. Instead, she sat, her head turned slightly to one side, staring out of the small, slit-like window, which offered a small light into the dark interior.

He could see the intensity in Morrigan's stare as she drank it all in. He would have done the same, he supposed. Soaked in whatever he could of the tapestry of enemy life around them. He hoped what she saw would further convince her, even if she did not yet realise it, of the life that awaited her outside the Order, if she so chose.

How foreign it must seem to her, he wondered. Was she used to bustling streets filled with colour, noise, and life? A mostly content and peaceful city, going about its daily business in collective harmony?

In that mountain camp, life had been harsh, close to starvation and peril, with only darkness to guide. A life he pitied her for, having experienced it so briefly. He could hardly imagine if he had had to grow up there, how bleak his own outlook on life would be.

Skies above, I hope I am not a fool for pushing this.

It could easily go so wrong. Right now, she would give him no grace or time. He had no doubt that if he called for her power to be unleashed and armed her, she would gut him, destroy everything within reach, and flee.

He could hardly blame her for that, he supposed, on the basis of her life and what had passed between them, but releasing her from behind tangible bars felt altogether like releasing a wild, caged beast. Unlocking the cage. And opening it a crack – more than enough for it to escape. And yet he had to if he were to stand a chance of turning her. Leading her away from that darkness and towards the light.

He would not be able to convince her if he kept her caged.

As his father had said when he had proposed the idea, "You cannot earn a beast's trust if you whip it."

Speaking of beasts... Vasili frowned. *The rat. She left food for a rat?* She puzzled him more and more. She would gut him without a second thought, but she spared a crumb, starving though she probably was, for a mere rat.

Vasili remembered their encounter with the mountain lion that fateful day Morrigan had taken him to the dragon pits in the mountain valley to feed the hideous, twisted, and stunted beasts within. Upon the path had appeared a huge mountain lion, standing higher than Morrigan on the inclined ground and ready to pounce.

It had been drawn by the scent of the meat, Vasili guessed. Its attention had fixed on Morrigan. She had frozen, her black dress utterly still against the crisp, white snow. The beast had crouched onto its haunches, ready to leap at her, its terrible jaws wide and waiting to snap her tiny neck.

Neither Vasili nor Morrigan was armed – save with sorcery. Vasili had raced forward on instinct, but before he could gain more than three steps, the beast had sprung. Morrigan had moved quicker, as fluid as water. There had been a blinding light, a sizzle, and a yelp.

The beast had tumbled to the floor, landing on a scramble of paws, before it shot off into the brush, leaping up the mountain on powerful, muscular legs and into the sparse tree cover above them. Morrigan, her cheeks balled with red and her eyes flashing with fury, stood ready and waiting – but the beast did not return. Only the scent of singed fur lingered.

She had scared it but not killed it. Vasili had thought that interesting at the time, that she would kill an animal for ritual sacrifice, or kill a man or an elf without blinking, but not needlessly an innocent creature in the wild.

She had turned upon him then, lashing out with her vicious tongue, as though he had seen beyond a chink in her flawless armour and she could not abide it. She would show him no ounce of humanity, but to a creature, she was not entirely beyond warmth and compassion? She made no sense.

The carriage soon ground to a halt, for it was not far to Vasili's parents' townhouse, and he helped her down. The pair of them were hidden from view of the street by the side of the carriage, parked close to the gate, and the bodies of the Kingsguard who stood in formation around them. They would stay to guard the house, handpicked by Elyvia in haste at the High Council's change of plans for their prisoner. House arrest was a different beast to a secure cell.

Elyvia arrived moments later upon horseback, out of breath and her cheeks as red as her cloak. She said nothing, nodding a greeting at Vasili as he led Morrigan up the steps and through the front door. Elyvia would ensure the house was sufficiently warded against any outside threat – and Morrigan. Vasili held the door open for Morrigan. She uttered no thanks. Inside, his mother awaited.

To him, Harper had always seemed soft, motherly. So rarely had he seen the hard grit inside that served her in the High Council. Now, he saw it in the unreadable expression she wore upon seeing Morrigan, which settled into calculated assessment, and in the power of her posture, standing tall in her domain. He knew, mother or not, she would brook no dissent, least of all in her own home.

"Welcome, Lady Morrigan," Harper said, inclining her head. "I am Lady Harper of House Ravakian, and it is a pleasure to make your acquaintance." She paused, but Morrigan did not reply, glaring at Harper as though Morrigan were a dog and Harper her master, ready to beat her.

Harper pursed her lips before she continued. "I acknowledge you have not the usual guest privileges, but whatever comforts we have are extended to you under the terms of your custody. You will have a private bedroom and bathroom, and one of our servants will attend to your needs, should you have any.

"You have fresh clothes and a bath drawn upstairs. We eat thrice per day, and you will join us for each meal. Guards will accompany you wherever you go, save to the latrine, where you may have privacy. Our home is warded inside and out. You are not permitted your magic, nor any weapon here. We expect that you respect your custody and bring no harm to anyone here lest you be returned to your cell in the castle. Do I make myself clear?" Harper's voice rang out, hard and unyielding.

Morrigan remained silent.

"Do I make myself clear?" Again, this time deadly and quiet.

Morrigan gave the smallest nod she could.

"Good. Go, wash. It will soon be lunchtime. And you, son." Harper allowed the flicker of a smile to creep in before her face smoothed once more into impassive authority.

"I'll show you to your room," Vasili muttered. He led Morrigan up the stairs onto a landing. "These are my rooms." He gestured to the left, and then the right. "And these are yours. If you wish to gut me, you'll know where to find me."

He had purposefully had Morrigan placed in the rooms opposite his own. He would sleep sounder knowing she was close – that perhaps he would hear if she decided to cause a fuss. Perhaps he wouldn't hear anything. She was as silent as any assassin, he would bet. As she glanced between the two doors, he wondered if she was thinking the same thing.

"Go. Wash. Dress. It will be time to eat a proper meal, and then you can rest."

CHAPTER 16

Two elven Kingsguard soldiers followed Morrigan into the bedroom. She glared at them, irritated that they would dog her presence. Beneath their helms, they remained silent, eyes glittering as they watched her.

Morrigan turned back to the room. Under her booted feet, smooth, polished, dark wood floored the room. So even compared to the rough stone she was used to. High windows allowed in bountiful light, even of the pale and feeble winter variety, bolstered by the golden faelights in elaborate wrought sconces on the walls.

More than that, even though there was no open fire, it was so pleasantly *warm*, and that was something she had never found in the wind and chill-chased halls of that underground fortress, not even in a pile of paltry old furs in her pallet each night. The chill never left, but here...she began to tingle as the warmth reached into her core. Here, she would not sleep on a pallet with worn and patched furs, but in a *bed*, a real bed, piled high with soft, sumptuous covers and pillows in royal blue that invited her into their embrace.

Morrigan gritted her teeth and strode to the bathroom.

"Keep the door open, please," a guard reminded her.

She ignored them and slammed it. Quickly searching. A small window. She tried the sash. It did not budge. She cursed silently, stepping back as the guard threw open the door behind her.

"Door. Open." The command came through gritted teeth. She heard him step back, to give her some semblance of dignity and privacy, perhaps.

She did not acknowledge it. Her eyes dropped to the bathtub. No dented metal tub here, or old barrel with the top sawn off, filled with ice-cold water and the promise of a brisk bath. Moist heat rose from the white ceramic, filled with white foam.

Topped with white foam, she corrected, as she slid a hand in, through the softness of those bubbles and into deliciously hot water beneath. Hanging over the edge of the bath was a small washcloth. It was too inviting. The feeling of dirtiness crawled over her, deep in every nook and crevice, and penance be damned, she wanted to be clean. She didn't have to enjoy the heat, or the rose-tinted smell of the strange foam, but she was permitted to be *clean*, she told herself.

She hated it. Valxiron take her, she hated it. She had to. Damned would she be if she enjoyed any of it. How was it fair that these traitors deserved so much comfort when she had lived in squalor her entire life?

Her penance, her suffering, was a badge of honour, and it proved her devotion to her lord, which would serve her in his reign, but even so, it scalded her with rage to know that traitors and those who did not follow his teachings were rewarded thusly. She would make them all suffer the more to make up for it.

Before she could think too much of it, and with no shame or modesty for the guards behind her, she stripped and climbed into the tub, hissing with delight and pain as the hot water scalded her. Morrigan sank in determinedly, relishing in that pain – especially in the still half-raw wounds of her last self-flagellation upon her body. Her eyes closed in bliss for a moment, swept away by it, before she sat bolt upright, gritting her teeth against any pleasing sensation.

She made it a brisk wash, scrubbing herself with the washcloth until her skin felt sore with it and was pleasingly red when she stood to get out. Long, sopping wet, raven locks trailed across her shoulders and chest, down her back, as it clung to her. The scent of rose was overwhelmingly foreign to her. *Sickly and cloying*, she told herself. *Not sweet and perfumed.* A necessity of bathing, not a luxury. She did not want it. Had not asked for it. *That's what matters*, she stubbornly insisted, though to whom, she had no idea.

A folded towel that was so soft it had her gritting her teeth and cursing them all anew awaited her. She hurriedly scrubbed herself dry, as roughly as she could, and strode to the bedroom, ignoring the hurried motion of the guards, who spun around to give her privacy, one sputtering with embarrassment.

That elicited a wicked grin from Morrigan. She had no shame about her body – it was a weapon, a tool to be used, not an object of desire. That was their accursed weakness, not hers.

On a chair in the corner lay a folded pile of clothes. *Strange.* She had expected a dress at the very least, a hateful contraption of boning and lace, frills and sickening femininity. Instead...men's clothing. She held it up, frowning. A plain tunic of blue so dark it was almost black, a surcoat to match with golden embroidery and a sheen upon the fabric catching the light, plus some more coarsely woven trousers.

She wondered whom it belonged to. Still, it was practical. All the better if she had to fight her way out. That always remained a possibility, no matter that for now, she had decided to watch and wait, gather information, and determine weaknesses she could exploit.

She quickly slipped on the clothes and then donned her scarred boots once more. In contrast to the clean clothes, they were dirty and old, but they were hers, at least. Her own soiled garments had disappeared. With suspicion, she wondered where. They were of no value to her, but even so, she wanted them back. If nothing else, they were hers. The one reminder tying her to her identity and her home. Now, aside from her boots, she truly had nothing.

She trailed over to the dressing table, where a tarnished silver brush lay. Painstakingly, she combed out her hair, staring at herself in the oval mirror there. Blazing defiance and courage into her own grey eyes. Finding strength and purpose in the crescent scars that marred each cheek and marked her as the oracle's heir and Valxiron's chosen one. With deft hands, she braided her long hair into a practical plait, tying it off with a simple black tie, and shoved it over her shoulder.

"I'm ready." She stood.

In silence, her guards escorted her downstairs to eat. Her

guard was already lowering, she realised. She shoved it back up. It was still so foreign to be without the sense of magic, as though she had lost a sense in its own right, one of such crucial significance, its absence was a yawning void. It left her feeling perilously exposed and vulnerable, and she despised the feeling.

Her hand went to her hip unconsciously, but of course, there was no weapon there to reach for. Without blade or magic – forget clothing, *that* was as close to feeling naked as she could be.

A bright dining room with twin chandeliers dangling from the wood-panelled ceiling awaited her. A long table, with three settings at one end, cosily close, and Vasili and Lady Harper awaiting her. Harper took the head of her table, Vasili seated to the right of her. A spare setting sat to Harper's left, across from Vasili.

She bristled at the sight of them, nerves settling in her belly, and held herself taller, raising her chin.

CHAPTER 17

"Welcome Lady Morrigan. I trust your bath and your clothes were to your satisfaction." A faint smile curled Lady Harper's lips as though she knew she would not receive a polite reply, if she received any at all.

Morrigan followed a guard to the chair, sitting in it and biting back a curse when he tucked her in. She shot him a venomous glare.

"'Thank you' are the words you're searching for." Lady Harper glared at her. "You may not like us, and you may not wish to be here, but I expect your manners nonetheless whilst you reside under my roof, Lady Morrigan."

Her stare bored into Morrigan, who glared defiantly back.

Vasili squirmed, and his chair creaked. "May we eat, Mother?"

Harper pursed her lips, but as she turned to her son, her entire face softened with love. Morrigan watched that transformation with fascination. Never had her own mother regarded her with such tenderness. "Of course. I do not wish to keep you from your duties."

It spiked such rage within her that she spoke without thinking. "You are a disgrace to the Ravakian name," Morrigan hissed.

Ravakian. A name of old to be feared and revered in Valxiron's Order circles. The name so many of his grandmasters had borne. A name equal in standing to Mallory. Indeed, their houses had intermarried at times to keep the bloodlines pure. And now, all of those ancestors were reduced to this shadow of their former glory in this female.

Harper glanced up at her, not ceasing to butter her roll, oozing bored indifference. "Your table manners are ghastly. I would expect better from a Mallory. Why, you have worse etiquette than I, and I was raised in a hovel with no inclination as to my heritage."

Morrigan frowned. "What?"

"'I beg your pardon'," Harper corrected. "You heard me correctly. I grew up alone, orphaned, far from here, in lands without magic, fending for myself for the most part. This life was not something I knew of or could even imagine." She gestured around at the fine townhouse.

Morrigan gaped.

"Eat," Harper commanded and turned to the dish placed before her by a servant over her shoulder. Dishes appeared at Vasili's place next, and then her own. Unlike them, she had a spoon. No knife. No fork. It was no accident. Still, it irritated her. She had been planning to steal some of the cutlery. It would be better than nothing as a makeshift weapon.

Morrigan was still suspicious of poison or drugs, but she

was still hungry, and her raging stomach rumbled in dissent at her hesitation. They could have poisoned her already – but they had not. They had taken her weapons. They had smothered her magic.

All she had left was the strength of her own physical form, and for that, she needed *sustenance.* That convinced her enough to pick up her spoon. Silver and gleaming, not like the old, mismatched, and tarnished things they had eaten with in the mountain fortress.

These people had no rations in *their* city, Morrigan deduced, and she despised them for that. Upon the setting before her was a bowl of hot soup, thick and creamy, with a swirl of white and a leafy garnish in the centre. A slice of artisanal bread crusted with poppy seeds and smeared with golden butter waited on a side plate. A goblet stood at arm's reach, filled with wine – not even watered down.

Morrigan hated it all too. Hated the way the crust broke against her tongue. Hated the rich tang of the wine. Hated the way the pepper and tomato soup burst a flavour so good it *hurt* in her mouth. It warmed all the way down her throat, pooling heat in the core of her belly.

Still, she ate it all, wiping the crust of the bread around the soup bowl, not caring at Harper's raised eyebrow for her lack of etiquette. Etiquette be damned. She was starving. She had been starving for over two decades, and she would not turn down the chance to become strong now. Morrigan consumed every last morsel and drained every drop from the goblet.

"Thank you," she ground out in a reluctant mutter.

Harper dipped her head graciously. "I shall leave you."

She glanced meaningfully at Vasili, though what passed between them, Morrigan did not understand.

When she was gone, Vasili pushed his chair out. "Come on. Let me show you the garden. It's not large, and it's not particularly alive in winter, but you may use it for some fresh air and some solace."

Intrigued, Morrigan followed him in silence. He led her out of the dining room, along a lengthy hallway lined with paintings and with weapons on the wall. Twin knives. A great axe. A sword with a rune-marked blade. Old, but serviceable. All that she would need to arm herself, in any case.

Vasili turned to her as she glanced up at them, examining them. She glared at him furiously as her cheeks warmed.

"Don't even think about it," he said lightly. "This way."

She followed him through a wooden door into a glass-roofed porch. He stopped to snag a couple of cloaks from hooks there. He passed one to her. Fittingly black, and lined on the neck with some dark fur. She wrapped it around herself, fingers sinking into the soft wool and stroking the neckline as she clasped it.

In the depths of winter, it would be helpful for her escape. Morrigan did not intend to remain a guest of Pelenor for any length of time.

Then he opened the glass-paned door, and a whoosh of frigid air blasted in. She braced against it and dove outside, grateful for what felt like the first even half-free breath of air she had drawn in a while. In the warmth, her hair had partially dried, but against the base of her scalp, the rush of cold had her shivering in seconds.

Still, she welcomed it, taking another gulp and turning her face to the skies to feel the snow pepper her cheeks with tiny, iced kisses. The garden was small, like he had said, and devoid of colour in the late season. High walls enclosed it on all sides, with gardens to the left and right and a row of townhouses before and behind. No gates. No way out. No *easy* one, in any case.

"Was the weather often like this where you grew up?" He drew beside her.

She squinted at him, full of suspicion. Vasili's face was blank, clear of emotion, but that did not mean he had no ulterior motive.

"You grew up there – in the mountains, no?"

"Yes," she said slowly. "It was hot in the summer. Baking and dry. The winters are harsh there." *As you saw. Our people have little or nothing.* "We scraped a living. Our cause keeps us strong." She lifted her chin. *Why are you telling him this?* She berated herself.

"I see. That sounds…challenging."

"We have no choice." Her reply was as brittle as the icicles shearing from the gutters far above. "*Your* people persecute us. You force us to eke out our existences on the fringes."

He frowned at her, angling his body towards her. "*Your* people follow evil teachings."

Morrigan bared her teeth at him. "I will not waste my breath trying to educate you. You're an imbecile and a traitor. I know the truth."

"You think you do," he retorted.

"And you? You are happy with your truth?" she demanded. With a twist of satisfaction, she saw the quickly hidden uncertainty flash across him. She grinned darkly. "Don't speak to me from your high pedestal. I am the oracle's daughter. I have seen things you cannot imagine. One day, I will be the truth of our cause."

"What does that mean?" He fixed her in a stare, and she could see the turbulence raging within him. It gave her such satisfaction to know she could unsettle him so, even as a prisoner in his care.

"It means that one day, I shall be the torchbearer for our crusade. I will lead the charge. I will speak for our lord and master. And I will bring about his ascension, should my mother fail to live up to the task."

Revulsion curled his lip against her then. "You are mad. Utterly mad."

She laughed in his face.

"Have you ever even stopped to consider what *you* think, Morrigan?" he snapped at her, taking a step towards her so they stood a foot apart, and she was ensnared in his violet eyes. "Hmm? Have you ever stopped to consider that you have been groomed your whole life to think what others want and need you to think? Have you ever thought that just *maybe* the world view you have isn't shared by the vast majority of people and that maybe you're all *wrong*?"

"Have you?" she said slyly back, with no outward inclination that his words had slipped between the cracks of her armour to take insidious root, no matter how much she railed against them.

Vasili fell back half a step, and his fist clenched at his side. It was quickly hidden in the rippling fold of his cloak settling around him, but she had seen it. "Skies above, you're impossible. I'm trying to help you. When will you see that?"

"I don't need your help," Morrigan said, her words sharp.

Vasili huffed with disgust and shook his head. "I bought you a reprieve, Morrigan, but it's only good if you use it. This, all of this," he gestured around them at the garden, the house, "this semblance of freedom. Even that will vanish if you're too pig-headed to bend instead of break. I cannot shield you from any of it. I doubt your rat friend will be able to help you then."

She had no answer, save to bloom with indignation.

He cut in before she could speak. "I tire of your company. You have the freedom of this garden, our sitting room, or your bedroom. I suggest you use your time wisely." Without a further word, he clenched his jaw and swept past her. The glass door slammed, rattling in its frame.

Only silence remained, dampened by the falling snow. It had already left a dusting on her shoulders and soaked into her still damp hair. Morrigan's chest constricted, and she pushed away the uncomfortable feeling settling within her. *Freedom!* She whirled. And stopped dead.

Unheard by her, two guards had followed her and Vasili out. They now remained, watching her, stony-faced.

Morrigan suppressed a curse. She eyed the dagger peeking through the folds of the left guard's cloak. That was all she needed. Just a blade of any kind.

Vasili seethed as he left. Skies above, she infuriated him. Even when presented with an alternate version of reality that she could see, experience, *live*, right before her, she chose to deny it.

The helplessness of it overwhelmed him for a second, and he braced against the panelled wall of the hallway. *Can I do this?* Doubt flooded through him, and the tide of it was stronger than he could swim against. He closed his eyes against it, for what little good it did.

He had wanted to prove that she was not beyond redemption – that no one was. And yet, she would spite herself to deny him that. To deny herself a better life.

Maybe you're not up to the task. You're already failing.

Vasili growled and punched the wall. He spat out a choice curse and nursed his stinging fist – it brought no solace.

He ought to turn back. Try again.

For a moment, he paused, half turned back to that glass door. And then, with another growl, this one of annoyance – at her, at him, at the whole damned situation – he stormed upstairs.

Vasili could not face her again. Not when she had gotten so cleanly and easily under his skin. He needed to lick his wounds first. But deep down, he knew he could not give up on her. Not for her sake, and not for his.

CHAPTER 18

The entire forest of Emuir held its breath, as though in anticipation of the great eruption of power that was to come from the Singing that night. Dusk loomed, late and slow, and with it built the tides of magic that would wash through the forest. In small pockets, the Singing had started, crescendoing as the numbers swelled.

That day had also brought movement through the forest of a different sort – elves massing for the exodus to come and the conflict after that. A steady stream of bodies all wearing the deep green tunics of Emuir's guard and Tir-na-Alathea's warriors from further afield.

Emuir's collective Singing would commence as the sun slipped beyond the horizon, feeding the last of the sun's power into the magic that would be wrought before the new dawn. The sun had left the forest floor, casting it into deep, dappled shade. Not the shadows of darkness as had pooled at Lune, hiding that terrible blight, but warming, inviting, and soft. The dusk chorus of birds was in full crescendo, a concert in the treetops as Lief and Aedon prepared to don their borrowed outfits. El'hari had been kind enough to lend them both something more formal, sending one of her elves up to the treehouse with two boxes of carefully folded clothes wrapped in tissue paper so thin it disintegrated as they unfolded the packages on the balcony table.

Lief gasped. The fine fabric shushed as it slithered over itself, unfolding in her hands as she held the dress up from the shoulder pieces.

Ornate copper designs of a peony bloom surrounded by vines and leaves, one for each shoulder, and hanging from them, a sheet of fine, diaphanous fabric of sunrise and rose, so fine that it was practically gossamer. By practice, wood elves were hardly prudes, and yet for an elf more comfortable in the close-fitting, practical wear of her ranger's duty, it felt altogether rather more than she was comfortable to bear.

"I cannot wear this," she whispered, half mortified, half intimidated by the garment before her.

Never had she seen something of its ilk – except for adorning the ladies of the forest or the Queen herself.

"Of course you can," Aedon said lightly. "I should like to see you in something less serious – and grimy – for a change."

She shot him a look, but his snide humour had the intended effect, distracting her from the thought of wearing that before everyone. It was a Singing, after all. There was no more important time to a wood elf. It was her duty to dress in the finest she had – the finest that El'hari could lend her – to show the Singing the honour it deserved.

Lief gazed closer. Tiny jewels like fragments of water in a spider's web caught the light, glittering and shimmering from where they nestled, scattered throughout the dress. She held it to her figure cautiously. Ethereal vines in dusky pinks and sunrise colours chased up the garment, flowering off into ghostly blooms, half there and half not as the fabric shimmered under her gaze.

Perhaps it would be a tad long, especially if she were to be barefoot, as the Singing demanded. The elves rooted themselves in the earth, connecting as one to it. She would manage, somehow. She had repaired enough holes in her uniforms over the years to be at least half capable with a needle and thread, but Lief dared not touch this wondrous garment to see if she could hem it.

Aedon changed in the treehouse. She had barely even noticed his outfit, so entrancing was hers, and she looked up as he emerged. A lump formed in her throat. She had seen him in all manner of garb, and all frightful states, but never like that. Never dressed to perfection.

Forest green trousers hugged strong calves and thighs, and he wore a matching sleeveless, form-fitting top with pale vines chasing over it and gold embellishments on the buttons. He had slicked back his tousled, shaggy hair into something resembling order, which made him look like half a stranger, for she had hardly seen him without wild, unruly hair. He was entirely opposed to the grubby, thin, wasted prisoner she had initially encountered, now strong, full of vitality, and brimming with magic.

As she drew closer, Lief could see the oak tree that spread across his chest, bark and leaf details picked out in delicate embroidery, golden acorns hanging, and roots delving down past his navel. She rested a hand upon his chest, utterly speechless, her fingers teasing at one of the buttons. They were shaped like oak leaves cupping acorns, she could now see, each as tiny as her fingernail and intricately patterned.

Lief shook her head. Her finger traced the form of an owl taking flight from the oak. A lump in her throat hardened. El'hari had outdone herself for generosity. They did not deserve anything even half so fine.

He grinned, that familiar twinkle in his eye, and did a mocking twirl. "What do you think?"

She laughed. "You don't scrub up bad, my thief."

Aedon smiled at that. *My* thief, she had said. "El'hari honours us greatly. Truth be told, I thought we'd have to wear whatever shreds of clothing we had that we could patch together."

Lief wrinkled her nose. "I would sooner burn some of them than wear them." They still had some scraps of soiled clothing that had ventured underneath the nest-like bed in the treehouse. They would have to fish out and dispose of the unsalvageable garments.

"Indeed. Well, this does beat a soldier's uniform. I'll give it that. I'll go put my boots on and wait for you to change."

"No!" she said, tugging him back. "You can't. It's not permitted."

Aedon frowned down at her.

"Perhaps for you it might be different, but for us, the strength of our magic is aided during the Singing because we stand upon the very earth barefoot. Our magic connects directly to the dirt, roots, and life around us more viscerally."

Lief harrumphed.

"It's hard to explain. But perhaps, even though you won't be singing, you might be able to *feel* what I mean. What?"

she said, when Aedon did not answer and instead gazed at her with such tender thoughtfulness.

Aedon's lips twitched, a smile stretching across them. "I was just thinking…" He leaned in closer so his breath tickled her ear.

Her breath caught.

"…that you are most adorable when you wrinkle your nose like that, when you're mildly annoyed about something."

He kissed her ear, trailing down it to her neck, each press of his soft lips lighting a trail of fire across her skin. She did not know whether it was the impending Singing enriching the very air with magic and sensation or that she felt more herself than she had done for weeks now, but Lief could not help leaning into that contact.

"Don't," she warned. "Or I might be undoing your work and undressing you."

Aedon chuckled as he kissed along her jaw, his hands tracing down her hips. He tugged. "I won't say no."

Lief groaned. *Skies above and roots below, he is incorrigible.* She opened her mouth, about to acquiesce, when a deep, sonorous *boom* rang through the forest.

Her entire body reacted to it. Every hair on her body rose, and her very essence shivered with the raw power of that.

"What was that?" Aedon murmured, frozen.

"The Singing. It will begin soon."

Aedon groaned and pulled away. "Then I suppose I must let you change. Go on," he said, pursing his lips.

Lief laughed. "I'll be quick. And there's always after," she said, mischief dancing in her eyes.

Lief slipped inside the nest, her heart pounding and her cheeks warm. *Skies above and roots below, he's irresistible.* It was nice, she reflected. Nice to feel such warmth and care for someone else – someone other than herself – after so long alone.

She did not turn her thoughts away from Finarvon when his spectre appeared in her mind. That rushing torrent of hurt and loss already faded from its zenith, and for that, she was most glad. Tonight, whatever had passed between them, she would think of his memory as she Sang with the others – him and all who had given their lives in service of the living forest. The Singing was a time of renewal, of growth, and of life, but such things could not be done without all those who had come before.

Lief slipped out of her tunic and breeches and combed through her hair quickly, deftly sectioning and twisting it at her temple and pinning it at the back of her head so her hair was half up and half down – out of her eyes, so it did not annoy her – whilst the rest fell in natural waves of coppery fire down her back.

Gingerly, she slipped the dress on, stepping into it and shimmying into the delicate fabric, convinced that at any moment, she would hear a frightful tear. Yet, without incident, it was soon on. The copper peony blossoms rested naturally in the hollow between her collarbone and her shoulder. A strip of fabric fell across each breast, leaving a deep hollow right to her navel between them. The back matched, two strips falling, leaving most of her back bare in the centre. Gathered at her hips, then the dress tumbled in ethereal waves to the floor, where it pooled at her feet.

As Lief moved experimentally, the skirt fell in delicate

strips that moved around her like an eddying current. Her legs slipped in and out of the fabric with each step, the vines and flowers upon the design writhing and dancing with the movement and the tiny jewels shimmering like a sea of stars.

Lief smiled. Such was the beauty of the bounty of the forest. That was what this dress represented, or at least, a tiny fragment of that. Wind and dew upon a meadow at dawn. She stepped outside, still captivated by the gown, looking down at the skirt as it floated around her.

Aedon's gasp was not lost upon her.

"Lief." Once more, he was before her, and his hands found hers. "You look breathtaking."

Lief met his gaze and her cheeks warmed, unused to taking such praise.

Aedon shook his head, his eyes glossy in wonder. "I do not know whatever I did to deserve you. All heads shall turn in your direction, my fiery goddess." He pressed a gentle kiss to her lips. "Come. We must find you a crown."

"A crown?" Lief spluttered. "Don't be ridiculous."

"I'm not! Come on. I know just the thing." He tugged her with him across the deck and down the stairs. Her feet revelled in the feel of the smooth, warm, whorled wood beneath their soles as she followed him fleet-footed to the forest floor.

At the foot of the tree, in a small, sunlit glade, flowers tangled. Wild ranunculi, bluebells, and peonies. Aedon scooped up a handful of the blooms, turning away.

Lief peered around him, but he hunched his shoulders so she could not see. "What are you doing?"

"You'll see," he muttered, and strode over to a tree to hook off some dying vines.

After a few minutes, he turned with a beaming grin. He held out a crown of flowers and vines to her. "What do you think?"

Lief laughed. It was rough, truth be told, far from the mastery of anything the wood elves could manage so easily with the natural form, but to her, it was a gift of priceless measure. "I adore it," she said warmly.

Aedon lifted it, and she dipped her head to receive it.

"There. Now you are fit for a Singing," Aedon said, with such authority that she giggled. He had no idea what a Singing included, but she would show him.

Lief slipped her hand into his. "Come," she said and tugged him with her. "We don't want to miss any of this."

Crunchy twigs and soft, springy grass and moss were underfoot with each step. Roots below, she had forgotten how good it felt to connect with the forest underfoot.

Around them, a steady stream of wood elves moved towards the Singing. Lief did not know where to go, but it was obvious they did, and so she led Aedon, hand in hand, as they picked their way through the trees. She realised quickly that it was that stone arcade and the circle of thrones they converged upon.

They could not move for bodies when they arrived. The forest was full to bursting with elves everywhere, and the noise of them chattering and laughing drowned out all sound of the forest. It was a strange dichotomy; rarely had Lief been in the presence of so very many elves and been so unable to hear the life of the forest around her.

The sun's light faded from the depths of the forest, with the circle of thrones, in the clearing as it was, receiving the last rays and warmth. Around them, faelights floated, muted amber and gold bathing the forest around them. Fireflies danced like embers floating on the breeze, though of course, there were no fires, flames being forbidden in the living forest.

As Lief and Aedon arrived, in sight of those stone arches wreathed in ivy and vines, that slow, sonorous boom rang out again. It shredded through the chatter, and silence fell. All turned to the stone circle, and with the power of the crowd's attention, so too turned Lief and Aedon. It was time for the Singing.

CHAPTER 19

With the light of a fresh day and ten hours away from Morrigan's infuriating presence, Vasili hoped he was ready to face her again. She had beat him to the breakfast table but had not been served yet. By the scowl on her face, she was not impressed to have to wait upon him.

He slid into his chair. "Good morning."

She glared at him.

"Oh, I'm fine, thank you, and you? Did you sleep well?" he said, pretending she had replied.

She scowled.

He raised an eyebrow. *Nothing? Not even a smile? Skies above.* But, his resolve strengthened, he was determined not to crumble again before her.

A servant marched in with two bowls, which he placed before them.

"Thank you," said Vasili, giving the man a grateful smile. Hot porridge, thick, creamy, with a dollop of sweet, tangy strawberry jam in the middle, by the looks of it. Far from the plain and tasteless watery oats of his outpost.

Without waiting for him, Morrigan dove straight in.

Vasili took a more refined spoonful, enjoying the thick, stodgy mouthful. "We're going out today."

Morrigan stilled, spoon halfway to her mouth, and glanced up at him. "What?"

"You're never going to change your mind if you're here under lock and key. A cage is still a cage, no matter how much it is gilded."

She narrowed her eyes. *She's always so suspicious.* It was sad, in a way. That she had been raised to be so instantly distrustful of everyone and everything.

"We shall take a turn around the town. The midwinter markets are in full swing – I haven't been for years." Vasili smiled, a true smile of warmth that made her face fall, for some reason. "You can see the best of Tournai. It is filled with light and laughter and goodness at this time of year."

She still gazed at him like a dog who had been beaten, expecting a trick. He half expected her to protest.

"You'll still be bound, your magic suppressed, and we'll have guards, but we can otherwise walk freely." Vasili's smile darkened, and it had her drawing up with matching hostility. "If nothing else, perhaps it will arm you with knowledge you can feed to your people, should you see them again."

A glint passed through her eye then, but Morrigan said nothing, instead dipping her head back to her spoon to finish her breakfast.

Vasili noticed she sped up.

Good.

After breakfast, they readied. Morrigan shrugged on the dark, fur-lined cloak again. She left the hood down – the snow had ceased overnight, leaving a blanket upon the garden. She had checked, peering to the street outside through an upstairs window. The grey cobbles had been cleared, the snow swept to the side of the road to pile in massive banks, though the cobbles were still slick in places with ice.

An eager anticipation had her almost rising onto the balls of her feet, so keen was she to be off. Perhaps it was the food – she had been better fed in the past day than she had been in years. Or maybe it was the sleep – for that hateful bed had been divinely cosy and comfortable, and she could not remember ever sleeping so soundly.

The guards stepped forward to shackle her once more. Today, there were no all-purpose heavy iron cuffs. Instead, they had a chain, so thin that it looked insubstantial, joining two delicate bangles. Yet when they closed over her wrist, she felt the snap of power that came with them. It fizzled against the chords of her spirit, a threatening burn that told her, *you are contained*.

She bit back the bitter taste of bile. And swallowed a huff of disgust. It was all words, really. All words, and not even pretty ones. So what if he took her to roam the streets? Now her cage had expanded – from a cell to a grand house to a city. She was still, in reality, a captive. And this chain, that infuriating young elven male, this whole damned society would not let her forget it.

Her venomous gaze drilled into the young soldier who

restrained her. He fell back, blanching at the loathing she exuded.

At the first step she took, however, the ice claimed her. Her balance went as her foot slid out from under her, an involuntary shriek crashing past her lips.

A strong hand yanked her up by the upper arm. Morrigan struggled to her feet, finding solid purchase, and glared at her helper. Vasili. *Of course, it is Vasili.* No one else would dare.

She did not thank him.

By the set of his expression – entirely impassive – she reckoned he did not expect her to. Wasn't that how this worked? They hated each other, and it wasn't about to change.

Morrigan set her jaw and lifted her chin. Captive or not, she was the daughter and heir of the oracle. No matter what they did to her worldly body, they could not cage her spirit. She would look, and she would see, and every morsel of information she could glean would become a weapon she would turn against them at the first chance she had.

Vasili watched her carefully as they strolled down the street, winding towards the market.

She ignored him.

Utterly silent.

Yet, he did not miss her eyes. They were keen and shrewd, absorbing everything around her.

For a moment, he wished he could see inside that mind of hers, to know what she truly thought. To answer the deep-seated question inside him – was she salvageable from the darkness that was so much a part of her that it came as easily as breathing?

For now, all he could do, despite the limitations of her custody, was show her. Show her the truth of his life in the hope it might sway her to see more than her own.

"You can do this," Icarus' voice floated into his mind, the dragon stirring far away in the dragonhold, ever present since their parting.

It gave Vasili strength. And so he wound through the streets, showing her the sights of Tournai, from the bakery that fed the city's poor for free at the lowest levels, to the famed forges of Guild Master Landry, Captain Tristan's father, who crafted the finest weapons in the realm, to the academy of seamstresses in a beautiful arcade outside the castle, where anyone with proficiency to study could gain a bursary apprenticeship.

He talked and talked and talked, and she listened – or at least, he hoped she did. Morrigan did not speak, watching everything around them with an imperturbable expression as she silently paced beside him, flanked by guards in all directions.

CHAPTER 20

Morrigan smelled the markets before she saw them. Something pungent, rich, and warm, with a hint of spice.

"Mmm, can you smell that mulled wine? Cinnamon and cloves with a dash of honey is my favourite. How about you?" Vasili glanced over. He had been peppering her with questions, but she had not replied to a single one, nor acknowledged any of his prattling. She had listened to every word most carefully, despite the bored impression she exuded, taking each bit of information and filing it away, never knowing when she might need to use it again.

He continued after a pause. After realising that of course, she would not answer. "We can stop for a drink. It would do us good, I think. Even with my cloak, the cold sneaks in."

The guards murmured their agreement, and Vasili chuckled. "Aye, you lads had best get one. I appreciate you traipsing round with us. Specially you, Indik, with you getting long in the tooth and all now."

"I'll give you long in the tooth, the cheek of you! It'd be rude not to." The grizzled soldier who responded clapped Vasili on the shoulder with a familiarity Morrigan had not expected. Such insolence would have been harshly punished; she could not imagine a bare soldier daring to do that to any lord's son or grandmaster in her world. And they laughed as though equal on some plane. She did not understand.

They walked through stalls that crowded the wide street leading into a square.

For a moment, the engulfing presence of so many people, and the hemmed-in nature of the stalls, overwhelmed her, and she fought back the instinct to dash away. Instead, she forced herself to open her senses even more, to take in this plethora of new information. The people that milled around her – or at least, outside the small bubble created by their ring of guards – were charged with positivity, smiling and laughing with those whom they walked with, in conversation, occasionally stopping at the stalls around them.

Stalls that held all manner of wares. Handcrafted wreaths of pinecones, winter boughs, and a plant with red leaves she had not seen before to her left. On the stall to her right, carved wooden ornaments and figurines of everything from bears to a dancing girl. The next one was candles, and a scent of sweetness washed over her from the lit candle burning there. On the next one, soaps, just as fragrant. The one after that, bolts of fabric. The next...it went on and on. Never had she seen such a visual feast of craft.

In the mountains, what time or luxury had there been for craft? None at all. It seemed so natural here, but to her, so intolerably indulgent that these people had nothing better to do with their time than play and make, whilst her people *suffered* for every morsel that passed their lips, every moment spent to survive. Her amazement soured as anger prickled up instead. It wasn't fair. None of it.

Her gaze snagged on an armourer's stall. On the shining, brand-new daggers there and the un-scuffed, pristine scabbards. She held back a moan. Damned that she was so close, but not close enough to grab one – not without being seen and restrained immediately. She walked past, with Vasili still prattling about goodness knew what – in the face of the sensory overload before her, she had quite forgotten to listen to him amongst the hubbub.

Vasili steered her towards a stall burdened with evergreen boughs and red berries, brightly lit with lanterns and boasting a rowdy crowd around it. He was careful not to touch her, for which she was glad. She did not have much choice, but if he tried, she would not hesitate to put him flat on his back, damned be the consequences. The chain rattled as she clenched her fist, and a dark chuckle escaped her, lost in the noise around them. Perhaps she could strangle him instead.

Now there's an idea.

"What do you want, I asked?" Vasili said slowly, obviously repeating himself, she realised. "From the stall," he added as she looked at him nonplussed.

"I don't," she said.

Vasili huffed and shook his head, muttering something under his breath. Leaving her in the circle of five guards, he pushed through the crowd, returning a couple of minutes later with two steaming wooden tumblers. He passed her one. She took it hesitantly. And sniffed the liquid inside.

Tangy and rich. It looked altogether too much like a cup of blood, sanguine in its ruby darkness.

Vasili was already in his cup, smacking his lips appreciatively as he finished a mouthful. "Oh, that is divine. A shame I only get the chance for a cup once a year when I'm on leave from the Kingsguard." He raised an eyebrow. "It won't bite you, you know. Drink. It's good."

Morrigan stared at him, and then at the cup. Hesitantly, she took a sip. Molten pleasure coated her tongue. There was no such thing as mulled wine where she had come from. Just a poor, watered-down wine to be served at ceremonial dinners. The grandmasters and the oracle kept whatever stock the Order had to themselves – she was lucky enough to get the occasional taste of a watered-down glass and nothing more.

But *this*, this was *painfully* good, like everything else she ate and drank in Tournai. As if the people here could somehow access a greater richness in every facet of their lives.

Her fingers tightened around the wooden cup, finding the grooves in the carved form of it. She looked down. Even that was a work of art. Flowing lines and stars, mountains, a moon. She stared at it dumbly for a moment. How easy it would be to sink into it all – to enjoy every moment and every morsel of this place. How tempting.

Morrigan hardened against that. With a vicious snarl, she hurled the still full cup at the floor. It connected with a *crash* she could not hear above the crowd, its ruby contents dashing over the boots of one of the guards.

"Hey!" he shouted at her, straightening and looming tall over her, his face twisted in a scowl.

She turned away.

"I'm done," she said through gritted teeth.

Not caring if they followed, though of course she knew they would, Morrigan forged a path back through the hateful crowd, back to her lavish cage. The silence of that was preferable to the life of the marketplace. It taunted her with every single sense it touched.

You could have had all this, it seemed to say. *Look what they enjoy, whilst you suffer.*

Except the voice it spoke to her with was her own.

And she despised that most of all.

"I need a knife," Morrigan said, her tone brooking no argument. She stared at Vasili's across the dinner table, resting so delicately upon the pristine placemat. She longed to lunge for it, but it was a mere dinner knife. Hardly sharp enough to cut cleanly.

She had no knife, of course. It had made eating slightly more difficult, but she would not stoop to asking for help. Not from the servants, and not from *him*.

A reflexive laugh burst out of Vasili. "I beg your pardon?" He looked at her, amused. He had been painfully unreadable that morning after the mulled wine incident, as though nothing had happened, continuing to prattle on about this and that as they wandered home and trying to pry any detail from her about her own life. It had been unbearable. She could not take it anymore. The pressure built within her, and she needed to bleed it out, quite literally.

"I need a blade. Anything will do, as long as it's sharp. A proper weapon."

"No," he said, laughing as he raised an eyebrow.

That made her see red, and she stuttered, "I—"

"If you think I will arm you, you are sorely mistaken, Lady Morrigan. I have seen what you can do with a blade – and truth be told, I fear what you are capable of without one. A fork will do. If you wish, I myself will cut up your food."

There was a glint in his eye that made her blood boil. The prat was goading her? How dare he.

"I don't mean for dinner. You would deny me my faith?" She scowled at him.

"Your *what*?"

"It has been weeks." Weeks too many. Her hand rubbed unconsciously upon the already fast-healing wounds upon her arm from her last self-flagellation. They were nearly gone. If they healed before she cut again, it would break a streak of thousands of days – she had lost track of how many – that she had proven her servitude and loyalty to the Order's master thusly. That would not do. Not in her own conscience, and certainly not as the oracle's heir. She was the example leading them all, even if they were not present to see her. She had to abide in spirit, too.

His eyes dropped at the movement, and understanding flashed through him. "Wait, you—"

"I need a blade," she insisted.

"You will cut yourself with it?" he asked, his gaze still snagged on her covered forearm – on what lay beneath the dark fabric.

"Yes. In service of my master. It is required." She did not want to explain herself to him, damn it. She would not give him any more of a window into her faith than the ungrateful wretch had already received by the grandmasters' misguided orders.

"No," he said flatly.

"You would deny me?"

He looked at her, frowning, as though the answer were obvious. "No," he said slowly. "I would *protect* you. I will not arm you so that you may harm yourself or anyone else here, Lady Morrigan. A calling that dictates you maim yourself is barbaric and ought not be practiced."

Morrigan hissed at him through bared teeth. "Infidel."

"*Heretic*," he warned her, folding his arms. She was the minority, and Valxiron was no god. "I will not do it. Make your peace with that and be grateful. Good night, lady. I will see you on the morrow."

Vasili pushed away from the table and left.

Her guards closed in once more.

Morrigan growled, the only sign of outward frustration that she could – would – allow through the cracks. They exchanged a glance, which she did not need to try to understand. They feared her, and she was glad of that, at least. If nothing else, she had lost everything, but she had not lost her fearsome presence. And, in a place so foreign to her in more and more ways each moment, she at least had that in her power.

As she retreated upstairs to the relative privacy of the bedroom – or rather, for a few moments of actual privacy in the bathroom – Morrigan relived that morning at the market. Being surrounded by the whirl of happy faces, the swell of chatter ripe with laughter, the sound of instruments and song in the background – it was such a world away from all that she knew.

It cleaved open a pain inside her that she did not want to acknowledge. *What if...?* She could barely give words to the thought, to give it any power over her. What if he was *right*? What if *this* was the reality of the world? What if everything she had been taught and told, lived and breathed, vowed and practised, was a *lie*?

CHAPTER 21

*A*edon and Lief craned their heads, trying to see through or over the crowd.

A flicker of movement ahead.

The thrones, Lief was certain, had been empty from what she could see, but now they were filled with the dozen of lords and ladies of the forest. They stood as one. Solanaceae foremost amongst them.

The Queen's gown was burnished gold, falling from Her like liquid sunlight, with a cape rippling behind Her so sheer it was like the breeze itself. At Her brow, a golden crown twined, a single stone of clear diamond hanging, and a halo of light as ethereal as the stars behind Her sparked off its arcing curves.

Solanaceae was tall and regal, emanating power, and so too was Her court. From afar, and not in the midst of their bone-chilling scrutiny, Lief could drink in every detail she could see of them all, these elves that were half as wild as the forest and more powerful than she could ever dream of.

It was so silent that even the forest had stilled. Not a bird sang. Not a beast moved. Not a tree rustled.

Boom. It shook them all once more. The very earth creaked and groaned beneath their feet.

The last of the sun's rays passed over the horizon.

Solanaceae opened Her mouth and Sang.

Rich and mellow, the melody rang out, lonely and haunting for a single moment before Her voice swelled with one, then ten, a hundred, then a thousand more.

Lief found her own mouth opening, answering the natural call of the Queen and Her forest and entering the flow of the Singing. Magic swelled within her, hers, those around her, the very Queen's, and the forest's itself, until she sank into that kaleidoscope of energy and knew herself no more.

Aedon felt like a sycamore seed tumbling in a gale, such was the force of the magic around him. It flowed through him, and yet he was not a part of it swirling and undulating around him, bringing light of its own to the darkening forest as the elves around him actually *glowed* with the force of it.

The scent of it, overlaid with the warm moistness of the forest and its perfume of flowers, stung his nose, that magic prickling him.

Around them, after the unnatural stillness, the trees swayed once more, caught in a dance, their branches writhing and leaves rustling. Aedon could feel their magic, deeper rooted and slower in the ground than their fleeting, bright, elvish keepers.

He wanted to close his eyes and sink into the flow and simply enjoy the Wellspring of power drawn from the reserves deep under their feet, but he could not take his eyes away from her.

Lief *shone*.

Her warm skin glowed, her freckles overlaid in bronze. Her amber eyes were molten like her peers, and her copper hair was fire in the faelights. With her arms half raised and that enchanting, insubstantial dress wreathing her, the loose bolts of fabric and her sheet of hair swaying to a wind not of that world, she looked like a forest dryad of old from the legends he had once heard. An enchanting being of power and beauty, at one with the life and forest around her.

Aedon could not measure how much time passed as they Sang. He watched, and he drank it in like a mortal starving for dinner, feeling that magic bathe him with life and warmth as the forest bloomed anew around him.

It did feed the forest, for the very ground writhed and heaved under his feet as new life pressed and pushed out of the soil. He could feel the magic humming through the earth through his bare soles.

New vines snaked around the trees. New leaves sprouted in that canopy high above, filling in the cracks through which the last remnants of daylight could be seen. Flowers grew from buds and burst into bloom, weeks of growing condensed into mere moments with the power of the forest's gift.

Aedon thought he had never seen anything so breathtakingly beautiful, and he did not want it to end. Yet, at last, as the sky overhead darkened and a web of stars watched over them all, the Singing diminished until once more, Solanaceae Sang alone, and then too, She finished.

With the last note and the cessation of that music, Aedon felt like something in his soul had sheared away. That beauty, cut off. The sound of the forest, once rich and deep, sounded poor and scratchy after such rich fare. Around him, the light of the Singing faded, sinking into the wood elves' skin, the trees, the leaves, the flowers, the forest floor. And then expectant silence laced the forest.

CHAPTER 22

Vasili spent the next days wandering through the city with Morrigan, showing her the fabric of his life, of his people, of their ways. To him, normal, and to her, so foreign. It pained him to be away from Icarus for so long when they had just reunited after such a painful separation, but he could not leave his mother's household at the mercy of Morrigan.

He was no fool.

It was evident in every hard line of her body, every coiled muscle, every suspicious glance that she would still rather gut him and disappear than renounce everything she stood for. He could not be angry at that; she had the same determination he did to fight for his cause. It just so happened they were on opposing sides.

"We're going to the dragonhold today," he said evenly, betraying none of his inner anguish at the physical separation he felt from Icarus.

Her gaze sharpened on him. Glittering. Covetous.

The Order of Valxiron had possessed dragons. *Possessed.* The word felt dirty even unspoken in Vasili's mind. Dragons were not chattel to be owned. The partnership of rider and dragon in the Kingsguard was an entirely different matter – willing on both sides.

What the Order had done was nothing less than barbaric.

They had raised stolen dragon eggs, keeping the dragons in pits without adequate nourishment or exercise, feeding them with magic so that the resulting dragons had been weak, stunted, and twisted, with no wild instinct, yet not tame enough to handle, too cruelly trained by their masters.

In the assault upon the mountain fortress, the Winged Kingsguard had exterminated them all. No match for a true dragon, wild, free, and willing in partnership with the Kingsguard. It had been a mercy for the tormented beasts, who would have been unable to survive in the wild or captivity.

Vasili knew that Morrigan would be *highly* interested in the dragons of the Winged Kingsguard. He hoped she would see what a true difference it made when they were wild, free, and willing – rather than covet them for the same twisted purpose as before.

"Did you help to train the dragons?" he asked. He kept his tone light, casual, his attention away from her, glancing around the street as though he took no real interest. It was the way, he found, to draw things out of her. Slowly teasing, things that did not seem to be of any real consequence, inviting her to lower her guard fraction by fraction. Learning about her and her way of life. *Understanding* her.

He had not gained anything that the High Council would deem valuable, he supposed, but he could build on the foundations. *If you don't run out of time.* He did not have long left, after all, before the High Council took any choice in the matter away from him.

"No. Grandmaster Hadir oversaw that." Distaste coloured her tone, and Vasili had to bite down on another question. If he asked once, she answered. If he delved further, she clammed up. This dance between them was painstakingly slow.

He glanced at her and nodded. "I suppose you won't have seen many dragons up close, then." He phrased it more of a statement than a question.

And received a noncommittal grunt and a shaking of her head, so tiny it was almost imperceptible, in return.

"You're in for a treat, then," Vasili said, smiling at her.

She lifted her gaze to his, her expression as guarded as ever. Yet in the time Morrigan had been in the Kingsguard's custody and in the care of Vasili's house, he could see the physical difference in her.

Morrigan's pale, drawn, waxy skin had begun to take on a more glowing pallor, and her raven hair was more lustre-filled than limp. She had filled out ever so slightly from receiving such improved nutrition, and it softened the harsh lines of her face and body, smoothing over hollows and jutting bones, creating a hint of future curves under her borrowed clothes where only hard muscle and bone were now.

Can she feel the difference? Surely, she felt stronger and healthier, Vasili reasoned. Or perhaps she had not realised. Perhaps she did not want to.

They walked in silence the rest of the way, Vasili matching her step and guards before and behind. He was closer now to her than he had been before, arms swinging side by side, almost brushing. Even so – he knew he would be foolish to let down his guard.

The wrought doors opened to Vasili, silent on well-oiled hinges. Warmth streamed out from inside, prickling his frozen cheeks, and he hurried inside with Morrigan on his heels. The tunnel was dark, an adjustment after the pale light of the snow-laden sky outside, but slowly, his eyes adjusted to the familiar dimness of the faelights set at intervals in the rocky walls.

Beside him, Morrigan ran a hand across the wall as they strode, and he wondered if she were marvelling at the melding of dwarven and elven tunnelling, enhanced by the gouging scratches and fire-melted swirling patterns through the rock. The place was old, resonating with magic that felt like *home* to Vasili in the same way Icarus did.

"Can you feel it? This place?" he asked her, his voice echoing. He wondered if, with her magic stripped from her, she could still sense it.

"Yes." There was a bite of curiosity in her voice.

"I always like to think that each dragon and rider who came here left the faintest impression of themselves behind – that over the millennia, it wove together to create this tapestry of old magic. Here, I hope you'll see what dragons are meant to be."

Light bloomed ahead – the end of the tunnel – and Vasili sped up, Morrigan doing the same beside him. Icarus' presence was intoxicatingly close. And then they were out.

Morrigan stopped dead, gasping involuntarily in wonder at the sight of it before her, the giant void in the mountain rising all the way to a summit far above. It was still warm, the artificial magic mixing with the resident dragons' heat to create a layer of sweat on the back of Vasili's neck.

He loosened his cloak, appreciating the stray breeze that curled past them, instigated from high above where a dragon launched out of one of the caves to soar down to them, gliding in lazy circles. Vasili craned his neck up, grinning. Icarus.

Beside him, Morrigan had paled even further at the sight of his glorious emerald wingspan and the glittering, rough scales of his belly. He was not yet fully grown, but even so, he was bigger than half the runts the Order had caged.

The smooth, rocky ground shook as he landed before them, a gust of wind sending all their cloaks flapping like a flock of birds taking to the wind. Icarus folded in his membranous wings and approached them. Vasili stepped forward easily, his hand rising to cup Icarus' muzzle and slide along his cheek.

"*I missed you,*" he said into the dragon's mind.

Icarus shuffled, a wordless acknowledgement of the same. And then he looked beyond Vasili, his predatory eyes fixing upon Morrigan. He stepped past Vasili, his tail slithering on the rock. Vasili turned.

Morrigan was entirely frozen before the dragon, who lowered his muzzle to her, his shoulders standing above her head, even on all fours as he was.

"So, this is the female," he said. "Morrigan." He tested the name on his tongue and rumbled. He had barely met her awake – only when she had been trying to kill the pair of them in battle. He had since carried her unconscious to return them all to the Winged Kingsguard's custody.

"It can speak?" she whispered.

Icarus growled. "It?" he spat, leaning closer and baring his fearsome teeth in a snarl.

Morrigan flinched, and Vasili did not know how, but she became even more tense, bending backwards as though she could escape Icarus, yet without ceding a step to him. Her eyes fixed upon the dragon before her, and in their depths, terror mingled with greed as they scanned over the creature, resplendent in his shimmering emerald scales, his horns worth a king's ransom, and his lifeblood even more.

Icarus rose up before her on his haunches, spreading his wings and flexing his claws. "I am Icarus, and you would do well to treat me with respect, elven female. Now, whom do I have the pleasure of meeting?"

Morrigan started at his expectant stare and curled herself into a bow, not taking her eyes from him. "Lady Morrigan Lilika Bellatrix of House Mallory."

"Much better." Icarus lowered himself once more, snuffling at her. "You smell of darkness, Lady Morrigan. It does not become you."

She frowned at him but had the wise sense not to answer back to a creature with teeth bigger than her hands. "Our dragons did not speak," she said to Vasili.

"They were lesser creatures, thanks to their breeding and lack of care." He did not drop his attention, not even when she gritted her teeth at the veiled accusation.

"Did any of them survive?"

"No."

Morrigan clenched her jaw. Who knew what she thought of that? Vasili could only wonder. Was it sadness at their passing, fury at their loss, a blow for the fighting fitness of her people?

"What of my people? You took me captive. What of them?"

Vasili shifted on his feet. "Some dead, some fled, some captured."

Her nostrils flared. She nodded rigidly. Perhaps she had expected little else. What more could he say? That they had all ridden off into the sunset and become fast friends? They were mortally opposed in every single value. The Order was a real threat to everything his people held dear, not least of all their lives and safety.

It prickled at Morrigan, that enduring sense of unease, as Vasili returned her to the townhouse. The feeling was born of the shattered contrast between their two worlds. The damnable lure of his. The crumble of hers. How could it be that the settlement in which she had spent almost all her life was simply gone and all those within it captured, dead, or fled? She could hardly conceive of it.

Already, it felt like a fading dream in the place she now was. A nightmare of sorts. One that she pushed and pulled at – one she longed to forget, and one she knew she had to uphold. If she turned her back upon it, she would be a worse traitor than all those who had bowed to Pelenor or fled.

The dragon, Vasili's partner, whom she had met that day, seemed to be yet another metaphor for the difference between their worlds – hers, withered, stunted, tainted, and his, strong, whole, and thriving.

Pelenor was so different to what she had been raised to believe. Not sinful, dark, and corrupt, but one that, on the surface and threaded below it firmly, was wholesome and at peace, where its people lived and thrived in safety and comfort.

She saw too how Vasili treated others and was treated by them. With mutual respect, kindness, warmth, affection, humour. Never had she known those things – to give or receive them.

Damn it! She ground her teeth – and ignored Vasili's sidelong glance.

Vasili steered them both to the dining room, where a small meal had been laid out. Fresh breads, cheeses, sliced cured and honey-smoked meats, with a bowl of winter fruits. The smell made her mouth water.

The food was a distraction as much as anything else. She fell upon it, half into a slice of buttered bread before she realised that she had not even sniffed or tried to taste the meal for a trace of poison. A curl of unease fingered through her. Was she softening? Leaning into the traitorous feeling of *trust*?

She would still rather kill him than trust him, surely? Yet that wary part in her, the beast untamed, knew instinctively that he would not hurt her, for personal gain or other, unlike those in the Order she knew. It made all the difference. Already, she could feel the ever-present tension singing along every taut nerve fading with each hour that her survival, she herself, was not threatened.

That tension was her cloak of safety. The edge that kept her alive.

She wanted it back.

Without that cloak, she had to face the terrifying possibility that everything she knew, everything she was, everything she upheld was *wrong*. How could it be? And yet everything she had experienced here was so real, and moreover, it refuted her existence. The threat of that shook her to the very core.

And, as a reflexive "thank you" bubbled up her throat as a servant cleared the dishes away, she clamped down upon it, gritting her teeth so those two hateful words could not escape. She would not let them. She would fight back.

That was all this was. A fight. Another kind, more insidious than any she had yet before encountered. One built of kindness, meant to dismantle her one stone at a time. It could not win. She could not allow it.

She would break him first. However she could.

CHAPTER 23

Slowly, the natural noise of the Tir-na-Alathean forest filtered in once more. The dusk chorus had crescendoed with the Singing, and now the soundscape of the night was entirely different, with the hoot of owls, the shriek of foxes, and the rustling of small, quiet things.

That noise was soon drowned by the swell of conversation from the wood elves, who began to drift away around Lief and Aedon. Ahead, Solanaceae and the elves upon the thrones dispersed, moving into the crowd. Elves cleared paths for them, and bushes and trees leaned out of the way to allow the Queen passage wherever She desired.

Lief sensed all of this with her eyes still closed, so deeply rooted was she still in the forest and its many threads of life. Each breath of the fresh, sweet air was a gift, and her toes curled happily in the loam at her feet. Fresh shoots tickled her ankles from the things that had sprouted during the Singing.

She did not want it to end. Still, she could feel that old

magic fading into the earth beneath her feet, sinking further and further. Back into the Wellspring deep beneath Emuir that fed the capital's power. She followed it, her consciousness chasing it into the ether, taking the last remnants of the wonderful, honeyed warmth it had left.

At last, when Lief sensed that those around her had departed, she opened her eyes. He stood before her. So silent, she had forgotten he was there, still half in and half out of her body from the otherworldly experience.

Aedon.

He waited, patiently watching her without comment. As though he understood that something profound had occurred, not just in the forest around them, but within the very depths of her soul, the hollows of her marrow, the shards of her being.

A sigh escaped her lips as the last of that magic slipped away, and she fully snapped back into her own consciousness. She had savoured it as long as she could, the rare experience that she had never experienced with such power before. A legendary event.

Aedon watched her still. She did not speak.

Lief glanced around the forest, taking in each new life – ones that she had sensed as pinpricks and tendrils of light appearing in her consciousness, breaking forth from the darkness as the Singing coaxed them into being. Before, the forest had been wild and wonderfully beautiful. Now, it was incandescent. Life bloomed *everywhere*, even on a dead log they had stepped across before the Singing. Now it was a carpet of mosses and mushrooms, and fresh cobwebs already glittered upon it.

Lief still did not want to break the relative silence with

anything as uncouth as her voice, so sharp and unmelodious it would seem after such a wondrous Singing. And so she took Aedon's hand and wordlessly led him into the forest, to the light and life of the party that now reigned.

Amongst the cheer of the wood elves, at last, it felt right to speak.

"That was..." Aedon trailed off. His steps faltered.

Lief shot him a half-smile and stopped before him. "You cannot put words to it, can you?"

"That's exactly it." He knew she would understand.

"I never thought I'd see the day when you were speechless." Lief's grin widened.

"There's a first for everything," he said with a cheeky glint in his eye.

"Come on. There'll be a feast now, and dancing throughout the night."

"This lasts until dawn?"

"If you can stay awake that long," she said daringly. The spirit in her made something in his core tighten.

"I do not wish to sleep when I have such a ravishing sight before me," Aedon said and bowed. As he rose, he offered her his hand, and she laced her fingers with his. She was boiling hot, some remnant of the magic that she had channelled and coaxed, he supposed.

"Then let us eat, and dance, and be grateful." And, for the first time in many weeks, he saw the truest, happiest smile from the depths of the contentment in her soul, and he could have wept with joy at it.

She begins to heal, at last.

They followed the crowd to a magnificent feast on tables that creaked and groaned under the weight of the dishes upon them. Served upon platters of bark and glass, leaves and crockery, everything made from the bounty of the forest, Aedon devoured it visually. The smell hit them as they drew closer. Warm, rich, nutty, sweet, earthy, *delectable*.

The two of them loaded up a bark platter to sample titbits of each delight together and retreated to a private bower under the draping canopy of a weeping willow beside a tumbling hill and far from the centre of the revelry. In the distance, a lake glittered under the moonlight sky. Glassy and smooth, it reflected the web of stars, like a pool of diamonds in the darkness of the forest.

Aedon propped himself in a nook amongst the tangled roots and offered a hand to Lief, who perched beside him, lowering the platter to the ground between them.

"This is heavenly," Aedon said with a contented sigh. He shook his head. After so long imprisoned, and then the fraught peril of the flight from Lune and all that had happened since, it seemed like the first true moments of pure happiness and ease that he had had in what felt like a lifetime.

Now, the quiet shushing of the draping weeping willow branches around them was a soothing percussion alongside the distant trail of stringed and wind instruments that teased the night, squeezing through hollows in the conversation and hubbub of elves feasting and revelling around them. Somehow, under that tree, they had a bubble of peace and privacy away from it all, like the *bomas* they had fleetingly shared in their travels through the forest.

Lief picked at a morsel from the plate and, kneeling, leaned across to offer it to Aedon. He opened his mouth obediently, and she placed it inside. The moment the mushroom hit his tongue, rich flavour burst across it. Earthy, sweet, with a hint of garlic and smooth with butter.

Aedon groaned in delight.

Lief licked her fingers and chose one for herself, scooting closer. She swept one into her mouth. "Oh, that *is* good."

"Not as good as the view I'm getting," Aedon said, smiling.

In the shadow of the tree's canopy, she was dimmed, pale in the darkness, that dress still offering a slight shimmer, the sheer fabric sliding over her skin. How he longed to peel it off and worship her, thank her for everything she had brought to him. Happiness, in its purest form, and the desire to live once more. Without her, before her, that spark had been long lost from him. And, stars above, he did not want to lose her – and risk losing his thirst for life once more.

In his moment of peace, a frisson of fear wormed. Soon they would leave this haven. Into peril they would likely fly once more. What did that mean for them?

"What are you thinking of?" she murmured as he gazed out over the lake, unseeing that beauty. "You look troubled."

Aedon turned to her and smiled, but it did not reach his eyes. "I'm worrying, that's all. Probably about nothing. Possibly about everything." He winced. "I'm sorry. I don't mean to spoil a perfect night."

Lief slipped her hand into his – she had cooled from the raging inferno that the magic had elicited within her. "You're not spoiling anything. Come, share your cares with me."

Aedon shifted and sighed. "I think I worry about what

happens when we leave here. This has been a balm upon so many wounds, for us both."

Lief nodded in silent agreement, sliding closer.

"We may face a storm out there, and a part of me wants to remain here, with you, and exist in this peace instead." He reached a hand between them, resting his fingertips on her hip.

"You and I both." Her hand slid up his chest.

"I worry too, I think, what if things change? Between us."

She looked at him quizzically. Skies above, his palms were clammy and his throat so scratchy and dry, he felt as though he could not speak, damned be it. He cleared his throat. "I mean to say, Lief na-Arboreali, I do not wish to be parted from you again, nor hide what is between us. I love you."

Something within Lief quivered at those words. The visceral feeling behind such a simple statement. One she felt too. He had elicited such life within her when she had felt lost beyond reach.

"I love you," she breathed. It felt euphoric and terror filled to admit to.

"If you will have me, I would be yours." His voice was half a whisper and half a growl, husky and low, as though he were also scared to voice it in case she rejected him. "I cannot promise anything – I do not know what tomorrow will bring, where we will find ourselves, and what circumstances will test us, but I know I want to face all things beside you."

A lump formed in Lief's throat that was a struggle to speak past. "I want those things too," she choked out, giving voice to such fragile thoughts from his own courage to do so.

"You've spoken so fleetingly of them, but I want to see your family, visit your village, see where you grew up." Her parents and brothers lived in a remote region in Tir-na-Alathea, far from the Queen's court. "I want to see that simple life, rooted in the forest. A good life. That is what calls to me. That is what my heart yearns for. To truly understand you and where you came from."

No one had said such things to her before. No one had truly seen her, warts and all, and accepted her. Wanted more.

"I want to see Pelenor. Where you call home," she said. "I want to see all the places you've been, all the places you and Valyria flew."

"I want to learn to glamour – properly."

That made her laugh with the unexpectedness of it. "Only if you tell me all your stories, General of the Winged Kingsguard and Legendary Thief of Pelenor."

He chuckled, rich and warm. "It excites me to dream that all of this shall be possible."

"It is possible. You are free – as free as you will ever be, and soon, so will I." She had not told him of her plans, half-formed thoughts to step aside from her role to adventure the world with him. She leaned closer and whispered the hints in his ear.

He gaped at her, stunned into silence. "Truly?"

For a long moment, the darkness that faced them both was forgotten, pushed aside in their tangible dreams for a future shared.

"Truly."

Aedon smiled, radiating pure joy. "I adore you, Lief na-Arboreali. More than the rising sun. More than the wind of a flight upon dragon-back. More than these delicious mushrooms."

She snorted at that one.

"It was worth waiting every single torturous night in that prison to meet you. I cannot wait for all these things – with you."

Lief's shy joy swelled his heart. The darkness waited out there, but it be damned, he would not let it steal this fleeting moment of joy before they were forced to face it once more.

"When all is said and done, I am yours, and you are mine," he said, a slight inflection at the end betraying the doubt and the question within him that somehow she would yet deny him.

"I am yours, and you are mine," she repeated.

Skies above, his heart would burst with love.

Aedon dropped her hand, and both of his hands slid to her waist. He pulled her to him, and their lips crashed together as they wound each other in an embrace so tight he could not breathe. Beside them, the food lay forgotten as their anticipation and excitement swept away the overshadowing darkness to come for a few glorious moments.

CHAPTER 24

The full might of the woodland realm of Tir-na-Alathea was ready to leave its borders and step into the mortal lands beyond – and Lief and Aedon with it. With the wood elves' ability to evanesce, they could cover weeks of travel in a day or so. Aedon did not know whether to feel glad that there would be less waiting – and time to worry – or more nervous that the danger was now so near.

Gone was the fine dress of gossamer and magic. Gone was the tunic of tree and root. Gone was any sense of carefree jubilation in the moments they had shared that night.

Now, hateful circumstances had parted them once more, as inexorable and inescapable as the tides. Aedon could not see Lief, but he could feel her. They had kept open a mental link between them. She was somewhere behind him, off to the right, with Kinear's *cinq* – or rather, new *cinq*, since he had buried half of his unit at Lune.

Unease oozed from her. Trepidation at what was to come.

Yet an undercurrent of excitement of that great unknown and all the adventures and experiences it would bring.

His own feelings mirrored hers, though for slightly different reasons. This was it. Standing on the knife edge between familiarity, comfort, safety, and freedom. But with that freedom came the unknown. Danger. And facing the ghosts of his past.

CHAPTER 25

Time. Vasili had run out of it.

The High Council beckoned, quite literally. He had had his days, and they had slipped through his fingers, squandered, unable to be kept, like water running through a crack in a dam.

His heart thundered in his chest, and it was tight, each breath a fractured, forced beast trying to escape from the clench of muscles that locked him whole. It was freezing, but he boiled. Beside him, in chains, Morrigan stood, silent and dark. She had retreated into herself once more. Gone were the tells that she was beginning in any small way to open up.

He had needed more time. Perhaps, eventually, he might have managed to break through to her. Yet he did not have until *eventually*, he had until now – and he had failed. Dread clutched him unyieldingly as he worried what that would mean for what came next for her and for all of them.

The doors ahead clunked open, held for them by silent

guards who watched them with implacable eyes. Vasili turned to Morrigan.

"Please," he said, his voice low and urgent.

She turned those silver eyes upon him. This close, he could see the gold flecks within them. Fitting, he thought; they were ice and fire, like her. Passion and vigour, coldness and steel. If only she could turn that to the path of lightness, what greatness she could achieve.

"Please do as they say. If nothing else, you have lived with me these past days. You have seen the truth of this realm, myself, my people, the world outside your Order. I *know* you have begun to think differently about everything, even if you do not choose this way yet. Trust in that doubt in your path. Give it a chance, scary though it might be to choose something different over what you have always known." He did not dare ask her to trust him. She would buck that immediately.

"I'm not scared," she bit out. There were no tremors in her voice, just edges as hard as she. Her defences were up once more. What few she had.

The High Council was waiting. He could not delay. Vasili led Morrigan inside the High Council chamber, where the full weight of the council waited. Two dozen bodies.

His parents were there, somewhere in those lines of tall, dark robes, but Vasili's focus had gone, and they were a sea of vague faces. All his attention was on Morrigan beside him. The way she stood, shackled, stripped of everything, and yet still her chin was high and her stare defiant, strong, before the weight of their attention.

He admired her for it. That she was no coward, even now, alone and weakened before her lifelong enemy.

"Young Lord Ellarian. Report." Lord Halkian's command rang through the echoing space.

Vasili straightened. "Lady Morrigan has resided under house arrest with me these last days. Her conduct has been impeccable." *Mostly.* His tongue stuck to his mouth, something in his throat swelling. He could not, did not want to speak. His motive had not been as ulterior as his given task. He had wanted to save her for her own sake – but he had been ordered to infiltrate her defences for their own.

He hated himself with a surge of hot regret and anger at the words that spilled from him, detailing their activities and his observations of her.

Beside him, she was utterly still.

He knew that with every word he irrevocably scattered what tiny grains of trust had built between them.

"That is all well and good," Lord Halkian said dryly, "yet I note that you do not detail to us anything of *use*. Order position, troop numbers, tactics, and so on?" His glance was derogatory, stripping what little dignity Vasili felt he had left.

Vasili shook his head. His heart sank. He had not only failed himself, he had failed her, and he had failed all of them. "I need more time," he said, but it sounded weak, even to him. She would not yield to him. He would gain nothing, just a temporary reprieve for them both, after which he did not know what would come to pass.

"Denied. You were granted a boon on the requests of both Lord Ellarian and Lady Ravakian"—Vasili's parents had indeed put their own goodwill and reputation on the line to give him the chance; he had failed them too—"and the time allotted has elapsed. Matters are so serious, and they move too quickly for us to consider granting you such a slow-moving strategy."

Strategy. As though she were nothing more than an object to be broken and conquered. Skies above, she was standing right beside him. He did not know who he was angrier with – Halkian or himself. Shame stung him, warming his cheeks.

"Dismissed."

That word needled into him. Vasili bowed respectfully, forcing his expression to smooth over. He lingered one extra moment, glancing at Morrigan, but she did not move to acknowledge him, her attention fixed upon Halkian. Silently, Vasili stole out as Halkian spoke, listening to every word the council leader said.

But then he was outside, and the doors silently shut in his face.

Not caring for the guards who stood there, not caring for the huddle that had accompanied him and Morrigan to the council chamber, and not caring who else might see him, he turned and rested his forehead and palm upon the cool wood.

"Step away, please," the guard to his left chided him.

Vasili clenched his jaw, but he complied. What other choice did he have?

Voices still rang out inside that sealed chamber. He could barely hear Halkian now. Anxiety raged within him. The tone inside was cool and hard. Unyielding as it rose in volume. Demanding.

And then the screaming started. Wrathful. Defiant. Female.

Morrigan.

CHAPTER 26

The Silent Sisters were as Aedon remembered them. Vast tors of stone towering into the sky high above them, lost to the swirling mists of a snowstorm.

It had been weeks since Aedon and Lief's previous passage there with the *centime*, just before the horror that had befallen the unit at Lune. Their tracks had long been hidden in fresh snowfall, but they approached the same way, from the forest.

The entire legion had paused to cloak in warmth at the Tir-na-Alathean border to repel that terrible chill, so far removed from the customary humid heat of the living forest. Something far more insipid sent chills crawling down their spines.

The darkness seeping from the place.

Unseen to the mortal eye and lurking beneath the blanket of pure white snow, the place was a paradox. Outwardly light to the eye, but it hid terrible power. Power that Aedon recognised with sickly horror. Power he had never wished to sense again. Valxiron's.

As they neared the tors, the legion's movements echoed off the silent stone, that muffled blanket penetrated by the steps of thousands of feet surrounding the place. Queen Solanaceae drove to the heart of the tors with El'hari at her side and a mass of bodies following behind, Aedon amongst them.

He could practically feel that darkness pulsing beneath his feet, threatening to suck him in and under like a dark lake. Aedon steeled his nerves – and the contents of his stomach – against such unhelpful thoughts.

"Here," Solanaceae's low voice hailed. "Fetch the elf."

El'hari forged back through the crowd of Solanaceae's guard to fetch Aedon and beckoned him forward.

Aedon followed her to the Queen's side.

As before, the snow formed a perfect circle around a spot of bare, blackened earth. Earth that crawled lazily with symbols that oozed fire and darkness and poison. The heart of Valxiron's anchor.

Aedon recalled the last time they had seen it – he and Lief. He had not told her of its presence when she had not perceived it. He had not wanted her to fear it as much as he did, but that presence had haunted him since. It resonated into his very blood, for it was something he had encountered long before. Even before his imprisonment in Tir-na-Alathea. El'hari's brother had given his life so that Aedon could destroy the anchor they had found – and live to tell the tale.

Destroy it they had. Damned be it, Aedon had never

wanted to encounter it again. Every fibre of his being urged him away from it.

"Yes, my Queen?" he murmured, no hint of his inner turmoil upon his voice.

"It is time. Let us end this. With my magic, and your fire, we shall scour it from this good green earth, and never shall it find hold here again." Solanaceae's lips curled into a growl, revealing a pointed canine.

He admired Her courage in the face of unknown darkness. The last time She had faced Valxiron ascended to his power, it had been almost impossible to defeat him, and they had not the weapon that had destroyed him then.

Even She had deserted Her usual ethereal garb and opted for more practical leathers and cleverly made delicate and yet strong plates that would protect Her, should it come to battle. He had never seen Her armed that he recalled, yet upon Her back She bore twin blades and at Her hip, a dagger. She looked fit for war.

Did Solanaceae expect such trouble that She feared too? Aedon, of course, did not dare ask. She would probably sooner smite him than admit to such weakness. Probably being *definitely*.

Aedon inclined his head and stepped beside Her.

"Fall back," She commanded. Behind Her, elves obeyed immediately, carving a distance between them like a knife through butter.

"Be ready." Under thunderously slanted brows, She captured Aedon within Her terrifying gaze. He could do little more than jerk his head in some semblance of a nod. Aedon's heart thundered too much to speak, and if he opened his mouth, he thought he might vomit.

He let forth an involuntary gasp as Her magic erupted. Powerful, more powerful than ever he remembered – or perhaps it was simply that he stood before Her, bearing the brunt of Her storm. Aedon knew that, had it been turned upon him, he would have been obliterated to ash and dust in an instant. He felt the precise moment that Solanaceae pinned down the key rune that held the enchantment of the anchor together – like the anchor Aedon had defeated so long ago with the help of El'hari's brother.

She pulled on it, hard. Separating it viscerally from the quagmire of sorcery around it, even as it squirmed away, attempting to evade Her. Her power focused on that singular point. More and more, She pushed, burning at it, tearing at it, shattering it.

"Now!" Solanaceae howled, hunched over the void before Her. The wicked contrast between the light of her magic and dark of the void threw Her beautiful face into savage, animalistic relief.

Aedon called forth the building fire within him. Now, there was no room for fear, only action. Aedon stoked the inferno, sending the flame of his dragon's gift higher and channelling it out through clawed hands, focusing on that same point as Solanaceae.

Outside their circle, a ring of Song crescendoed to a deafening roar, the magic of that breaking through the barrier of Solanaceae's magic. Joining with it. Melding. Strengthening. A people, pouring themselves unbidden into their Queen.

Such power, it was heady, and Aedon reeled in it. He planted his feet deeper into the frigid snow to stop himself toppling over, bowled away by the sheer strength of it and almost losing whatever sense of balance he had, overwhelmed by the rush on his senses.

That darkness did not die unchecked, however. A sudden pulse sent a black shockwave through the gathered crowd.

Then Aedon did fall, crashing into the snow, entirely disorientated for a moment. His flame guttered out.

The Queen's focus was momentarily distracted. The Song faltered, then shattered – and the darkness erupted around them.

CHAPTER 27

Morrigan trembled inside as Vasili stepped away. If she had felt vulnerable before, now she felt stripped of all defences. No matter that she blazed outward defiance; inside, she knew how truly alone she was, and, as much as she hated to admit it, she was scared.

He had compromised her already, imperceptibly and yet inexorably. She had been plied with comforts and fine food. Respect and measured patience. Exposed to a life entirely different to that which she had always known. And a part of her, she had felt, she had known, little by little, had softened. Day by day, a little more, like night bleeding into daybreak, uncurling and brightening.

Hope.

Morrigan had started to hope. To dream. To imagine anything outside what she had known. More than that, she had begun to survive without her magic and her weapons. Existing just in her purest form, whatever and whoever she was. Daring to dream that maybe she did not always need to be so hard-edged and surrounded by spiked walls of her own making.

Now, that seeping weakness that breached her, and it would be her downfall.

The doors shut behind Vasili, sealing him outside, with an ominous boom that struck right to her core.

She stood before those faceless elves, who all stared down at her from their high chairs with impassive superiority. The floor around her was bare, and it felt like for a moment, she was the eye in a storm – something brewing and about to break.

The one in the middle, the one Vasili had deferred to, Lord Halkian, rose to his feet and stepped down from his chair. She did not like the look of him. Perhaps because he reminded her so much of what she knew of people – uncompromising hard edges inside and out. Something in him carried himself like a grandmaster of her Order, with the same weighty status. The same ego. She could see it in the sneer of his mouth and the glint in his eyes as he regarded her.

"Lady Morrigan." Her title sounded like a mockery in his mouth, as though he degraded her without even saying a word or laying a hand upon her. "You have been treated well, as a guest of this city and of Pelenor. Your time comes now to decide how you wish to be treated henceforth. You have a simple choice. Tell us what we wish to know, or it shall be taken from you."

Dread sawed through Morrigan, stealing her breath. Her chest felt stuffed with something, and she could not draw air. What had he said? He would take it from her? He could not. Surely. Vasili had reassured her it was against the laws of their land. Indeed, had he not prided himself upon it? That although her people practised such barbaric methods, his people were far above that? And, as much as she tried not to fear anything, her walls were deep, high, and jagged for a reason. No one got in.

No one.

"*Halkian,*" Vasili's father, whose name she could not remember in the blanket of fear at Halkian's words, protested.

Lady Harper stood beside him, her eyes burning into the back of Halkian's head. Others stood, until half the chamber had moved.

Something fluttered low and deep within Morrigan. Something conflicting. These people, whom she did not even know, would stand for her, when she would have annihilated them without a second thought?

At the unexpectedness of it, her seized chest eased for a moment, and she gasped in a breath before that tight noose of fear closed around her once more. Doubt curled in her belly, of who was right and who was wrong, and that grey kaleidoscope in between the two.

"You cannot surely stand on the side of the Order of Valxiron," Lord Halkian said. He stared in turn at each member of the High Council who had moved.

Half of those who had stood or shifted settled slowly back into their seats at his attention. Leaving a mere quarter standing.

Halkian's widening smile was triumphant. "I believe that this demonstrates sufficient support, Lord Ellarian."

"You cannot," hissed Vasili's father. "If it were not bad

enough that it goes against our own laws, Halkian, she is but a young woman."

"She is the oracle's heir, not an innocent girl. We are at *war*. That supersedes all." Halkian practically shouted now, dominating them all, but his next words were quiet, cutting through the silent chamber. "If there are no other objections?"

Lord Ellarian, Vasili's father, looked so like his son in that moment that Morrigan could see the same defiant streak Vasili had inherited, present in his burning stare and the clench of his jaw. His attention drifted around the council chamber, and she saw the moment his shoulders sagged when he realised that he did not have enough support to quell Halkian's intended action.

Morrigan already stood rigid, and somehow, she locked even further yet, every muscle tensing as Halkian approached her. She dove deep into that pit of herself, but it had been scoured and smothered, and she could feel no essence of her magic there. No blades had she.

She stifled the cry that slipped out, of terror and desperation, of fury and hate, but Halkian heard it, and he smiled with such cruel savagery that she knew once he sank his claws in, she would not be able to fight back.

"What is your choice, Lady Morrigan?" Halkian asked, his voice icy and quiet.

He asked, and she could tell the answer he wanted her to give. This man *wanted* to break her. She had thought, from meeting Vasili and seeing such intimate, close details of his life, of the men he interacted with, that perhaps men here would be different. That *people* here would be different.

But, as she looked into Lord Halkian's merciless eyes, she

knew that had been a deluded desire. People were cruel, no matter what walk of life they came from. Darkness and sin took them all.

She shook her head, because words had entirely failed her. No. No. *No.* She would not give in to this, to him. Morrigan stood tall, raising her chin, even though it felt like baring her throat to the jaws of a lunging wolf, and sank her claws into what shreds of courage remained tattered and drifting inside her.

Lady Morrigan was loyal to her people. Loyal to their cause. Loyal to Lord Valxiron.

A few weeks in enemy hands could do nothing to change a lifetime of that, no matter that she had not hated her waking time in Vasili's company as much as she ought. Vasili had betrayed her, exactly as she had expected, and Lord Halkian would flout the laws of his own land to see her broken.

They were no better than the Order they professed to hate.

She rose above them all. She alone was dedicated to her cause. When the grandmasters had fled, when her mother had vanished, when her people had routed, and died, and surrendered, she alone had remained, a bastion to the cause, to whatever end.

To *this* end.

She would not desert it now.

Her eyes fluttered shut, as though trying to protect her from the inexorable threat that drew nearer. Her hands clenched around the chain that bound them. She could feel it building within the elf opposite, a great tide of power, ready to be unleashed upon her, and she was powerless to face it.

Halkian loomed over her.

Through her closed eyes, the shadow of him blotted out the light there.

Morrigan clamped her lips shut. She would not give him the satisfaction.

And then he struck.

It was lightning fire, and a scream ripped from her as his magic savaged through her. Unnecessarily cruel, and she had not expected less, having taken the measure of the man, but she had not envisaged, not been able to imagine that *this* would be how it felt.

He battered at her walls, shattering them in a few smashes. Without her magic bolstering them, a swell of her own strength to meet him, suppressed by the hateful cuffs, she was powerless to stop him.

Her obsidian walls came tumbling down, and he crashed into her mind.

It was excruciating as he scoured through her, invisible claws rending her as he dove without mercy into the tides of her being. It was so overwhelming to her senses that she could not hear the scream ripping from her own throat, tearing it red hot with pain. She could not see. She barely felt the slam of her knees into the cold stone as her body gave way before the onslaught.

Her face was frozen in a wordless howl, her body rigid, her hands locked into tortured claws as she braced against it, but to no avail.

Lord Halkian strode through her mind at will, taking what he desired – and she could do nothing. Were those hot tears slicing down her cheeks? Morrigan could not tell, watching from within herself in horror at the memories and thoughts he helped himself to. Watching powerlessly as he violated and degraded her without mercy. Ripping each thought away from her desperate grasp to be examined.

She lay on the floor, the feeling of cold stone upon her cheek breaking through the maelstrom for the briefest moment, like the sun finding a chink in the clouds, before it slipped away again. Morrigan felt naked before the council in a way that felt tenderly, painfully raw. She cared not for her physical form, but for the privacy of her inner self...it felt as though he had scoured her dry, as though all the council could see inside the wasted husk that was left.

Unbidden, for she had not the strength to recall or prevent them, hot tears wet her cheeks, pooling on the stone, as she lay there prone, utterly spent by the painful invasion.

Her interrogator had taken everything.

Not only the precious and hateful memories of her carving chatura pieces as a girl, sitting in the woods, dreaming of a full belly and a warm hearth – craving a cuddle from her steel-cold mama before she understood anything of duty and oracles – but the other ones too. The locations of the Order of Valxiron. Their strategies. Their planning. The truth of their mission. The identities of their grandmasters. In the end, last bastion or not, Morrigan had delivered to the enemy everything they needed to know to break her people once and for all.

The blackness, when it came, was a welcome relief. Not from the pain and the indignity and the shock, but from the shame and self-loathing that clawed its way up her throat like bile.

CHAPTER 28

Vasili could do nothing but listen from outside as they broke Morrigan, sharpening his hearing with a simple charm – and half wishing he had not, for how it rent his heart to hear the fullness of what passed within. His eyes stung with hot, angry tears, and regret that he had not been able to prevent it clogged his throat. They picked over what she had yielded to them for the following hours. Hours in which she was silent. Worry raged within him. He had been on the receiving end of such a savage invasion, and for a fraction of the length of time.

In what state would he find Morrigan? Was she damaged by Halkian's brutality? He could not see how she would be intact. The screams had been shards of pure pain. He did not imagine she would stand idly by as they picked over the tatters of her being. If she could speak, she would, which meant...

Vasili's thoughts spiralled. He could not contemplate the worst of them all. That she might be dead.

He could do nothing but pace and listen and reel in the antechamber, like the council inside as they scrutinised everything Morrigan had ceded so unwillingly to them and took in the ramifications.

It was nightfall by the time they finished – with the High Council meeting, and with Morrigan. Vasili still waited outside, like a dog for its master. Hungry and persistent.

The moment the doors clunked open, he perked up, rushing forward – to fall back as a stern-faced Halkian and his retinue marched out. They did not even so much as glance at Vasili scrambling out of their way, so far beneath their notice was he.

Without challenge – or rather, ignoring the warning call of the guards upon the door – Vasili rushed in, crying out when he saw Morrigan lying prone upon the floor.

"How long as she been like that?" he called indignantly, not caring that his tone was insubordinate.

His mother was already halfway to her across the space, and he could see fury in the tight lines of her face. "Too long. Get help – a healer," she shot at the guards who had rushed in to stop Vasili. She turned back to Morrigan, kneeling beside her. "Damned be that egotistical bastard."

Vasili raised an eyebrow. He had hardly ever heard his mother curse.

"She's freezing." Harper shook her head, gritting her teeth as she pulled Morrigan into her arms, as though she were a daughter and not a dangerous and mortal foe. A flutter of warm magic chased around her and settled into Morrigan, bringing some colour back to her drawn pallor.

"What now?" Vasili asked his mother quietly, his attention focused on Morrigan. Would she be beyond further use? Would she be sent to rot in the cells – or worse?

Harper set her mouth in a firm line. "What happens now is this young lady comes home with us. Lord Halkian," she sneered, "did not specify what was to be done with her, and that ambiguity shall be his loss. We were forced to cede to him today, but I will not maltreat her now. The girl has been through quite enough. She'll be tended to at our home until such time as I see fit to take Halkian's opinion on her welfare."

By the tone of her voice, *'never'* was the answer that Vasili expected on that count. Relief bloomed at her words, however. Morrigan would be safe and comfortable with them. He had not wanted to send her back to the cold, dark cells – not after Halkian's punishment – for her own welfare and to assuage the guilt that crushed him. Had this been his fault?

It settled unpleasantly in his belly. This had been his fault.

"Son?"

Vasili started. Harper looked up at him, frowning, Dimitri hovering close by.

"It's not your fault," she said quietly, and he realised he had spoken aloud.

His throat was too constricted to answer. *Yes, it is*, he wanted to say.

"I'm proud of you, Vasili."

"We both are," added his father.

"You acted with integrity and decency, no matter how she treated you in turn. You tried to give her the benefit of the doubt and protect her, despite that, even though it might have been more than she deserved."

Then why do I still feel like I failed?

CHAPTER 29

Gone was the white of the snow at Aedon's feet and swirling above all their heads. Inky blackness surrounded them. An inescapable void.

Ash clogged his throat, and Aedon retched upon it as it stole all moisture from his mouth and filled his nose with death and devastation.

An animalistic shriek of inhuman rage pierced that darkness. Solanaceae, somewhere in that nothingness around him.

Aedon's stomach flipped. Into his fire he poured himself and, taking a huge, shuddering gulp of toxic air, pushed out. That flame flickered before him. The void was an anathema to it, and it tried its utmost to quench him.

With a roar, he pushed his fire harder, his fingers rigidly curled like claws around the flames in their midst. He would not let that darkness take him. He would not let it *win*. His hands shuddered under the strain of it – the pressure of that magic, smothering him into oblivion, and the desperation feeding his fire, because he knew that if it went out, they might well be done for.

His fire blasted outwards, crackling and sizzling, a thousand tiny explosions and sparks as it cascaded against that black sorcery. Light bloomed before him, pure and bright as sunlight, and as his fire touched it, it strengthened tenfold, as though fed with pure air.

Solanaceae's savage face appeared from the darkness before him. Her mahogany hair gleamed dark and bloody in the ruddy light. She looked like a warrior of life and death with the contrast between that and the leafy, life-giving green of Her armour.

He met her molten eyes. In them, a wordless challenge raged.

Fight or die?

Aedon accepted it.

Fight.

In the same moment She exploded, so did Aedon. Energy blasted out, sending them all tumbling to the ground. Aedon was lost in the blackness shrouding him and the Queen, the surprise of that magic's vigour knocking his breath from his lungs, winding him. He sucked in an agonizing breath.

It seared into Aedon. That toxic, dark sorcery, burning into his lungs, more painful than any flame. But around them, it burned to ash, and through the void he saw shafts of white breaking through – the snow outside, or perhaps Solanaceae's light, or maybe both. He could not tell, still stunned and dizzy.

His fire lunged at that darkness, which tore into tatters like fabric floating on the wind, those pieces becoming smaller and smaller as they disintegrated and burned into nothing, chased into oblivion by his fire and Her light.

The Singing once more crescendoed around them as Her elves recovered and rejoined the fray once more.

Upon the ground, in that dark pit, those sluggish, sanguine symbols writhed, as though trying to escape their inevitable fate. But they could not. Snapped one by one into nothing, devoured by light and fire and Song.

And then there was nothing. Silence fell – or perhaps it was the absence of the cacophony. An expectant air upon the crowd of elves.

Aedon's chest heaved, taking life-giving breaths, the air now free from that poisonous vitiation and searingly fresh and cold. Across from him, straightening, a heaving chest also betraying Her exertion, Solanaceae stood. Cold fury was in those molten eyes, but it was not directed at him.

He followed Her gaze.

Down to the circle free of snow upon the ground.

Now he understood what felt so different. So clean. That taint of dark sorcery was absent.

Gone? he wondered.

Aedon could not see a single one of those dark marks, nor feel the power that had throbbed there moments before, stubborn in its wish to cling to life there.

Her lips moved, and then he realised that the clamour of the explosion had deafened him. All he could hear was the ringing of his own ears. But he could see from the wideness of Her mouth that she too, Sang. Her hands rose so they stretched out, and he could feel that magic coursing through him.

That sound slowly filtered through the buzzing in his

ears, rich and melodious, searing into his heart such sweet joy and bitter sorrow in the same moment, he thought his heart would be entirely stilled by it.

Still, Solanaceae's hands rose, and with them rose other things. Living things. Roiling and carving through the frigid earth as though it were newly tilled soil, warm and ready for sowing. Impossible plants and flowers grew there as vines and shoots and saplings forged upwards, as tall as his knee, and then to his waist, and then, shivering as leaves grew and unfurled at breakneck pace, his head, and beyond. All the while, those vines and grasses, mosses and plants churned up the snow around them. Solanaceae took Her vengeance on death and darkness with life and light.

Aedon spun on the spot, gaping in wonder as those vines and climbers ascended the tors around them, sprouting heavy blooms that spilled out perfumes onto the air. An impossible contrast with the snow that surrounded them all, the winter of Pelenor holding firm on the land.

At last, Solanaceae ceased, and so too did Her people, their melody and their magic fading on the wind. She looked drawn, the cost of such magic great upon Her.

Relief swirled with nausea inside Aedon. They had been lucky. That darkness – he had felt how close it had come to prevailing.

Around them, an oasis of green and life now stood, choking the tors. Before them, that bare earth was now rich and grassy, a patch of snowdrops sprouting from the centre.

"He will find no purchase here again," Solanaceae said, satisfied, defiant against what had challenged them, Her voice betraying none of the risk that had almost ended them all. A wicked smile curled as She looked at the delicate, white blooms. It softened as She beheld the rest of their creation. "Here shall ever be an oasis for life and light."

Aedon had no words and could only bow. Around them, elves moved through the trees that were already taller than they, stepping carefully over flowers and past bushes and tangles of greenery as they marvelled at their creation and then departed.

"Your fire is most appreciated, Aedon of House Felrian," Solanaceae said, Her stare level. It was as close to a respectful thanks as he would receive. He could not remember the last time She had not called him "thief" or something as derogatory.

It stirred something within him that he still did not dare to aspire to. Hope. Hope that perhaps, despite his obligation to the Queen and Her refusal to truly release him, he was closer to true freedom than he had been before.

Solanaceae marched away without another word to him. "Onwards, to Tournai," She said to all and sundry, Her powerful voice ringing out with ease over them all.

Ah, yes.

Onwards, to Tournai. His sense of relief and victory faded. Aedon shivered. This was but one anchor. Who knew how many more existed?

CHAPTER 30

Waking was painful. Every inch of Morrigan felt as though she had been battered like tenderized meat, and pain sheared through her head like a knife.

It took a long few moments before she recalled what had happened. Her body seized up at the memory, spurring a wave of cramps rolling through her.

She groaned.

"You're awake! Morrigan." Vasili's voice was urgent and filled with emotion.

Morrigan blinked, slow and bleary-eyed, licking her dry lips – her mouth tasted of iron, oddly – and fisting the coverlet in her hands. *So soft. Wasn't this stone?* Sensory awareness overloaded her. It felt as though she had been scoured raw, and now even the slightest graze on any of her senses was too much, too jarring, too painful, like a raw nerve being tested.

But there it was, the kernel of truth nestled within. The

cause of it all. The deeply dehumanising violation that she had suffered. Any empathy for those who had also borne it at the mercy of the Order was washed away with raw fury before it could be acknowledged.

Morrigan hissed, propping herself up on her elbows and scrambling back from Vasili, even though she could hardly escape him, backed into the corner as she was. "You bastard!"

Vasili shifted in the chair he sat in, placed so close to her bed his knees bumped it as he moved. "I'm sorry, truly. I did not know he would go so far." He raised his hands to placate her, but it only riled her further.

Morrigan vaulted out of the bed, stumbling as her hands caught and shifted her centre of balance.

Bound.

They had bound her once more with that hateful, magical chain.

Morrigan screeched, molten rage pouring through her. She backed into the corner of the room as Vasili stood, approaching her slowly, his palms still raised to her.

"Morrigan, please, listen. I—"

"No!" she cut him off with a howl. "You are a liar and a traitor! I curse the ground you walk on. May your soul die, and may you suffer for eternity in sin!"

"It wasn't like that. I promise you, I—"

She could not hear him, her shriek was so loud. So loud that he blanched before her, stumbling to a halt.

She was right. She had been right all along. There was no good or evil. These people, Vasili's people, Vasili himself, were no martyrs, no do-gooders. They were exactly as filthy and sinful as she had been taught, and she knew but one way to deal with them.

I should have killed him the moment I had the chance. She would not delay any longer. She would not hesitate.

Morrigan charged at him, taking him by surprise. The cuffs and long chain gave her enough room to manoeuvre to throw a punch that sent him reeling – and a new world of pain shooting from her fist up her arm.

He went down with a cry and was back up on his feet in an instant. Wary and defensive, but not aggressive. Exhaustion and disorientation threw her next swing off. Granted, she was better fed than she had been in a lifetime, but without training to keep up her physique in recent weeks, it only served to make her feel slower and unwieldy.

She crouched and barrelled towards him again. He sidestepped enough to catch her with his arm across her belly, and he wrapped her into him, her back pressed to his front.

"Stop it, damn it!" he growled, but it made her fight all the harder.

She wrenched herself from his grasp, and when he tugged her back, she was waiting. With a feint to the side, she shoved him forward, wheeling behind him. In one movement, she looped the chain connecting her hands around his neck. And tightened. And pulled.

A standing mirror beyond reach showed her savagery in all its glory – and his surprised terror.

Vasili's eyes widened, and he retched, the cry in his throat choked off. His hands tore at the links around his throat, but he could not find purchase. She pulled, hating him, hating herself – she did not know whom she despised more, for it all blended into one churned-up cesspit.

Desperation was obvious in his widened eyes. Magic flared in his hands, and the chain and bracelets burned Morrigan, but she could not escape them. She cried out in pain as blistering welts seared into her skin, but still she pulled. What other choice did she have now but to keep going?

Vasili struggled, pulling Morrigan this way and that, and she threw her weight against the direction of his movement – until he surged with her, and together, they fell.

A blast of magic propelled them into that mirror, and with it, her cuffs fractured, the link between them clean sheared through. His magic was so wild in its desperation, it fizzled through the metal, eating it into nothingness, cuffs and all. Morrigan squeezed her eyes shut as the mirror shattered over the pair of them, landing hard enough to wind her. She moved on instinct, rolling away, but Vasili was faster. He launched himself at her, pinning her to the floor, his wrists like vices on her forearms, his weight dead upon her, so she could do little but twist and buck under him, her legs kicking out uselessly.

"Stop!" he commanded, his voice unyielding. This close, Vasili's hard breathing fanned across her face, his teeth bared and glistening above her. Her chest heaved. He shifted his weight, the sheathed dagger at his waist bumping into her hip.

Morrigan blazed defiance at him, but something akin to regret soured the edge of her enjoyment at seeing the burning line seared into his throat from where his own magic heating the chain had burned him.

The chain. Despite the throb of her wrists, she could feel the cuffs and the weight of the chain were simply gone. His magic, so urgently seeking to ensure his survival, had inadvertently freed her.

The promise of freedom throbbed through her, and Morrigan's heart missed a beat with the powerful temptation of it.

Morrigan knew what she had to do.

"What in the damn hells were you thinking?" Vasili snarled. "I am not your enemy!"

Morrigan spat up at him.

He gaped at her. "I tried to save you, damn it." He released her wrist to wipe the smear from his cheek.

"I don't need saving," she raged back at him. In one fluid movement, Morrigan wrenched the dagger from its place at his hip. A split second. And damn her, she hesitated. She knew what she should do. What she had to do. Thrust up under his ribs, through the soft flesh of his unguarded belly, straight into his heart. Fatal.

She punched it into his gut instead.

He grunted.

The sound resonated deep into her, like he had stabbed her too.

Their eyes met. She saw in them the flicker of betrayal. And the question.

Why?

Vasili convulsed forward, almost crushing her.

The current of adrenaline and desperation running through her tripled her strength. Morrigan shoved him off, rolling him away, the dagger coming with a sickly squelch, still tight in her hand. She stared at her hand as though out of her own body for a moment. It glistened red, the blood hot on her skin.

His blood.

"I had no choice! Damn you!" Morrigan scrambled to her feet, backed away.

Vasili curled in on himself, but he craned his neck up at her, face pale, blanched in pain as a dark wetness spread through his garment and sanguine liquid squeezed through the fingers that he pressed to the wound. "Don't," he ground out. A single word of a plea.

Don't do this.

He shuddered.

Morrigan turned and ran.

CHAPTER 31

Morrigan could outrun Vasili, lying bleeding out upon her bedroom floor, but she could not outrun the crashing guilt that chased her.

What if he dies?

She growled. What did she care if he died? He was a traitor. A sinner. They all were. It was nothing more than they deserved!

And she...Morrigan turned the hateful thoughts onto herself as she barrelled downstairs, slicing at a guard, as fleet as a passing shadow of black and steel as she dispatched him. He fell with a thud to the floor, but she did not slow or turn.

She was the worst of them all. She could have killed him. And damn it, she ought to have done. Vasili had been right there, at the mercy of his own knife in her hands, and with one plunge, she could have ended him.

Why did you give him mercy?

Her skin itched and crawled with self-revulsion. She

would have to punish herself savagely to atone for such mercy, such weakness.

Did I do the right thing?

She had no answer, for two halves of her vied to be correct. The dark side of her, she embraced, she understood, but that new facet of her, the one that felt more tender, more wild, more unfamiliar scared her with its potential for any sort of compassion.

You left him to die. He will die. That is enough.

It did not matter how he ended up dead. Why, a slow, painful death served him better.

Yes, that's right, she encouraged herself. *You did not show him mercy. You did not hesitate – you chose a worse way for him to suffer. That was right. You saved yourself.*

And yet that river of doubt wormed through her, a growing part of her wanting to turn back. To undo stabbing him at all.

Morrigan thundered through the front door and down the steps, snatching a cloak as she passed the hooks next to the front door. It was early morning, still dark, and mercifully unguarded. She leapt up onto the driver's bench of the carriage waiting outside and shoved the unsuspecting man off unceremoniously.

He crunched to the cobbles headfirst, cried out, and was still.

It was a small carriage, a single horse. Morrigan lashed it with the reins and whip, and it spurred into action, driving forward with such force it jolted her in the seat and she had to brace or tumble off herself.

"Yah!" she snapped, driving the horse perilously fast on the icy streets.

They careened down through the levels of the city, slowing as the streets clogged with other horses, carriages, wagons, people.

Her heart thundered with the rush of her own making and the threat of her escape failing. She had to escape, she had to. Now she had irrevocably burned whatever tiny bridges she might have built in Tournai, the only way was forward. The only destination was the Order. They would praise her, surely, for her noble efforts in flying their flag alone in the citadel of her enemies.

If they do not find out you betrayed them too, her mind insidiously suggested. Morrigan snarled.

"Get out of my way!" she shouted at a gaggle of washer-women holding up the traffic, huge baskets resting on their hips, scarves tying back their hair, burly arms exposed to the biting winter pre-dawn.

They shrieked as Morrigan forged through them with the horse, cutting a path without waiting and forcing them to dive out of her way or be crushed beneath hoof or wheel.

And then she was through them, thundering away once more – to become caught in a gridlock of wagons waiting to leave the city. At any moment, she expected shouts behind her, for the alarm to sound, for the portcullis ahead of her to lower, trapping her there for a punishment even more severe than Lord Halkian's invasion of her mind.

Yet nothing came. The gatehouse loomed. The portcullis was overhead, like iron jaws waiting to gnash closed upon her. Then she was through.

Trundling in the midst of all those wagons loaded with produce for other cities or empty to return to their homes.

The horse plodded obediently, its speed matching those around it.

No challenge came.

She wove through the slower carts, eager to put distance between her and the citadel yawning at her back, still too close for comfort, a wolf nipping at her exposed heels. They filtered agonisingly slowly to one side to let her pass, and then there was a way ahead clear for her to drive the horse faster.

When dawn came, Tournai was already falling over the horizon on the hills she passed between. Her ungloved hands were freezing, yet she did not dare stop, and her softening belly rumbled in mutiny at the lack of fare it had received, but she had nothing to offer it except her own hardened will. She would not sacrifice her effort now, so soon, so weakly.

As Morrigan tipped her hooded face to the sky, breathing the clean air, Vasili's blood still sticky on her hands, she did not know whether she wanted to laugh or grieve.

Freedom.

CHAPTER 32

Lief did not see the city of Tournai from afar, for the host of wood elves evanesced from the Silent Sisters, travelling on wind and shadow, right into the courtyard of the royal palace itself. Their numbers were so huge, they filled the space and spilled out beyond, snaking through the gate and out – what lay beyond, Lief could not observe.

Her first impression was of being *contained* by the grey stone, inside the high walls that rose around the space. It was constricting, confining, and a world away from the open forests and glades of Tir-na-Alathea.

With the height of the walls, what little daylight remained in the depths of winter seemed cut off, and shadows pooled as deep as the snow in forgotten corners. Overhead, the castle soared. Imposing. Dark. Cold.

It was so far removed from the warmth, light, and life of Tir-na-Alathea, and the organic structures that so seamlessly integrated with the landscape, that Lief could not help but stare, open-mouthed at it all – but with more horror than awe at how the Pelenor elves had crushed any natural aspects of the landscape there.

Around Lief, elves waited in silent, disciplined ranks, whilst ahead, Solanaceae greeted their unwitting hosts – elves garbed in dark cloaks. To Lief, pale, tall, and stern-faced strangers.

Apprehension coiled through her. What had she dreamed of when she had envisioned adventure? She had not known what to expect, that was for certain. *Did I imagine everywhere would be like Tir-na-Alathea?* Lief frowned at the thought. She rubbed her bare arms, glad for the shielding warmth of the magic she called upon to keep the winter chill away. Still, it had found its way insidiously into her heart.

She did not care for the lifeless cold stone of this place – and for a moment wondered if she had been right to follow that wild notion for adventure. And Aedon. Not when it meant leaving behind the forest – a home so integral to her that without it surrounding her, she felt as though a limb were missing.

Aedon's stomach roiled. It had been decades since he had stood in that precise spot, before the royal palace. A different elf in a different life. And now that life perhaps taunted him. Would it return? Was it gone forever? Here, he would find an answer to the question he had – what was to come next? He was scared of the answer.

The great doors opened, silver armour flashing as the guards heaved the giant leaves apart. Down the wide stairs strode a delegation from Pelenor's council. They made straight for Queen Solanaceae, who stood before silent lines of Her warriors. Aedon was a few metres behind and off to one side, hidden in the ranks.

He recognised the faces before him – like ghosts from a former life.

Lord Dimitrius Vaeri Mortris of House Ellarian. Aedon's once great nemesis within Pelenor's former court. And since the fall of Saradon, an ally. Their bond had been forged unbreakably in battle and blood – and in a shared care for Dimitrius' now wife, Harper. Aedon wondered if she too still lived, resided with Dimitrius, and what had passed of his once close friend. Something within him clenched at that. Here, of all places, he was most likely to see her. The closest remnant of his previous life.

Beside Dimitrius, as equally stern-faced, stood General Elyvia of the Winged Kingsguard. Once deputy when Aedon had held her rank. A respected soldier, and a good elf he could rely on. Would she even remember him? Recognise him?

A curl of unease loosened within Aedon. Maybe he had no idea what he was getting himself into. *Maybe you should have stayed hidden in the forest with Lief.* Life had been much more straightforward in her arms and without responsibilities.

Around them, half a dozen members of the council flocked, hastening to greet the Queen. Half new faces he did not remember or recognise. The other half were lesser nobles of the court whose faces seemed familiar, though he did not know them well.

The Queen, along with Her personal retinue, El'hari and

Aedon included, were whisked inside. As he ascended the once familiar steps, Aedon glanced backwards. Knowing Lief was present. But he could not see her amongst the faceless ranks of her kin, so many of them were there.

"*I'll come for you*," he promised her, sending the message across the mental bridge between them.

A pang of discomfort was her reply. No doubt, with their numbers so large, the Tir-na-Alathean warriors would be expected to stand and wait until lodgings could be found for them. Aedon, at the very least, had somewhere to stay – and Lief by extension – if the place still belonged to him. He had plenty of assets squirreled away. Enough to set up once more.

He wondered if those he had cared for still waited for him – or remembered him. After the fall of Saradon, Aedon had been acquitted of his crimes in Pelenor during his time as a virtuous outlaw, but still – he had been gone so very long, who knew what had happened to any of Pelenor?

Aedon followed the Queen and High Council to the council chamber. It was a large, vaulted hall that brought yet more uncomfortable memories, mainly of his time there serving King Toroth, the mad king. Toroth had been the last in the line of monarchs ruling Pelenor and a cruel elf whose bidding Aedon had abhorred to do and yet been bound to.

His heart stuttered as he entered and, his eyes drawn by a flutter of movement, beheld a familiar face. Harper. His once dear friend, their comradery forged through weathering the greatest of adversities together. In the decades that had passed, she had changed little, thanks to the long and blessed endurance of the elven race, but he could tell the difference as he drank in the details of her.

Her hair was longer and not quite so full. Her face lengthened, some of the plumpness of her youth beginning to draw tighter. She was sterner than he remembered, her eyes darker than before with the weight of wisdom she now carried.

She had not seen Aedon, had not perceived him. Her face turned to Dimitrius'. It lit up with a smile that soon faded into serious contemplation as she saw their guest – the Queen of the Woodland realm herself. As far as Aedon knew, the twain had not met since the battlefield decades before where they had cast down Saradon and, through him, Valxiron at his last rising.

They all should have known then, he thought in dismay. They should have realised that of course, that dark and powerful lord would not have had only one way to reincarnation.

"We welcome you and extend the hospitality of our hearth and hall to you and yours, Your Majesty," General Elyvia said. Before the Queen, all swept into low bows.

The Queen acknowledged them with a slight incline of Her head. "As well you know, I would not venture forth from my realm without utmost need, and such a time has come once more."

"Your messenger passed on some brief detail," Lord Dimitrius acknowledged, shooting the general a troubled look. "Enough to cause us concern."

"Then I shall not lean to brevity to ensure you understand the full weight of why my people and I felt such urgent need to come." Solanaceae stared out at the council. "A mirror, if you will. I shall show you."

One was speedily procured from the palace and laid

gently on the floor. The huge rectangle reflected the vaulted stone arches of the ceiling above, decoratively carved with dragons, flames, and clouds.

Aedon looked away as the mirror's surface darkened to ash. He knew what was to come, and he did not desire to see it unfold again in the light of day. He still saw it enough in his nightmares. It seemed to take an age before She was done and the tale was shown. The darkness that had taken Lune, encroaching throughout her realm from the dark blight emanating from Valxiron's hidden anchor, and the danger that it posed.

"This is a grave blow," General Elyvia said at last. She still stared at the mirror, though once more it reflected the innocuous ceiling. "Valxiron rising anew. Unimaginable. I wish it were not so, but I cannot doubt you, Your Majesty." She shook her head, without words for a few moments. "We have our own dark news, but perhaps it pales in comparison to this."

Aedon's attention piqued, and he lifted his head to stare at the general, safely hidden still within the ranks of Solanaceae's personal guard.

"The Order of Valxiron masses once more," Elyvia said. "We discovered in recent weeks a hidden citadel in the eastern mountains. They are dealt with, but their grandmasters and oracle fled, along with a relic of alleged priceless value – Erendriel's remains."

A chill crawled through Aedon at her words. *Surely not. Could this be a coincidence?* He did not believe in them.

The very air crackled with oppressive energy like the calm before a thunderstorm broke as the Queen drew Herself up with ire. "You speak truly? Erendriel's rest is violated?" Solanaceae's nostrils flared, and She took a step forward.

Elyvia, to her credit, did not fall back but nodded. "I am afraid it appears so. We are, at present, determining the truth of those accounts and where the grandmasters and oracle may have fled to so we may understand how strong our old enemy truly is before we face them. Yet, if you bring us news of the true darkness, Valxiron himself, not only his puppets..." Elyvia shook her head, unable to finish.

"It is darker than any of us yet feared," the Queen said scathingly. "We faced his anchor at the Silent Sisters. One of your own was of greatest help in defeating that darkness, and at Lune. Without his fire, we may not have prevailed. Aedon Lindhir Riel of House Felrian, come forth."

Aedon's breath ceased, his chest constricting in panic. But already, before him, ranks of wood elves parted. Leaving him exposed. Open.

He forced himself into one wooden step, and then another.

The pale, shocked faces of the council were frozen before Aedon as he raised his chin and stood as tall as he dared, garbed in the armour of the wood elves of Tir-na-Alathea. He swallowed and met Harper's eyes.

She looked as though she had seen a ghost. Her lips parted, and her eyes fixed upon him with slack wonder.

"It was my honour, my Queen." Aedon bowed to Solanaceae, but when he stood, his attention returned to Harper across the vast space.

Aedon could see a shine – of tears glistening in her eyes.

Harper closed her mouth and swallowed. Something

intense and unspoken burned in her gaze, and her expression softened upon him.

The Queen spoke once more, and both of them dragged their eyes away from each other.

"I grant him his complete and unending freedom in response to his noble defence of my realm and the depths of his bravery."

Aedon stilled, and he was certain he had imagined the words, but Queen Solanaceae regarded him impassively for a moment before She turned away to continue – as though she had passed comment on the weather, not the fortunes of his whole life.

Roaring filled Aedon's ears as he focused on remaining standing. *Free.* That was what she had said, no? *I am free.*

The Queen continued, but he barely heard.

"...appreciate the unexpectedness of our arrival, but I saw no course of action less extreme that was justified. We will not rest and rise too late, speculate and fail once more. I have no doubt Valxiron moves to power once more, and that if he had two anchors that we have yet faced, there will be many more – in addition to his foul supporters, who breed unchecked, it appears."

She glared haughtily around at them all, as though She stood Queen in their council. "We must combine all efforts to stop him before our disarray and complacence becomes our downfall."

Shattered silence greeted Her declaration.

CHAPTER 33

Red hot pain speared through Vasili. He could not breathe for it as he curled in upon himself, clutching at the source of that pain – where Morrigan had stabbed him.

She stabbed me.

Vasili could scarcely believe it, shock sending him numb for a moment. As if it were not bad enough that Morrigan had tried to strangle him with her chain – his neck throbbed, the painful chokehold mixing with the sting of his burning skin where he had broken the chain to save himself and enabled her attack and escape in the process.

He tried to move, but it was too painful. Vasili gritted his teeth and tried again. He had to try. Fury rose in him – at his weakness, at her forced ultimatum, which was nothing less than he ought to have expected. It veiled a rising fear of what she would be capable of now she was free, for he did not expect to find her anywhere in the house.

Grunting with the strain of his injury, he glanced down. *Red.* So much blood. The floor became the ceiling and then the floor again as his senses swam. Outside, a ruckus grew, but it seemed to come from far away, drifting further, and with it, so too drifted Vasili as he slumped to the floor and knew no more, his lifeblood slipping from the wound Morrigan had inflicted with his own dagger.

Blissful nothing first greeted Vasili as he awoke. A slight tug of soreness in his belly pulled him in from the untethered clouds through which he slowly floated. The indistinct sounds around him seemed thick, muffled.

They solidified into voices, ones he recognised. *Mother. Father.*

"Oh, thank goodness," his mother huffed, and before Vasili opened his eyes, he could feel her familiar cool hand upon his brow. For a moment, it threw him back to a distant memory of childhood sickness.

He groaned as he opened his eyes.

It all flooded back.

Vasili kicked off the covers atop him, scrambling up, before hands pushed him back onto the bed in which he found himself. His own, he realised after a moment of confused thought – for he had just been in Morrigan's bedroom. Except now, it was daylight, whereas it had been dark. And he had been stabbed – the pain, it had overwhelmed him. There had been so much blood. His last tendril of thought had been that it was *too* much, and maybe he would not wake again. The confusion stalled him. What had passed?

"Rest, son," his father said. "You've had an ordeal."

"Morrigan! She's escaped – we need to find her!" Vasili struggled against his father's and the healer's hands holding him down.

Again, they shoved him firmly back into the bed – but, at a growl of protest, allowed him to prop himself up on his pillows.

"We know," said Dimitrius gravely. "She's gone."

Vasili gaped at his father for a moment before a flicker of movement behind him caught Vasili's eye. General Elyvia.

Vasili's heart sank like a stone. If the general had come... *I'm in serious trouble.*

"What happened?" asked Elyvia, but her tone was not unkind. Still, her scrutiny made him squirm.

In a low voice, Vasili recounted what had passed until the moment he had known no more. "What now?" he dared to ask, his gaze crossing all of theirs – a wall of inscrutable faces from his mother, to his father, to the healer, to Elyvia.

Elyvia clenched her jaw. "She's gone. A guard and your carriage driver were seriously injured, though they will survive, and of course, you were too."

Vasili wanted the bed to swallow him up. "It's my fault. I'm sorry," he whispered.

Elyvia shook her head, her teeth still gritted. "Her choices are not your fault, Vasili."

But Vasili shook his head. Guilt surged through him, hot regret causing his throat to clog and his eyes to burn as tears of shame prickled. He had thought the two of them were finally beginning to reach some shaky kind of understanding, a truce, perhaps, but Vasili knew he had been entirely wrong.

Of course, you could not shake a lifetime of faith. Like I did, she's been biding her time. I betrayed what little had built between us. No wonder she fled.

His own betrayal, called by his duty or not, had been the last shred. It had been the kindling that had sparked her explosive wrath. She had seen an opportunity and taken it.

But... The insidious thought landed. *She spared me.* He replayed that horrific moment again and again involuntarily. Vasili knew Morrigan was well-schooled in the art of death. She had had the perfect opening to end him, and yet she had not taken the opportunity to thrust a killing shot. She had mortally wounded him, but in such a way that he had a chance of survival if someone found him in time.

A chill settled over him.

Had that been her intended consequence? Had she intended to give him a fighting chance? But, in the end, had she left it down to that – mere chance? Was it mere chance that he had been found and saved in time?

"Where is she?" he dared to ask.

"Long gone," Elyvia replied. "We found the carriage abandoned far outside the city. Our wards checking her power will have disintegrated at that distance. She will be restrained no more. Doubtless, she evanesced away as soon as she could. She could be anywhere now."

She has returned to the Order. He did not want to voice the thought aloud, but he reckoned they all thought the same. *She has gone where I cannot follow.* He had failed, and he would not receive a chance again to turn her to a better path. The bitter guilt of that stabbed into him like his knife – only this time, it savaged him over and over. Vasili curled over into himself.

"What will happen now?" he asked, his voice muffled.

"War."

A frisson of movement fluttered around them all at that ominous word.

Elyvia spoke, but her tone was quiet, the hint of apology upon it. "Morrigan yielded all the information we needed to move against the Order. Most significantly..." Elyvia sighed, and her shrewd glance assessed Vasili, as though deciding whether or not to divulge more.

"The oracle is the key to it all. Within her lives the very spirit of Valxiron himself, like a master to all other anchors. She is more dangerous than ever we feared – but if we can destroy the oracle, we can destroy Valxiron."

Vasili gaped. Morrigan's own mother, the oracle, a greater thread than any of them had known. Did Morrigan hold any of that dark power? Unease curdled within him.

"With her escape, we also lose whatever small bargaining chip we had – and the element of surprise. We must be ready to mobilise by the close of midwinter celebrations. If the Order moves first, they may raise more of Valxiron's anchors, and then..." Elyvia trailed off as though she did not want to contemplate what that meant.

Midwinter. He had almost forgotten about that, so absorbed with Morrigan as he had been. The invite to a family dinner seemed an age ago now. Vasili sat up. "I'm coming."

Elyvia raised a brow.

"Please," Vasili said, strengthening that word with a plea

in his tone. "I have to make this right. I'll be fit enough to fly. Right?" He looked to the healer.

The elf nodded, though worry clouded his face. "Yes, but I would ask that you exercise caution. Magic healings are nothing short of miracles, but you will still be tender, and you will need to understand how to move with the new scar tissue. Some muscle was severed, so this will need to be strengthened carefully."

"Of course," Vasili said automatically, but his mind already raced. *War.* And, if he found the Order, perhaps he could yet again find her. Perhaps all was not lost.

That evening, Vasili made his way to the dragonhold, following the trail of seething terror and worry that Icarus blared in all directions.

"You!" Icarus snarled. "You always get into trouble when I am not there to help!" He gnashed his teeth. "I told you she was terrible news."

"All right, all right," Vasili said wearily, stifling a yawn. Despite the aid of magic to heal his body, he was exhausted from the day's events, for such healings took a physical toll, and the emotional one lurked too, deep and unhealing under the skin.

He rested his cheek on Icarus' muzzle and closed his eyes.

Icarus whined softly.

"It's all right, my friend," he said, even though it was not.

Icarus' answering huff told him the dragon was not fooled either.

Vasili sighed. "What is the truth, Icarus? We are so opposed, and I believe my truth wholly, and she hers, yet only one can be true. So who is right and who is wrong?"

"Does it have to be so cut and dried?"

"What do you mean?"

"Can it be neither and both?" the dragon answered cryptically. "Each person's truth is different. What we feel is true to our being. What we acknowledge may not be. What you think is her truth may not be her real truth – she is not bound to bare her soul to you honestly. Besides which, are we all not permitted to bear flaws? What we think is our truth is a tapestry of many weaving threads, some true, some not, to form all that we are.

"Perhaps both of your truths can be true, or at least fragments. It does not make one less valid than the other. That is the beauty of this life's journey, is it not? Testing each truth, one by one, seeking answers, adjusting course each time, evolving, until we find such answers as resonate within ourselves and without."

Vasili chewed over the dragon's words.

"But..." They each had such opposing world views. Even down to the origin stories of Valxiron himself, to Erendriel. They could not *both* be true in their current forms. He could still not discern which one was correct – how very wrong one of them was.

"But nothing. Think on it," chided Icarus gently. "We grow, we change, we evolve – if we are wise. For wisdom is not in the destination, but in the journey. Perhaps part of your journey, and part of hers, is how you can each influence the other to distil your truths."

Icarus spoke as though there were a future to be had

there. Perhaps between Morrigan and Vasili, whatever that looked like. But Morrigan had fled, and war came, and despair roiled within Vasili as hot tears erupted, because he did not see how both of them would survive it to embark on such a profound journey.

CHAPTER 34

"Well met, Junior Librarian." A sardonic voice echoed through the vault. *Sylvestri di Niani Verdiatris*, The Book of Gateways, or more commonly called amongst the librarians, 'Sylvio'. A grimoire that had saved Venya's life on her illicit and misguided quest to rebind an escaped grimoire of incomparable power and danger. He was also a grimoire that was as untrustworthy as he was sarcastic. In other words, very.

Venya thumbed the brass token in her pocket. Back to her normal duties she had returned with relief several days ago, but it was the first time she had encountered Sylvio since their misadventures.

"Good morning, Sylvio," she said agreeably, not rising to his usual taunt of her inferior rank.

She moved along the shelves to his bay, where he rustled at her presence, pages fluttering. His chain, securing him to the shelf, clinked as he moved. The violet of his new binding caught the faelight, glimmering with faint iridescence.

"What do you think of my new binding?" he said, oozing smugness. He fluttered his cover open and shut as much as the padlock and chain allowed, his silver corner accents flashing as they caught the light. On the cover was embossed text in shimmering silver to match – his name, but in a foreign alphabet that Venya had not yet learned.

"Magnificent, of course." Sylvio always did like an ego boost, and she would oblige. He had saved her life, after all. Besides which, he knew about Nyx, which the First Librarian most certainly did *not*. She had no intention of Sylvio dropping her in even more bother.

"Quite, quite," he said, immensely pleased, ruffling his newly cleaned pages. Last she had seen him, he had been blackened and dirty, with a myriad of scars and scratches marring his binding. He had been in a disgraceful state – thanks to his surprisingly noble and stalwart efforts to save her and the Athenaeum from the fiendish clutches of the escaped beast.

She was glad that he had been fixed up to even better than his former glory. He wouldn't be able to moan at her then – rather, perhaps, she would consider that he owed her for that, as much as she owed him for keeping the secret of her little *companion*.

"What brings you to my fine, dusty shelf today, young librarian?" Sylvio affected a bored tone – he never liked to appear too interested in anyone else, Venya knew.

"I just wanted to check to see how my favourite grimoire is doing."

"It's taken you long enough," he said sniffily, slamming his covers shut.

Venya winced. "Yes. After our, um, escapades, I was

punished. I haven't had my token for a month." She held up the brass token between her first and second fingers before slipping it back into her pocket.

"Punished, you say?" Sylvio sounded positively gleeful.

"Yes, thanks for caring." Her reply was acerbic. "I've been stuck in a stuffy, windowless vault for a month without any sight of the sun."

"Oh, I wonder how awful that's been." He dripped sarcasm, and too late she realised the error of her words. Sylvio had been in that position for centuries.

"You're a grimoire," she reminded him.

"I still like to feel fresh air on my pages, young lady." His tone became less hostile. "So, if you ever decide to have any more *adventures*, you'll know where to find me, hmm?"

Venya grinned. "Not likely. I have to toe the line for a good long while now. I'm still in trouble, I reckon. But thank you. I mean it. I wouldn't have survived without your quick thinking and your incredible skills."

Sylvio rustled open, fluttering his pages happily. "I'm rather magnificent, yes. I can find anything in a pinch, you know, if ever you need my services. It would be far better than wasting away on a dusty, old shelf century after century."

Chuckling, she returned to her duties, feeling lighter than she had done for the last month, her punishment finally served – but in a darker corner of her heart lurked an unassuaged hunger to know more than her current rank allowed. It would be *years* before she got her hands upon grimoires as fascinating and dangerous again.

Venya sighed.

Patience definitely wasn't a virtue she possessed.

As she returned to the surface, away from the vaults in the depths below the mountain, a familiar tendril of presence crossed hers.

Venya stopped dead.

She had not felt it in a year, since last mid-Winter.

I'm imagining it. It cannot be.

She ran upstairs, her light boots slapping against each stone step as she raced towards the atrium, where—

"Ven!"

She stopped dead. In the centre of the large space, a familiar figure awaited. Dark cloaked, tall, stern, and severe – more so than she remembered him.

"Vas!" Venya raced forward to her twin brother, and Vasili enveloped her in a mighty embrace, but it was so much weaker than usual. Normally, he so strong he lifted her off her feet, and he would swing her round in a circle and set her down. Now, he grimaced as she stepped back.

Gods, when did he get so big? Her brother had not been so fearsome the last time they had seen each other. She took him in – the fresh bulge of muscles packing out his once lean and gangling form, the hollowing of his cheekbones and set of his brows making him appear more like their father Dimitrius than ever. And yet he could barely embrace her. *Is he injured?*

"I forgot how much you look like Mother," he said with a laugh as he took her in. "Your hair grew."

"It's been a year. You didn't write for ages!" Venya said accusingly.

Vasili's face fell. "We have much to speak of. I have been...*indisposed* for a while, shall we say." Between the bond that linked them as twins, the one that had severed in their adulthoods and separation of their physical selves, she could feel the truth of his words in the seeping unsettlement that crossed the bridge between them.

"Is all well?" Unease settled within her too.

Vasili shook his head. "We cannot speak of it here. Tonight. A family dinner. Mother insists – you know what she's like."

"All right." Venya's curiosity piqued at his cryptic message, with a tinge of apprehension lacing the edges. "Are you well?" she asked quietly.

This close, she could see the dark shadows pooling under his eyes, the worry in his drawn brows, the tension from his stiff form.

He paused. "No," he said after a moment, and she knew it was the truth.

Venya leaned in to kiss him on the cheek. "It's good to see you, brother."

Vasili caught her hand as she stepped back and gave it a squeeze. He shot her a faint smile. "Likewise. More than you know. There was a time when I thought I would not see you again." He straightened, and she could see the will it took to stretch that smile wider. It did not light his eyes though. She was no fool.

He cleared his throat. "Tonight. Dinner. Seventh bell."

"I'll see you there, brother." Venya smiled in return, but it was hollow too as that lengthening unease coiled and turned unpleasantly in her stomach. What in Pelenor had passed that was so terrible her brother would not even speak of it to her?

CHAPTER 35

*R*eleased at last from a fraught council meeting, Aedon escaped with all haste into the courtyard. Much as he wanted to reconnect with Harper, Elyvia, even Dimitrius, he needed Lief more.

Free. The word burned through him, hot and feverish, so fleeting he thought it would disappear.

Still, the silent ranks of wood elves waited in disciplined lines, unflinching as sleet pelted the courtyard. Aedon stifled a curse under his breath. Some had started to filter away, being led by soldiers of Tournai to lodgings. Aedon forged through the heart of them, following that tenuous connection to Lief.

As he appeared in front of her, she sagged with relief, at last allowing herself to crumble from the excruciatingly uncomfortable, straight-backed posture she had held herself rigid in for hours. Already, the pallid daylight began to fade. Thanks to the magic of their Queen, she would be warm, but not dry. Her copper hair was plastered to her head, tendrils curling down her neck, across her cheek.

Their eyes met, and she did not need to say anything. He saw the mute plea within them. For her to be free, even momentarily, from the charade that now bound them.

"She freed me," he blurted out, not caring who stood around them, who could hear him.

Lief frowned. "What?"

"Your Queen. I am free, truly, without conditions. She said it before the full council." A lump settled in his throat. "It's over." He wanted to sag, crumble to the ground in relief, as though a weight he had not known he carried had been lifted. They were still bound by obligations, tied around them like ropes, but the most binding and suffocating of his own had been lifted.

"Come on," he said. They had to get out of there – he needed to, and he would not leave her behind. He tugged her out of line, and she followed him hastily out of the courtyard. Yawning shadows engulfed them – and a blessed respite from the freezing, driving gift of the winter sky – before they passed out on the other side and it pelted them once more.

Aedon followed the shadow of the castle walls before he dived into alleyways. Despite the time that had passed, he did not step false, following the streets down and across a level until he found the archway he sought.

It seemed that everything and yet nothing had changed. The same buildings, the same cobbles, the same features of the city, though different shop fronts. The potholes on the main road had been repaired with new paving. None of the faces they passed did he recognise.

The city was decked in its finest for midwinter, the lamps and storefronts festooned with evergreen boughs, red berries, and poinsettia, the scent of pine and mulled wines twining up the streets, and the air full of the cheer and chatter of a people in celebration for the turn of the dark winter into the coming of spring.

Into a small courtyard they passed, with a leafless birch tree in the centre of the cobbled space, hung with bobbing faelights. Aedon hurried Lief to a weathered door on the other side of it. He needed to paint it again. He could have huffed with amusement.

What else had he expected? He had been gone over a quarter century. Of course the red, peeling paint would need redoing. But no matter – he did not care for such a trivial thing in that moment. He had no key, only the power of his own magic. The door had a single brass knob in the very middle of it, formed in the shape of a small dragon devouring its own tail.

Free. I'm free. The thought kept surging into the forefront of his mind.

"Where are we?" Lief asked, shadowing his steps closely. She hunched her shoulders, though it made no difference against the driving sleet, and craned her neck up. The courtyard was surrounded on all sides by the statement multi-story buildings of Tournai. Built upon the mountainside, with a dearth of ground space, the buildings had risen higher and higher over the centuries to accommodate a growing population. Here, the pale grey stone of the houses was five levels tall. The sky far above was a narrow square.

Aedon did not answer. She would see in moments – he hoped.

He stepped forward and placed a palm on that knob, wrapping his fingers around it. It still felt familiar, he realised with a strange flutter in his stomach. The way the decorative patterns in the brass bit into the whorls of his fingers. The metal was freezing cold, but under his touch, it warmed with the flare of magic.

Please, he silently implored. Hoping the place would be his. Hoping that his estate still endured. That with his disappearance from his old life, it would not have been sold off to goodness knew who.

Click.

The door gave before him. Protesting on unoiled, aged hinges that had not been opened by any other hand since his. But it had opened.

Aedon laughed with relief and shoved it open. "Come on," he said to Lief, turning and smiling at her. "Here's where we shall stay. I extend to you the full hospitality of the House of Felrian, little though it be."

"This is yours?" Lief wrinkled her nose as she passed under the dark shadow of the doorway.

"Aye," Aedon murmured. He felt strangely untethered, somewhere between the present and the past as he climbed the steps inside, coaxing small faelights into bloom in the web-covered sconces upon the dark walls.

Up he led her, right to the top of the building. No doors came off the stairs or the landings, but at each level, a tall window threw baleful winter light half-heartedly into the depths of the building. Lief trailed after him, the soft *shush* of her hand on the railing the only sound aside from their footsteps.

At the very top of the last flight of stairs, a wooden door

barred the way. At Aedon's touch, magic flared, and the brass handle clicked and turned, opening inwards silently. Aedon crossed the threshold.

It was as he remembered – and yet not.

White ghosts greeted him. Sheets covered every inch or furniture. They were not white anymore but covered with a layer of dust and starting to colour in the light. But still, it was his. Exactly how he had left it.

"What is this place?" Lief asked, brushing past him. It was a large, open sitting room. Through doors, there was a kitchen, a bedroom, a bathroom, and a balcony overlooking the city from the vantage point of what seemed like an eagle's nest.

"Home. Or at least, it once was." He frowned. It felt bare and utilitarian. Perhaps it was the harsh light of winter that stripped any warmth from it, or perhaps, perhaps his feeling of what 'home' was had entirely started to shift. Perhaps he now found himself more welcome in the forest, or perhaps it was just with *her*.

Aedon marched to the empty grate. There were still some logs in the basket beside it. It was frigid, and though he could warm it with magic, some part of him longed for the comfort of firelight to lend any kind of life to the place. Soon, a roaring fire blazed, and Lief moved closer, groaning with delight as she held out her palms to warm upon it.

"Come. Let me see if there's any linen." Aedon had not planned to be back. He had cleaned and folded everything and then put it back in the cupboard. But when he opened the cupboard, stale air wafted out. He sighed. The towels and bedsheets were unsalvageable.

"Sorry," he said ruefully. "Looks like we're down to

basics." Regardless of how long they were to stay, he would have to source some fresh bedding, towels, clothes – everything – if they were to find any comfort.

He wandered through the kitchen – every cupboard stripped bare – and the bathroom – where the bath filled with dust, not bubbles – and then the bedroom. The bed, stripped, was home to a vast stain and the stink of rot. Aedon glanced up and groaned.

"Oh, dear," Lief said faintly as she slipped inside.

"It wasn't like this when I left it." Aedon sighed and turned away from the gaping hole in the ceiling where storm damage to the roof had eaten away in his absence, come through, and destroyed the mattress. "Best laid plans. Perhaps we are better off not staying here after all."

He turned on the spot, surveying the sheet-covered sofa and lounger. This had once been his haven, but in that moment it felt foreign. *I do miss the forest. It has become more of a home to me than these walls.* It was an unsettling feeling – a sign of how much he had changed after all that had passed since he had last stood in that spot.

"I'm sorry."

Lief glanced quizzically at him. "Whatever for?"

"I can sense you do not feel at home in this city. I cannot blame you. Once, I loved it, but now, I am not so sure. There is far more to Pelenor than this place. Grassy plains, tangled gorse moors, sprawling forests, deciduous and coniferous, wetlands, seas and shores, mountains. So much of it is wild."

"Hmm. I simply do not understand how people can live in the city, barred behind stone, when there is all that out there."

Aedon smiled faintly. "Reality is made by people, and

then it is adopted as an absolute truth, I suppose. Everything you see here, all of it, was decided by someone, and no one stops to question why it is so."

Except, after so long away from this place, now he was beginning to question. *Is this life what I want to return to, even if it still exists in its entirety?* A leaky roof and some mouldy sheets could be sorted with relative ease if he wished it.

Lief opened her mouth to reply but did not speak, instead furrowing her brows at a crashing sounding from downstairs.

"What in the blazes?" Aedon muttered and strode to the stairs.

CHAPTER 36

Lief followed Aedon downstairs. Someone hammered on the door like their life depended upon it. Who would even know they were there?

Aedon pulled open the front door as Lief clattered down the last few steps after him. She halted on the bottom step, hand curling around the cap on the newel post.

A woman stood in the doorway. Her hand hung in mid-air. Mid knock.

Past Aedon, Lief caught a glimpse of long, straight, raven hair. Pale porcelain skin. Silver eyes. And formal robes of charcoal.

There was a moment of silence as Aedon stared at the stranger, and she him. And then a strangled cry escaped her, and she threw herself at him.

"It's really you!" the elf cried, her voice muffled as she buried her face into Aedon's shoulder, her arms encircling him in a fierce embrace.

Jealous rage, hot and vicious, surged through Lief –

doubling, and tripling, as Aedon picked the stranger up in a giant embrace and whirled her around on the spot. "I never thought I would see you again!"

"Thank the stars you're all right. Skies above, Aedon, what in the blazes have you gotten yourself into now? Last I heard..." The elf pulled away, her slim fingers still resting upon his upper arms. "We have so much to catch up on." The mirth and joy faded from her, worry and tension replacing it in the hard lines of her face.

Lief stepped silently down that last step onto the tiled floor. Who was this woman who behaved so overly familiarly with *her* Aedon? Old insecurities, born of Finarvon's betrayal, reared up, churning her surety into doubts and worries.

"I'm so glad you're here. I worried," the woman said. "All those years, every day, I worried what had become of you."

Lief could not breathe. It was as she feared. An old lover. Perhaps a flame to be rekindled, with her cast aside. Her chest hollowed.

"You must come for dinner. Today. It's mid-winter, and we have a feast you are welcome to share. I can assume you have no alternative? Come."

Aedon chuckled. "Gladly. And if you can offer lodgings, may I be so bold as to beg them? My own are rather poor after so very long absent."

"You are always welcome, my dear friend." She reached in to embrace him once more. "Come for dinner. Stay as long as you need. Dimitrius and I have plenty of room."

Dimitrius? Wait. Lief recognised that name.

"Harper, you must meet someone very dear to me."

Harper? It cannot be. Lief recovered her breath in a gulp as

Aedon turned to her, a beaming smile lighting him up with effervescent joy.

"Lief, *this* is the one and only Harper of the legendary tales, the very *Chronicles of Pelenor*."

The woman, Harper, scoffed behind him and nudged him in the arm. "You haven't changed, storyteller. Who, pray tell, is your friend?"

Lief did not think it possible, but Aedon's smile widened, his eyes softening upon Lief. "This is Lief na Arboreali. Ranger of Queen Solanaceae's woodland realm and thief of my heart."

Lief stilled. *What did he say?* They had so barely started to admit it to each other, and now, he threw it about publicly? Half pleased, half embarrassed, Lief felt her cheeks warm.

"It is a great pleasure to make your acquaintance, Lief na Arboreali," Harper said warmly. "I extend our hospitality to you as well." Her gaze slid back to Aedon, and she smiled coyly. "Stealer of your heart, eh? There's me thinking you were off to your doom at the Queen's hands."

"Oh, I had enough of that, don't you worry." Aedon retreated from Harper and offered his hand to Lief. She slipped hers into his uncertainly. "We have not long met, but what I have survived thanks to this incredible elf, and what she has given to me...well." Aedon squeezed Lief's hand and winked at her. "Perhaps that is another tale to tell."

Lief glared at him, a wordless plea not to divulge anything private between them. It all felt too new. She felt too fragile. She was unsure what they even were. Besides which, that pang of jealousy still curled within her, reluctant to fade. It taunted her.

How close were they? Does he still harbour feelings for her?

The way she had heard the *Chronicles of Pelenor* sometimes insinuated so. Already, she felt on the outside, not understanding the dynamic of their relationship and what lay in the unspoken gulf between them.

Harper guffawed. "Oh, there is much for the telling here. Come. You must come at once. Council has had quite enough shocks for one day, and we shan't be called until tomorrow morning now, when the first wheels are set in motion to figure out what on earth to do about it all. We may as well feed you up."

"Um…"

Harper chuckled. "Dimitrius will be there too. You two might not be adversaries anymore, water under the bridge long ago and all, and I know you do not long for his company, but I'm sure you can both put up with it for my sake. He's mellowed with age, you know, much like I expect you have." Her eyes twinkled with mirth at the subtle dig.

Aedon turned to Lief and raised his eyebrow. *Are you game?* he invited her silently.

She could hardly say no, not seeing the excitement within him, which she supposed she could understand, at seeing a friend he thought he would probably never meet in that life again. This was an altogether different adventure. One she had to steel her stomach for as she laced her fingers through Aedon's and allowed herself to be tugged along with him.

His lives had collided, the old and the new, as Aedon Lindhir Riel stood in the once familiar halls of Harper and Dimitrius' city home, a modest yet well-appointed townhouse in the upper circles of Tournai, close to the former royal palace where they both still worked as members of Pelenor's High Council.

"We have the Summer Palace, of course, and mainly reside there. But alas, we find ourselves both here on business now, graver than we could have imagined."

He remembered the place. *Lief would love it there*, he thought. Far from the city, on the northern coast, nestled in verdant lands, it had been a half-ruined and forgotten old palace, tenderly restored by Harper and Dimitrius. Perhaps one day the two of them could visit, if their hosts would permit – and if they survived. He would like to show Lief the greenhouse there, growing all manner of exotic plants and greenery.

Aedon held open the tall, slim door for Lief, who passed him.

Harper led them along a marble-floored hallway towards wide stairs carpeted in royal blue. "I'll show you to guest quarters now and have a bath drawn and fresh clothes found for you. We'll have something for both of you from Dimi's and my wardrobes, if that's all right."

"Clothing donations gratefully accepted unless you want us at the dinner table in unwashed war garb."

Harper chuckled. "No, thank you. We can find something more comfortable than that. Do you want quarters together?" she asked lightly, but Aedon did not miss the way her eyes slid between him and Lief.

"Yes," said Lief beside him, unexpectedly.

He offered her a small, crooked grin. He was unsure quite what they were, but for now, together was all that mattered. Before Queen Solanaceae, in all eventuality, probably tore them apart once more. He was as free as he had ever been, and yet it felt like the pair of them were still on a tight leash.

"If you'd be so kind," Aedon added. He shut the unhelpful thoughts away in a dark recess of his mind as he followed Harper up the stairs.

"Here. You can have this room. There's a bathroom attached – I'll send someone up with clothes. You look half frozen, you poor thing," Harper said to Lief.

"Hey! I'm half frozen too," Aedon protested.

Harper shot him a look. "And you are big enough and ugly enough to fend for yourself."

Aedon scoffed. "You know, I don't have to put up with this."

An involuntary giggle escaped Lief. She clamped a palm over her mouth.

Harper rolled her eyes. "If you can put up with him, I respect you all the more. I'll see you both at the seventh bell for dinner."

"Red wine, please. The good stuff," Aedon called after her.

"You'll get what you're given, you charlatan," she called back, with a rude hand gesture.

Aedon muttered to himself as he opened the door for them both.

"So, that's the infamous Harper?" Lief looked amused and a little thrown by the no doubt strange first impression she had received.

"Er, yes. Not whom I was expecting to see, but there she was in the council chamber with Dimitrius. Her *husband*." He laughed, and then frowned. "Life and times have moved on. I missed that too. I'll bet that was a beautiful wedding." He glanced around the room. It was warm, homely. Wood panelling, high ceilings, tall windows, soft furnishings. A four-poster bed stood beside him, and Aedon longed to sink into it, dinner be damned.

"Come on. Let's wash. I long to be free of this grime."

"So do I. I can smell you a mile off," Lief said dryly. She ducked, laughing, to avoid the feather-stuffed pillow he threw at her.

Warmth bloomed within him. He was *free*. Such an enormous thought he could hardly conceive it. Would he get to enjoy this – enjoy *her* – every day now?

CHAPTER 37

*S*nap.

She had felt it itching at the boundaries of her consciousness, but it stole Morrigan's breath when she crossed the final threshold needed – of the distance between her and her captors for their power to wane enough to break its hold upon her.

Her magic rushed in to fill the void, hungry as a raging fire, crushing as a drowning sea. The force of it knocked the breath from her as though she had tumbled from the horse. Despite bracing, her thighs tightening around the beast, the impact still sent her reeling forward over her mount, a guttural groan emerging from somewhere deep inside.

All other senses fell away, sight blinded, hearing obscured, touch scoured for a second as the pure rush of *magic* overwhelmed all. Morrigan sucked it in, as though it were a drink after a drought, for that was how she felt – parched of it.

The horse must have felt it too, for it writhed under her,

threatening to buck. Despite feeling as though she were dizzyingly drunk on power, Morrigan clung on. The carriage, she had unhitched miles back outside the city, as it had been too big and cumbersome for the beast to pull without exhausting. She had driven the horse hard after that. She was no keen rider – indeed, they had eaten the horses years ago in the mountains, for it had been that or starve – but she remembered enough.

She sent a surge of power shuddering through the horse, compelling it to still. What she did not possess in riding skill, she had in magic, enough to force the beast to comply.

"Aah." Morrigan tipped her face up to the icy sky, revelling in the power coursing through her, as familiar as breathing.

Can I? What of one of the most useful of her powers? Would she have the strength and ability to wield it to ensure her escape?

Morrigan stilled. Perhaps she did not need to slog endlessly through the gathering snows until she and the beast dropped of exhaustion and starvation. They had been going most of the day, and she did not plan to stop through the night, for fear of her captors reeling her in once more.

The traffic on the road had already thinned. She would be picked out easily. Even now, she was sure they were on her trail – they would be fools not to, and she did not think so little of them that she would underestimate them. Not after the conduct of their High Council.

She scowled. Morrigan reached deep into herself, feeling that well of power – as whole as the day it had disappeared. Perhaps even stronger, she wondered, as a result of the better nutrition she had at least received during her captivity.

Before she could dwell on the conflicting feelings she had surrounding that, because it opened the lid on more unsettling guilt about a certain Vasili, Morrigan sank into her magic.

Abandoning the horse there, in the middle of nowhere, Morrigan vanished into smoke and wind, leaving a delighted and dark peal of laughter behind her as she evanesced.

The mountain citadel they had abandoned would long be empty, Morrigan reasoned. She knew where they would go – as did the High Council, having ripped it from her mind. They would not have travelled far, not with the sick and the infirm.

In the north of Valtivar, the dwarven mountain realm bordering the east of Pelenor, were vast networks of abandoned caves, old mining networks long forsaken by the dwarves. There, she knew she would find them en route to a more permanent and defensible position. She knew they would, with the tidings she brought. Morrigan knew exactly where they would retreat to – the problem was, so did Pelenor.

She shook – from exhaustion, nerves, or the rush of power she had not felt in so long, she was not sure – by the time she reached the edge of the cave network. Weeks of travel on foot, but mere hours by evanescence. An ancient practise taken from the wood elves of Tir-na-Alathea and honed to perfection by the Order of Valxiron, who had adapted it so that it took power from the world, not the wielder, to sustain. Thus, it allowed feats so much greater than the body could endure – and thus, it allowed the Order to escape, where otherwise it might be a futile cause. Ever, the Order endured, no matter the odds. One of their mottos was to defend the cause, after all.

As I have, Morrigan thought proudly. Her eyes were gritty with tiredness, the rush of adrenaline from her escape long faded. Her whole body ached with a dull throb, her thighs burning from hours in the saddle and her lower back searing with what felt like a knife wound from the hateful posture.

Still, she stood tall and searched with her power once more for that familiar thread of magic that linked her to her people, as though she were a hound with a scent, sniffing out their very essence. *Strange. Did it reek so much of brimstone and ash before?* She frowned. Her magic was reluctant to seize it. Had so much changed in such a short time that she would feel like an outsider with her own people?

For a moment, she hesitated. Standing in that barren valley, below the snowline in a jagged canyon, where even the light struggled to reach, it was inhospitable and unwelcoming. A part of her, a part that she hated, longed to turn back, instead – and this would be her last chance – to soft bedding, warm hearth, and full stomach in that happier, wholesome place.

Morrigan nipped herself, a hard, twisting pinch on the wrist, to snap herself out of such weak thoughts. That was exactly why she needed to return. She was in danger of turning soft, damned be it. *Valxiron take me, if so, and I shall deserve every atonement.* Already, the cuts on her arms had healed. She would have to make fresh ones. Did she relish that now, or not?

Before she could curdle any of her thoughts into doubts, Morrigan disintegrated into shadow and wind once more, winding through the rocky canyon to the carved halls of stone that awaited.

A cry arose as she walked the last of the distance. No doubt they would be on high alert, ready to destroy anyone who approached. She needed to take due care to avoid that, for it would be a poor reward indeed after the trials she had endured on their behalf.

Knowing she wore the attire of her enemy, Morrigan lifted her chin and threw back her hood, letting her raven hair tumble down her shoulders and the twin scars on her cheeks stand out in stark relief below her blazing, steel eyes.

"The oracle's heir!" rang out around her from the few unfortunate bodies posted outside on guard.

"Open it," she commanded those who guarded the stone door.

They glanced at each other, as if unsure. Mortals. No magic ran through their veins that she could sense. A crack of her magic saw them both fall to the ground with cries of pain as she sent lightning fire through them.

"For your insolence," she snapped. "Do not make such a mistake again." She strode forward and pushed open the great, stone doors herself. Carved with dwarven runes she could not read and with mountains, moon, sun, and stars in relief upon the stone, it was a stark contrast to the pitch black that awaited her inside. She could smell the sharp tang of burning rags somewhere inside and covered her mouth with a gloved hand that carried the faint scent of rose blossoms.

In she strode. "Take me to the oracle and the grandmasters," she commanded to no one in particular. A soldier from outside hurried forward to lead her under the bobbing faelight she conjured to light their way. And then she followed him into the dark, steeling herself against what was to come, for Morrigan was entirely certain her trials were not over yet.

***

The three grandmasters and the oracle watched her as though they did not trust her. Morrigan supposed the feeling was mutual, but the open hostility was unexpected. *Have I not journeyed through hells to return to warn you?* she wanted to demand.

She set her jaw instead, standing tall in her borrowed clothes in the centre of their scrutiny. In the dark cavern, the echoing silence was crushing, every drip of water from the stalactites above onto the rough ground below amplified a hundredfold. Morrigan flinched as one struck her shoulder. It was damp in there and a different kind of cold to the dry scour of winter outside.

Dark, too. None of the baleful white glare of sky and snow, but an impenetrable blackness barely held at bay by paltry red faelights that cast everything into a bloody hue that grated upon her.

Had she become so accustomed to light in the city of her enemies? Damned be them for getting under her skin as insidiously as the dripping water carved through stone.

"You escaped." The statement was flat, the doubt within it clear.

"Yes, Mother."

"Oracle," her mother snapped. Of course, before the grandmasters in their obsidian cloaks and veiled judgement, status was key. She was a woman in a den of men, and only Valxiron's bestowed gift kept her any kind of equal with them.

"Oracle." Morrigan bowed deferentially, hovering low for an extra moment. Her mother was the vessel of their lord, after all. "I plotted my escape from the moment I awoke and took it at the earliest opportunity."

"You were in their captivity for weeks." Grandmaster Namir stepped forward, his dark eyes gleaming greedily as he took her in. "You must have a wealth of information for us."

"Certainly some." Though much of the early part had been spent in ensorcelled slumber, she had, after all, seen much of the city in her final days in captivity. Why did it sting her with a feeling of betrayal to spill all of it to her own people? She pushed the thought away. "I can show you."

She sent a tendril to each of their minds in turn, pushing a summary of her time there to the grandmasters and oracle. They drank it hungrily, poring over the memories. Seeking more. She would have to give them more. Still, somehow, she felt raw after Lord Halkian's probing. She did not want to endure that again, nor any semblance of it.

She did not expect Grandmaster Hadir to step forward. "You stayed with Houses Ellarian and Ravakian." His mouth was thin with ire. Namir and Hadir were both disgraced sons of House Ellarian – Vasili's step-uncles, as it happened.

"Yes."

"Then we shall need to examine your memories for any and all details."

Morrigan flinched, stepping back as he advanced.

"You would deny us?" Hadir hissed, looming over her.

"I would not deny Lord Valxiron's true servants or cause anything," she defended, though the barb lay veiled in her words, for she did not consider Hadir and Namir as pious as they ought to have been. And in that moment, she knew she had no choice but to bare herself and show them it all. She stood tall and closed her eyes. "Do it."

They dragged it out of her as harshly as Lord Halkian, leaving her forgotten, shivering, and retching on the floor afterwards as they pored and picked over each memory, significant and insignificant. How was it that they had violated her just as savagely as their mutual enemy?

Morrigan held back the prick of hot, angry tears and hoisted herself to her feet, still trembling, glad for the crutch of her magic's power to keep her with enough energy to stay conscious this time. To keep hold of perhaps some little shred of dignity. Hoping they would not see some of the doubts that percolated within her.

Her mother Bellatrix, the oracle, shot her a glance veiled with disgust. Morrigan steeled against that, smoothing her face into an impassive expression. How much contrast was there between her own motherly relationship and that of Harper's warmth towards Vasili. How much she did not know she had craved that, not the endless coldness and punishment.

"You look ridiculous," Bellatrix remarked scathingly.

Morrigan swallowed. "My own garments were taken. This is all I have."

"Well, they shall have to do. We have nothing here."

They had had nothing at the mountain fortress. Here,

they had less than, Morrigan thought, but she kept that to herself.

The grandmasters ceased their muttering and turned to view her with suspicion. "How do we know she is not ensorcelled? A traitor in our midst?" Namir said, tipping his head to regard her under half-lidded eyes.

Morrigan wanted to laugh with derision. Namir, talk of being a traitor? He had betrayed his country when she was still a babe in swaddling. And he had the nerve to speak thusly of her?

"We can examine her at greater length, if you wish, Oracle," Hadir suggested, his face unreadable.

"I am no traitor!" Morrigan exclaimed hotly.

"Perhaps, perhaps not," Namir replied.

She turned a hate-filled glare upon him and burst out, "I am more loyal than any of you cowards! You turned tail and *fled*. You left us all to die rather than stand and fight for your cause." She bared her teeth, resisting the urge to spit on the ground before them, because that would be even more unforgiving and punishable than her insubordinate words.

Even so, Hadir strode forward and struck her a harsh backhander across the cheek that sent her careening off balance. She caught herself and glared up at him, a hand to her smarting face.

"Oracle's heir or not, you will not speak so to your grandmasters, girl. Get out. You will atone."

It was a promise as much as it was a threat.

Morrigan turned and marched out, straight-backed, determined to not let them see a shred more of her anger as she clenched her shaking hands into fists.

Morrigan had found a corner to curl up in, far from any others. It was a dank, dark hole with nothing but a nook to rest in, off the wet ground that constantly trickled a steady stream down deeper into the mines. It did not feel like home – not like the mountain fortress had either, she had to admit, for home was an unfamiliar concept. She wondered if her things were still there in her cave, what little she had, anyway – a change of leathers, some spare garments, that dark dress of her mother's – or whether it would all have been lost to plunderers rampaging through after battle.

It did not feel as homely as Tournai, either. She had wandered the tunnels. Poorly stocked, with few provisions, and the tell-tale signs of starvation amongst the hollow-cheeked Order members lurking in the dark tunnels. Fear of Valxiron kept them in line, but she wondered if they had a breaking point. She knew now not to expect dinner that night. Perhaps not even breakfast.

As if in protest, her stomach rumbled.

Morrigan sighed, nestling into the hard rock with only her cloak for comfort. Her people deserved better than the dark, fetid, abandoned caves. They deserved more than being forced to hide and skulk. They deserved, surely, all the comforts the Pelenori had. Perhaps they would not seem so weak and downtrodden as now if they had full bellies and warm beds.

There was none of the warmth – physical or camaraderie – that she had witnessed in Tournai. She clenched her eyes shut as though it could shut out her own thoughts and gritted her teeth. She had liked that, and she hated feeling as though there were a hole in the midst of her chest at returning to the crushing isolation and fraught survival of the Order of Valxiron. Was this the cause she had fought so hard to return to?

The call came after dark, a clamour that arose, echoing down the tunnels and causing such a din that no one could miss it.

Morrigan awoke groggily from a fitful sleep. Wakefulness flooded her after a moment, edged with nauseating anticipation.

Rumour and fact mingled, growing with the telling, as the whispers of war chased down the old halls. It was time to move. Time to prepare for battle. Pelenor had challenged, and the Order of Valxiron would meet it.

CHAPTER 38

A lump formed in Aedon's throat as he entered the formal dining room, guided by Harper.

Dimitrius awaited inside the door, tall and dark as always, but his eyes crinkled with a smile of genuine warmth as he reached forward to clasp Aedon by both arms and then gather Lief's hand up to dust her knuckles with a gentle kiss.

"I never thought I would see the day, but, Aedon Lindhir Riel, it is *good* to see you."

"And you," Aedon replied. "I hear you've mellowed in your old age?"

Lief gasped at his rudeness, but Dimitrius chuckled darkly. "Still an ass, I see."

"Why change a winning habit." Aedon grinned.

"Come. I would like you to meet—"

Aedon gasped, cutting Dimitri off. His host turned, revealing a young pair of elves the very spit of Harper and Dimitri.

"Vasili and Venya, our son and daughter," Dimitri said,

gesturing to each in turn.

Aedon turned bright eyes upon Harper, and she smiled shyly. "We could not exactly write to tell you," she said by way of apology.

Aedon guffawed. "No, quite. My goodness." They had all thought, when he surrendered himself to Queen Solanaceae's punishment, that he would be dead in a blink.

Aedon crossed to the two young elves, taking them in – and they shifted awkwardly under his scrutiny. "My apologies." He shook Vasili's hand and bowed to Venya. "It is the greatest pleasure. You cannot know how truly I mean that."

He could not help but stare, longer than was polite. It was uncanny, and for a moment, he had thought himself stepped back through the reaches of time to when he had first met Harper as a young and untested woman, for Venya held the same awkwardness in her of a woman growing into herself, who had yet to recognise and learn her untamed power.

Beside her, her brother Vasili looked as surly as a young Dimitrius, the same fine features, dark sleek hair, and violet eyes. Much younger than Aedon had first known Dimitrius and, he hoped, better educated to avoid the same straying path.

Aedon turned to Harper. "Your daughter is the spit of you, my friend. The very image. It brings back memories."

Harper smiled warmly. "And Vasili is just like his father."

"Well, nothing's perfect," Aedon shot at Dimitrius, who gestured rudely, winking at his son as Vasili threw him a baffled look.

"Don't mind this old scoundrel, Vasili," Dimitrius said pointedly. "A dear friend of your mother's, and so we are cursed to suffer his lack of manners too. Come, sit. We have much to catch up on after so many decades parted."

They settled around the table, with one seat yet unfilled.

"Guests first," mouthed Harper as dinner was served and Dimitrius' hand inched towards the serving ware.

"I'm hungry," hissed Dimitrius.

Aedon stifled a chuckle as a pointed glare from Harper stopped Dimitrius' complaint.

Lief gave him a side-eye.

He muttered, "Be yourself. Relax." He could see the tightness in her shoulders – she had no idea how to respond to these new people, to the familiarity of the joshing they gave each other. "Mmm," he said. "Smells delicious." Winter berries gave a tart richness to the aroma of gravies, meats, and roasted root vegetables that soon loaded the table.

"Fair midwinter, and may the sun soon shine on your face," said Harper, raising her wine glass in a toast.

They murmured the toast back to her, and then Harper and Dimitrius waited as their guests took first portions before Dimitrius at last dove in, piling his plate high.

Lief thanked Aedon quietly as he served her from the dishes upon the table. A tremor of nerves still wracked through her.

How was it that she had faced everything from the blight of a dark evil to a giant arachnid, unarmed with little but her wit – but she was frightened of *dinner* with strangers? Her cheeks warmed, and she hoped the smattering of freckles across her cheeks hid any bloom of red.

It was simply that she already felt like such an outsider.

She had heard tell of the *Chronicles of Pelenor* – for the saga was told in their land, and Aedon had furnished her with more – and it felt entirely out of body to be dining with two of the elves who had featured so heavily in that woven tale. It had always seemed like just a story. Now, watching Aedon's easy banter with Dimitrius, seeing Harper's warm treatment of him, she felt a stranger, and it unsettled her, turning her stomach.

Still, she automatically forced down a mouthful of warm, rich, tangy gravy with a mouthful of potatoes, not wanting to waste the food that Aedon had generously – annoyingly so – heaped upon her plate.

Beside her, he tucked in with gusto, unaware of her worries.

A bicker broke her reverie, and she looked up. Harper admonished Aedon and Dimitrius, "Honestly, the pair of you are worse than children."

Dimitrius guffawed at the look on Vasili's face. "I think our son is embarrassed by us, darling."

Vasili flared as red as Lief felt.

Harper must have noticed her discomfort. "Don't mind these two," she said snidely. "Always rivals. It seems they're still regressing."

Lief offered a tentative smile.

Aedon swept an arm around Lief. "Oi. Do you mind? I'm trying to impress her. I can't have you dismantling my heroic and utterly charming facade."

Lief snorted at the same moment as Harper and batted at him.

"Oh, I can tell she's not going to take any of your crap, Aedon," said Harper, eyes twinkling. "Good for you, Lief.

Don't you mind him. And Aedon, you keep her if you know what's good for you, all right? It's about time you settled down."

Aedon grumbled in good humour and waved Harper away, shooting a wink to Lief that made her blush.

Talk flowed back and forth across the table, each there curious to know about each other's lives. Lief found herself drawn to Harper's daughter, Venya, for there were no libraries in the living forest, with tales mostly passed down in story and song, and impressed by their son Vasili. A dragon rider – she had never seen a dragon, but she had heard fearsome tales, some from Aedon. She was not sure she wanted to, in all honestly.

And she found herself plied with questions, hesitantly telling details of Tir-na-Alathea and her life in the forest, with Aedon hanging on every word, even though he had heard half her tales before. It left her oddly flattered, for amongst such noble company, she had felt like nobody.

Soon enough, however, their conversation turned to darker tidings and the reason for Aedon and Lief's unexpected visit to Pelenor. After that, the food lay forgotten, and pudding was turned away as they conversed deep into the night.

When they parted, the moon was high, veiled by the dark clouds outside, and as Lief trudged upstairs with Aedon, it felt like every step held an extra weight in the knowledge that there was much darkness to endure before they would be able to enjoy such a peaceful evening.

On the morrow, the High Council would meet – and then Aedon, Lief, Harper, and Dimitri would soon scatter to the winds again as battle called.

CHAPTER 39

After the midwinter dinner, Venya felt troubled to say the least. Whispers of darkness haunted her light footsteps back to the Athenaeum, and she found herself glancing back along the well-lit city streets more than once as though something followed her. It did not – just her own worries nipping at her periphery.

The Order of Valxiron.

She had heard tell of them – from her family history, from what she had read of modern history, and from her brother's determined quest to clear their family names and see the Order vanquished for good.

She tightened her cloak around her yet again, warding off the wintery chill which felt even deeper than usual, until at last, she reached the wide, dais-like steps of the Athenaeum. Gratefully, she hurried inside.

A fitful night's sleep awaited her, haunted by the beast from the vaults that she had secured with Nyx's and Sylvio's assistance, and shadowy forms in dark cloaks, crackling with despicable sorcery.

The next day, Beatrix caught Venya on the way down to lunch.

"No time for that, Vee. Nieve's called a meeting of the entire Athenaeum in the atrium. It must be serious. Come on." Beatrix snagged her arm and tugged her down the hallway in the opposite direction to the vaults.

Venya's intuition prickled. It could not be a coincidence after the conversation topics of the previous night's dinner, surely? Nieve had not called a full meeting without notice in the several years since Venya had joined the Athenaeum.

With the growing swell of librarians filling the hallways as word spread and they diverted to the atrium, soon Venya found herself carried along by the flow, Beatrix unusually serious-faced striding beside her, hissing questions in her ear that Venya could not answer.

They filed into the Atrium. The enormous, glass-roofed space that had been deserted save for Venya and Vasili the day before was now crammed full of bodies and warming quickly. Usually, the atrium was used for stargazing, astronomy, and astrology, for the ceiling also retracted. Today, the glass and steel contraption was closed. Thick snow clouds swirled overhead, and the glass was already white with its load.

At the head of the atrium on a platform standing waist-high above the tiled floor that led to stairs, which ascended in graceful arcs to the roof, stood Nieve. First Librarian. Her silver hair gleamed in the cold faelight in the space, reflecting bright white from the snow falling above.

Nieve seemed drawn, sterner than usual, and her hands were clasped tight before her as she waited without speaking. Librarians streamed in until the space was so full that an unlucky few crammed the corridors outside.

The rumour-filled murmurs and whispers hushed to an expectant silence as Nieve straightened, glancing across those upturned faces before her. Her gaze passed by Venya and Beatrix deep within the crowd.

Venya shivered. Last she had faced Nieve, it had been with the full force of the First Librarian's disappointment, disapproval, and frustration at Venya's recklessness. Now, she was glad to find anonymity in the ranks of her peers.

"I have grave news to share with you all," Nieve began. Her voice was husky and low, but effortlessly it sliced through them all, so keen was their respect for her and so utter the silence, allowing her words to reach every corner of the huge space.

Nieve's hands clenched together before she woodenly parted her hands, forcing them down to hang at the sides of her black and gold robes. "There is no pleasant way to break such dark tidings, nor would I ordinarily wish to burden our youngest and most novice members with such, but I feel I have no choice. I would do you the respect of being honest with you. You deserve that much from me."

She sighed, and for a moment, she looked tired, burdened by something terrible. Trepidation wormed through Venya.

"Our oldest and gravest enemy rises once more. The Darkness of Altarea is in ascent. So too rise his Order, his most loyal and noble supporters, from the shadows in which they have hidden for so long. Darkness stirs at the borders of our lands – and I have seen it. Our neighbours of Tir-na-Alathea have had great evil blight their realm, and it nips at ours, from the threat of both the Dark One and his followers.

"Some of you will be blessedly young to remember the Fall of Saradon, a quarter century ago. Many of you are not. Many of you remember, and it is why I feel such a heavy heart this day, knowing that despite the sacrifices made then, we did not truly prevail. We pushed back the darkness. We did not extinguish it.

"But now, we must do so. We have a rare chance, and it cannot be squandered. The anchor of power that the Dark One used to tether himself to life until the moment came for his ascendancy was not alone." Nieve's eyes slipped shut for a long moment. She recounted what Venya had heard, of the potential for Valxiron's power to be spread so greatly through the accursed anchors, that he might never cease returning – unless all the anchors could be destroyed.

Silence greeted her, a deep carpet of shock upon those gathered in the atrium.

Venya suspected that only the high respect for Nieve held by all those present saved it from descending into a panicked furore.

"It was a shock to me too," Nieve admitted gravely. "Yet we cannot allow ourselves to be cowed by this grievous revelation. Rather, we ought to use it to fuel an urgent hunt for answers. I have offered our full services to the High Council in this matter."

She spread her arms wide, and a note of pride crept into her voice. "Here, we hold the collective wisdom of our entire realm and some of the cleverest minds it possesses. I have no doubt whatsoever that, when we put out collective minds to this, we shall triumph in finding answers.

"From this moment, until otherwise instructed, our collective effort shall be focused on several key tasks to aid the efforts in locating these anchors and the remaining supporters of the Order of Valxiron and in defeating them with certainty."

The whole room seemed to straighten as one, standing tall and proud, ready to serve. Beatrix's gaze met Venya's, and she could see in her friend the same mix of fear, anticipation, and excitement that she felt.

"Firstly, we will seek to find a way to locate any and every anchor that Valxiron may have left behind. Secondly, a way to destroy them. Third, I want a comprehensive list of every place the Order could yet be hiding under similar glamours to the one they employed in their mountain fortress, and then ways we can dismantle those glamours so they may not hide from us any longer."

Nieve's hands clasped before her once more, almost lost in the obsidian folds of her amethyst-trimmed robe. "The finest minds and strongest magic users in all Pelenor and Tir-na-Alathea will be turning their attentions to these pressing problems. Let us aid them. We simply have no time to lose. One of Valxiron's anchors has already stirred. By the grace of Queen Solanaceae of the woodland realm, it is vanquished, but there is no doubt. This is merely the first. If we wish to maintain the peace that we have so carefully cultivated these last decades, we must do all we can to avert this looming crisis."

With a few more words, Nieve sent them all away, and

the atrium became a flurry of movement once more. A furore broke out as the revelations crashed through them all.

Having some forewarning from the family dinner the previous night, Venya remained silent, bearing the brunt of Beatrix's outpouring of thoughts, worries, fears, and ideas as they returned, like so many others, to the common rooms to react to the news and digest the enormity of their tasks.

Venya soon excused herself, feeling the wriggling of the tiny mouse in her pocket. She needed to escape the noise and pressing claustrophobia of being surrounded by so many, all clamouring to be heard.

"I left my gloves in my room," she lied to Beatrix, interrupting her friend, who had not stopped chattering for the last half an hour. A headache threatened the edges of her mind, biting hard. "I'll be back shortly."

"Oh." Beatrix blinked. "All right. I'll see if I can find any promising records in the catalogue room." Beatrix stood and smoothed down her robes.

You and a hundred others, thought Venya, but she did not say it, nodding and smiling instead. No doubt the place would already be full of bodies combing through the records for one grimoire or artifact to stand out.

She slipped upstairs to the blissful, cosy quiet of her bedroom and locked the door before sinking onto the bed with a grateful huff and closing her eyes.

Nyx wriggled out of her pocket and transformed. A few seconds later, the wet nose of his puppy form wormed under her hand resting upon her knee. "Well, that's not good."

Venya laughed. "Er, no." It was indeed serious if the Athenaeum was compelled to become involved. Her smile faded. "I'm scared, Nyx." And it was true – she was. Down in the pit of her belly, something unsettling lurked. Her life had been peaceful, predictable. Venya had only ever wanted to live and work in the Athenaeum, able to potter and learn from the grimoires there, and one day ascend to the position of First Librarian.

"I don't know anything of darkness, or war, or...any of that."

Nyx harumphed and squirmed closer so his head rested in her lap.

She fondled his ears just the way he liked.

"It is something to fear – I will not pretend." Nyx's words sent a shard of uncertainty into her core.

Her fingers stilled.

"In my long lifetime, I have seen such things. Suffered them, and escaped them, in many forms. But always, where there was light, there was hope. If you allow yourself to crumble at the faintest sign of life diverging from your intended path, why, you shall never achieve anything, least of all First Librarian."

Venya bowed her head. Did that make her a failure? Not wanting to engage with anything threatening? She had always been such a mouse, just like Nyx had once called her in frustration. Was being a librarian simply another way to hide away from the world until it forced her hand otherwise?

"I know you shall not, though."

A ray of hope punched through that uncertainty.

"Look at how well you faced the beast in the vault." Pride coloured Nyx's voice with rich warmth. "I bet you did not expect yourself to rise under such pressure, hmm?"

"No, I didn't," Venya mumbled slowly.

"Then consider how you can do the same. You might not

walk upon any battlefield, but your contributions shall have merit, Venya. What are your strengths?"

"I..." Venya did not know. Strengths were things she rarely dared to think about. Weaknesses came easier. Shy. Awkward. Uncertain. She slammed down on that insidious voice before it could batter her anymore.

"I think creative. Resourceful. Conscientious. An eye for detail, and an astounding memory. A gift for tongues. A rapport with otherwise untameable grimoires. The list is longer than you realise, I believe."

"Thank you," Venya forced out in a whisper as warmth bloomed in her at the kindness of Nyx's words.

"You ought to believe in your own capabilities more, my dear."

Venya swallowed. "What can be done, though? What can we – *I* – do?"

Nyx sat up, his wagging tail swishing across the bedcover. "What you do best. Librarian-ing."

Venya let out a snort. "That's not a word."

"I just made it a word," Nyx retorted airily, giving her a side-eye. "My point is, play to your strengths. You've been set a problem, nay, a challenge. Forget about the fact that it might in reality be cripplingly terrifying and approach it like any other task you must complete for your work. How can you find the anchors? How can you destroy or negate their magic? How can you unearth the strongholds of the Order?"

"Find..." Something niggled at Venya. Something small but insistent. Something that would not be ignored. She frowned.

"See. I see that right there. You've got something."

"I don't know," Venya moaned. "I feel like I've forgotten

something quite important." She chewed on a hangnail, but the thought would not coalesce.

"Then, Mistress Venya, I suggest you think harder."

Venya did what she did best when mulling over a particularly complicated problem. Entirely ignore it. The best course had always seemed for her to throw herself into something else and let the original problem percolate in the recesses of her mind. At last, something usually emerged, better formed than it had been and pliable enough to work with.

After a morning of combing through the unbearably crowded catalogue room to no avail or peace with Beatrix, she retired for a solitary lunch break in her room, finally picking back up the elven poetry she had been translating from old Tir-na-Alathean scripts – a cryptic warning, as it seemed to be.

The after-lunch bell rang, booming sonorously through the whole building, magically amplified far beyond the scope of the brass bell in the outer courtyard. It startled Venya out of a trance-like reverie. She gazed over the lines transcribed on the page, one painstaking letter, word, and phrase at a time, with many a crossing out and correction.

Venya frowned as she read it anew. Her lips parted with surprise, and bell and duties be damned, she rushed to translate the very last line.

No. It cannot be. How had she stumbled upon this? In a book of the oddest collection of Tir-na-Alathean snippets of folklore, instruction, and fact, she had not expected this. It had innocuously nestled between pages on everything from how to cook a local dish known as *tirol*, to how to use music and magic to coax forth life, to how the court of the woodland queen operated hierarchically. She finished translating. Her handwriting was a scrawling mess in her excited haze of recording her scramble of thoughts.

Venya read it again.

She consulted the original text once more – for she had already made so many corrections – trying to scan it through for sense, to make sure that she had not missed something after all. That this was, in fact, worthless gibberish, not a potential priceless snippet of information, because the latter seemed beyond possibility.

But there it was. Undeniable before her. Venya's insides quivered with barely suppressed anticipation as she read it again. No mistakes could she find in the translations – that she had not corrected.

"Venya?" Nyx lifted his head from where he lay curled up against her pillow.

"I think I found an answer." The parchment shook in her hand. "One of them. Perhaps. Maybe."

Alert, Nyx cocked his head, waiting for her to elaborate.

She quoted:

Under boughs where dhiran and elves dwell,
There roam dark beasts so deathly and fell,
Where none can tread for fear of falling
Into claws, teeth, and stings ensnaring.
Steer clear of glades silent and bereft,
For those places no elf came and left.
In life and fyre and Song be solace –
Back to shadow and ruin they chase

*All things ill of this world and beyond,
To the grim bowels whence they spawned.*

Venya looked to Nyx, that parchment tightly between her fingers as though it would disintegrate and take all answers with it.

"Don't you see what this is? According to Aedon, this is precisely how he and the woodland queen defeated the anchor at the Silent Sisters. They used 'life and fyre and Song', didn't they? The power of the wood elves, in their Singing, and Aedon's fire magic. Doesn't that tell us everything we need to know? Perhaps they *already* have a way to defeat the anchors?"

"Why, Venya, you might be onto something there," Nyx said excitedly. "You must take this to Nieve at once!"

But Venya stilled. She pressed the parchment close to her chest. Something else had unlocked within her mind. The thought that had been percolating, maturing like a butterfly in a cocoon. It too was ready to emerge from chrysalis.

A hiss escaped her.

"I have one more thing to do first."

CHAPTER 40

Venya's heart pounded as she stood outside Nieve's office, waiting for her knock to be answered. For a moment, it was louder than the constant fall of boots upon the stone floor as throngs of librarians passed to and fro in their quest for answers.

"Enter," Nieve's serious voice called from inside.

Venya steeled herself, straightening, and slipped inside. In the cool, dim interior, shrouded in shadow by the snowstorm still raging outside, Nieve was almost lost behind a stack of papers, books, and grimoires piled high on her desk.

"Venya. How may I help you?" Her serious face softened, but her smile was tired, her eyes dim.

Venya swallowed. Hoping she was right. She did not want to be a disappointment to the First Librarian. Again.

"I found some answers I think may help." She marched to Nieve's desk and handed her the parchment. "I've been translating a small book from the upper levels, a Tir-na-Alathean volume."

Nieve's brows rose at that. Such volumes were rare, even in the Athenaeum. It was fate or fortune that Venya had stumbled upon it. Venya had thought fortune at first, but the more she considered it, the more she wondered if fate, if such a thing existed, were instead at play.

"I-I think it's right. I'm sorry it's so messy. I'm learning the tongue, and the alphabet is deceptively confusing," she babbled before clamping her mouth shut. She cleared her throat. "That is to say, it may confirm that how Queen Solanaceae defeated the anchor at the Silent Sisters was not chance after all, but potentially how it may be achieved time and again, should the opportunity present."

She watched as Nieve's gaze flicked across the lines, down the passage. Then again. And a third time. "Do you have the original text?" Nieve paused to glance at Venya.

Venya handed her the small book, a battered old thing which would be so easily lost in the library's vast collection. She had found it when searching for another tome months before. It had been shelved in entirely the wrong section of the library – far away from the sections written in other tongues – and that curiosity had led her to pick it up. The beautiful, flowing script had enchanted her.

Nieve flicked to the bookmarked page. It was unceremoniously marked with a scrap of torn paper – all that Venya had had to hand. For moments that yawned into seeming eternities, Nieve cross-examined the book and the translation.

"I will confess," she eventually murmured, "I am not fluent. I shall have a Tir-na-Alathean assist checking this. However..." She glanced up at Venya once more, a fresh hunger burning in her eyes. "I think you may be onto something. Perhaps we shall simply confirm what the wood elves know, but even so, that in itself has value."

"I'm not sure they do know, ma'am. Last night, I had dinner with my family." Venya trailed off, chewing her lip. How much should she divulge? "Aedon Lindhir Riel of House Felrian was present."

Nieve arched an eyebrow. She knew of Venya's family connection to the High Council.

"He disclosed how they had fought the anchor at the Silent Sisters, and the impression I received was that the combined use of magic, fire, and Song was a coincidental success rather than a deliberate one. I believe this knowledge might aid the Queen in Her ongoing strategy."

"Noted." Nieve nodded. "I shall have the translation verified at once, and then take the information to the High Council and the Queen." She stood – faltering when Venya did not give way before her.

"There's something else, ma'am," Venya whispered.

Nieve did not answer, her silence indicating that Venya continue.

"You tasked us with locating things, and, well, I think I might have an answer for that too."

Something akin to pride flashed across Nieve's face.

"I know of a grimoire. Sylvestri di Niani Verdiatris. The Book of Gateways. With the... *incident* last month," Venya said delicately, "he was instrumental. He has a knack for finding things, you see," she rushed out, before her courage could entirely desert her.

"He's magnificent, actually. I don't know how he does it, but somehow, he can find things and open a gateway to take the seeker to them. That's how I found the beast roaming the vaults and how I trapped him in the cage. It was Sylvio. He hunted down the beast and transported me there, and he manipulated his gateways to trap the beast in the precise pocket of space and time that was that cage. He can find anything, he says. I just visited him in his vault, and I know his ego can be overinflated, but I think I might believe that it's possible. Ma'am."

Venya subsided, her cheeks fiery hot.

Nieve blinked at her, wordless for a long moment. Then she laughed. "Venya, I have never heard anything quite so hare-brained and fanciful." Amused, she shook her head.

Venya crumpled.

"No, you mistake me, my dear girl." Nieve's gentle hand upon her shoulder transferred some strength back to Venya. "I am astounded at your resourcefulness and ingenuity. You have such a way with the grimoires. I do not know whether it is perhaps your sorcery or your manner, but they take you as they do not take to anyone else presently here. It is a gift of great honour, you know. Sylvio hasn't talked to another librarian for thirty years – not since he spoke to me, in fact. Consider me impressed. Are you certain of his abilities?"

"I spoke to him myself, ma'am. I can fetch him if you like."

"Yes, I should like," Nieve said firmly. "Bring him here at once, whilst I seek a translator to verify the accuracy of your translation. I shall find the truth of his skills. And then, just perhaps, he can find *anything*." Venya could hear the urgency of that possibility on her voice.

Anything at all.

Like hidden Orders.

Like concealed anchors.

CHAPTER 41

Venya's heart hammered as she stood in Nieve's shadow upon the snow-covered plain outside Tournai, at the eye of a storm of tension waiting to break. Thousands stood around her. Soldiers of Pelenor. The wood elves of Tir-na-Alathea. The full High Council. The very Queen of the woodland realm herself. And, wheeling above them, the Winged Kingsguard.

It was precisely why she preferred to hide away in the Athenaeum – standing before a crowd was her worst nightmare, and already, she was unsure whether she wanted to vomit, or pass out, or both. First Librarian Nieve flashed her a kind smile, though it was tinged with seriousness, not quite banishing the frown from her eyes.

Venya listened, head tipping back and forth as different council members spoke – her parents too, at times – of things she had little understanding of. Of seeking hidden strongholds of the Order of Valxiron, of using the memories of Lady Morrigan, her brother's prisoner, who had mysteriously escaped, leaving her brother mortally injured.

Venya had felt terrible for not knowing until the Midwinter dinner what had happened.

Vasili was there with the general of the Winged Kingsguard, their dragons standing behind them, tall as several men, in the general's dragon's case. Her brother looked as drawn and worried as she felt.

"It's us," Nieve whispered, jolting Venya out of her thoughts.

A rush of pure fear shot through Venya. She was not certain she could move.

"Don't worry," Nieve said soothingly. "You may need only speak to Sylvio."

Venya forced her legs to move and tugged the grimoire with her. Sylvio floated, bobbing in mid-air at shoulder height beside her, pulled on the thin silver chain. It was the most silent Venya had seen the acerbic grimoire, who ordinarily liked the sound of his own voice too much to remain quiet – but Nieve had quashed his ego with a stern warning.

A gust of freezing air blasted them both, and Sylvio grumbled beside her. Somehow, despite the severity of the situation, that cracked through her brittle veneer of fear, and her lips trembled in the shadow of a smile.

"I thank you, High Council, for your faith in us," Nieve said in her even, measured voice, betraying none of her own feelings, but Venya could see in the way her hands clasped together, knuckles whitened, that she was less than calm inside.

Venya halted in Nieve's shadow, with Sylvio bumping her elbow. The horizon wobbled as Venya drew in a large breath, hyperaware of the attention upon her. She could not breathe with the weight of it, sat heavy upon her chest. *Pull yourself together*, she chided herself, trying to force in a breath and stand taller. And banish the warmth from her cheeks.

They had spoken at length with the High Council – or rather, Nieve had, with Venya mostly silent and even Sylvio suspicious and subdued. The poem Venya unearthed had been shared, much to the Queen of the woodland realm's interest. Venya had found Her *terrifying*, and that day had been glad to leave.

Over the next days, they had tested Sylvio's capabilities, and sure enough, he had passed with flying colours. Just as he had done for Venya in the vault, he could open portals to different places at will, which others could step through – though Venya, this time, would remain behind, for which she was glad. The Book of Gateways indeed.

Twinned with Morrigan's distinct memories, Sylvio's power would be truly tested today. Could he open a gateway to the Order's new location – and could he transport an army there?

CHAPTER 42

*I*n the midst of the wood elves, Aedon's bumped shoulders with Lief. Half hidden by their cloaks, his searching fingers found hers and laced together. They stood on the small rise, still and watchful amidst the Tir-na-Alathean wood elves.

Queen Solanaceae stood far from their position, in the centre of the maelstrom. Her hair was braided in a coil upon her head, laced with gold and vines, a half-living crown. Her body outfitted for war, cloaked like the rest of them, the warm terracotta of her neck standing in pale contrast to the rich purple of her cloak, borrowed, as all the wood elves' winter attire had been, from Tournai's reserves. Every army casket raided. Every domestic cloak-maker compelled to hand over their stock to ensure the army did not die of cold before its task was complete.

From what Harper and Dimitrius had told Aedon, they would be going to colder and more inhospitable climes. Aedon had borrowed a set of clothes from Dimitrius –

slightly ill-fitting, as Aedon was the shorter and stockier built of the two, but needs must. He was grateful for them all the same. Harper's attire adorned Lief. Gone was the sleeveless tunic of her people, suitable for the light summer weather. Outside the forest of eternal summer, midwinter had just passed, and the clutch of the cold was months from over.

Aedon should not have been there, technically. No longer a member of the Winged Kingsguard, and no longer in the service of Queen Solanaceae. He could have turned tail. His fingers squeezed Lief's. He would not leave her to face whatever came alone, for she was still bound to serve.

Kinear had not been pleased, but he had hardly had a choice if Aedon wanted to accompany them out of his own free will. Aedon suspected only Kinear's respect for his conduct and assistance in Lune dissuaded the *cinq* leader from making a more vocal objection. And so Aedon would travel with Lief. To whatever end.

Before them, light flared.

Down there, Harper's daughter, the librarian, worked some grimoire magic – more than that, he did not truly understand. Only that it would help them travel an impossible distance in hardly any time at all.

The very air fizzled and rippled, sending waves through the view of Tournai beyond, as though Aedon looked at it underwater.

A prick of darkness appeared, growing by the second, ringed in swarming light that folded and undulated over itself like living gold and silver, circling a growing *nothing* that had Aedon's jaw falling open in wonder. In all his years, he had never seen anything like it.

A prickle of unease shivered through him at the power of the unknown sorcery before him. He could taste the tang of it on his tongue, feel the strength of it like the sun's heat radiating upon his skin, feel the chords of it call to the magic that flowed through him.

The city beyond was entirely lost to the giant portal, which flashed, silver as a mirror, before...Aedon blinked, and blinked again. *Impossible.*

A circle, perfectly cut, was suspended in mid-air, only it did not match. Through the gateway, he could not see what was really there – the city beyond – but an entirely different landscape. A never-ending boreal forest of pines and snow, with unfamiliar hazy mountains in the distance, lost under seething winter storms.

A horn blew the advance.

Through that portal they would march.

Aedon steeled himself and glanced at Lief. She burned intensity in the rigid lock of her body and the tension of energy he could feel singing inside her.

They had to make it through this. They needed to survive – both of them. To make it through to the other side.

Then, finally, at last, they would be free. Without illusion.

Please let me keep her safe, Aedon prayed to the unforgiving skies above as a bitter drive of hail began.

CHAPTER 43

Vasili's heart beat as loud as a drum of war. Warded against the cold, he soared far overhead, having flown through the breach with the rest of his comrades. A disconcerting experience if ever there was one, to trust to the magic of a grimoire, a being of sorcery, upon the word of his sister, her First Librarian, and the hopes of the council.

Yet they had survived and passed through from one winter landscape to another far more arctic clime. Passing through that door had felt like being impossibly weightless and immeasurably heavy all at once. Light and floating, pressured and squeezed. An assault on all of the senses, roaring and darkness and coldness and yet nothingness in the silent void. And then Vasili had passed through – to this place.

Beyond Pelenor's eastern border, far to the south, winter's grip was strongest yet. The mountains, an impenetrable set of steely teeth, were a barrier ahead of him – far beyond them, Pelenor. Icarus wheeled in the sky, Vasili atop him. In all other directions, a foreign landscape stretched. Vast, empty expanses of tundra and boreal forests, evergreens heavy with a permanent layer of snow and ice. Rivers snaked, frozen solid and silent, hidden under the blanket of white, and in the distance, Vasili could see the expanse of a lake, clear of trees and perfectly flat.

He was too high to see animal trails winding through that harsh and inhospitable landscape, but they would be obliterated anyway by the thousands of booted feet tramping relentlessly under him. Onwards, towards that barrier of mountains and their destination nestled upon the flanks of a peak.

On the basis of Morrigan's snatched intelligence, they made for an uninhabited and long abandoned dwarven colony on the far south of the mountain range. According to Morrigan's knowledge, it was the Order's refuge in times of trouble, with strength in stone and the network of old, dwarven tunnels and mines reaching deep into the mountains like a network of roots. Defensible and escapable.

Vasili wheeled at the tail of the formation of Winged Kingsguard riders, swinging towards the mountains again. That settlement clung to a barren, rocky slope far below. It looked as haunted and lacking in life as the rest of the landscape. Gone was the once fine dwarven town in the prime of its years, deserted when the seams of ore had run dry.

Now turrets crumbled, wood had rotted, and though the stone still stood tall for the most part, it was a shell of its former self, neglected and lost to time. Vasili wondered how the Order had found it and whether they had made use of it over the years, for as he soared over, he saw the cuts of newer wood patching over holes in a platform linking two parts of the battlements. A platform that had been far more recently repaired than dwarves had lived in those halls.

He could see it would barely stand up to the strength of a dwarven attack or perhaps even an elven one. Those halls were meant to repel goblin and troll attacks from the mountains – a threat that was long gone with the expansion of the dwarven realm Valtivar's patrols to banish the scourge of the mountains.

Now, the Order hid there, an insidious presence the dwarves had never intended to take those halls. As Vasili's attention scanned the settlement below them, Icarus doing the same, their senses mingled, becoming one.

"Good luck drawing the Order out from there," Icarus growled to his rider.

"Aye," said Vasili, frowning. "If they can retreat to a maze of tunnels, we shall be hard pressed to find them again." And he did not want that – not again. Not after the Order had simply disappeared when cornered in their stronghold, presumably through a similar network of tunnels and their leaders' abilities to simply vanish on smoke and wind with the skills of evanescence.

The alliance would have to draw the Order out, somehow. Neither side, the alliance nor the Order, had the time or resources to sit in siege, starving one or the other to submission, in such a harsh landscape.

This time, however, the Winged Kingsguard had something up their sleeve the Order could not see coming. A legion of wood elves, with an irate Queen.

Vasili watched from upon high as, far below, a lone figure on horseback wove through the uneven landscape towards the settlement.

Parlay.

A common courtesy, if nothing else. Vasili wondered whether the High Council thought it would work at all, for he was entirely doubtful.

He could see small figures congregating upon the battlements and upon one of the towers. He searched amongst them, though he was too far away to discern who they were. He wondered whether one was the oracle. Whether any were Morrigan.

As he watched, a surge of magic blasted from the stronghold's highest tower, spearing towards the messenger. The messenger must have seen it coming, for he dove to one side and ran.

The magic chased him, changing trajectory, until it was answered in an explosion of crashing fire – a defence that saved the messenger, who had time to dash into a copse of trees and vanish beneath their sheltering boughs in the middle of that no man's land.

Vasili's heart notched up as he watched the exchange of power. The Order had firmly rejected any notion of civility or negotiation – as they had all expected. Still, it dragged them all inexorably forward to the storm of battle.

With a horn, and then another, and then a dozen more, the call to battle sounded. Icarus roared with the other dragons, like thunder rolling from the heavens. The very sound of it shook Vasili, reverberating through his legs as he sat atop the dragon, and then shaking through the rest of him, until all he could hear and feel was that challenge.

The dragons wheeled around again as the land assault began – for they were to hold in reserve, at least for the moment. The roar faded, leaving Vasili's ears ringing. He heard cracks below, like the shattering of deep ice, ricocheting through the frigid land, ripping through the steady *tramp tramp tramp* of all those booted feet advancing.

What is that?

He scanned the ground but could see nothing. His attention returned to the stronghold. Searching, as he had been all along, for *one* person in particular. Pale skin. Raven hair. Steel eyes. Damned that he was so far away; he could not see Morrigan anywhere, but he felt it in his bones that she had to be there. Where else would she be, except in the fold of her people?

It was tantalising. Could he feel the smallest hint of her essence down below, muddied amongst the presence of so many others? Or did he taunt himself with her ghost? Was she already dead? After all, willingly or not, she had ceded all the Order's secrets to Pelenor, and her people were not a merciful bunch. Vasili knew she was in grave danger of being branded a traitor of the worst kind and punished accordingly.

Was it simply a deluded hope that he would find her before the worst happened? Perhaps she had not returned to her people. Perhaps she had fled. Perhaps she had tried and failed, and now lay cold and frozen somewhere under the winter snow, never to be seen by him again. He refused to believe it. She *had* to be there. He knew her. She would not forsake her people. Not now.

Distress carved a channel through his own fear as he sought her out to no avail. With the time for negotiation and truce passed, they were caught on opposing sides. Enemies. To the death. And despite that she had stabbed him, left him to bleed out, and vanished, he could not hate her. Not when he understood her.

Yet if she did not want to save herself, there was nothing he could do but watch on as she died.

"It will not come to that," Icarus said strongly, but they both knew it was a lie. He could provide no guarantee.

When the dragons of the Winged Kingsguard were ordered to unleash upon the keep, if Morrigan was not already dead, she would burn with the rest of them.

CHAPTER 44

Morrigan emerged onto the battlements, and her throat caught. She stopped dead in her tracks. Where not long before had been an ocean of white pricked by trees now surged a seething mass of dark figures as far as the eye could see over the nearest rise.

An army.

And as she looked, a flicker of movement caught her eye, and she glanced up. An involuntary cry slipped out, one that she strangled into silence immediately, lest anyone hear it and think her weak.

Dragons.

They wheeled in the sky, great, glittering birds, far larger than any of the mountain eagles she had watched as the sun had set early the night before. They gleamed dully. Morrigan found herself searching, though the low, harsh light stripped all jewel-like colour from them, for an emerald dragon – until a barked order from above had her scurrying onwards, across a battlement lined with serious-faced men and women, and up a spiral stone staircase to the top above.

As she emerged, she had a better vantage point yet. There was a dark tide of surging bodies, their scarlet cloaks like blood in the snow – and a throbbing well of power at their forefront, belonging to a woman of such unearthly magnitude, the commanders flanking her seemed so much lesser.

How had they come to be there? Morrigan reeled. It was impossible by any means that she knew, for the Pelenor could not evanesce in the same manner as some of the Order of Valxiron, for they did not practise the art. Of the wood elves, she knew nothing.

She stood, frozen, watching them advance, wrestling with the impossibility of it, when—

"*You!*" Lady Bellatrix screeched. She stormed to Morrigan and raised her hands, claw-like and brimming with crackling magic. "You brought them here, traitor!"

Morrigan's magic flared in answer, ready to defend, but as three grandmasters drew closer behind her mother, she knew she could not withstand them all. "No! Mother, I didn't—"

"I knew you were a worthless, unworthy worm, girl." Her mother's face was wild and savage, spittle flying and whites of her eyes flaring, as she advanced on Morrigan. "They are here because of *you*! You sang for them like the traitor you are."

"I did not!" retorted Morrigan hotly, shaking with fury and shame and humiliation. But she retreated half a step all the same in the face of her mother's and the grandmasters' vicious hatred, feeling altogether like a rabbit cornered by wolves.

"I am more devoted to our cause than any of you cowards!" Her cheeks were burning with the injustice of it. "I returned to warn you. Why would I do that if I were a traitor?"

"Enough!" snarled the oracle. "You were *weak*. You allowed them to wrest all knowledge from you, and thus, you are a traitor. You should have died before you gave anything, and I wish you had."

Morrigan felt like the breath had been punched from her with the vitriol of her mother's words, and she could not reply.

"I reject you! You were never enough to be my heir, and you do not deserve to bear the scars of this duty upon you." Her mother's gaze locked on Morrigan's twin scars, which she also shared, crescents upon each cheek marking them as Valxiron's favoured, his most loyal followers, and when times called for it, his own vessel.

Morrigan wanted to defend herself, but she could see how futile it was. They converged upon her in the limited space, and she could feel the power building within her mother, a darkness brewing, ready to erupt like a thunderstorm.

A gust battered them, and Morrigan looked up on instinct, her nerves fraught. A dragon, flapping as it wheeled overhead. A green dragon. Something in her somersaulted. Icarus. A flash of dark, streaming hair, a pale face filled with wide-eyed fear, soaring over her. Vasili.

He was alive. She had failed to kill him. Something sent her insides weak, threatened to buckle her knees.

Her mother turned. The grandmasters wheeled. She could feel the very moment they flooded with magic, preparing to assault a moment later, for her ears popped with the strength of it.

"No!" Morrigan screamed, anger and fear surging within her, even though she did not know why in Pelenor she ought to care for him, or the fact he had survived her attack, slim as the chances had been. Their gazes – Morrigan's and Vasili's – locked for a fraction of a moment, and then he dropped away, plummeting out of sight, taking evasive action as her mother and the grandmasters thrust an assault of magic in the dragon and rider's direction. She could not tell if the blast of her mother's magic had struck true.

Morrigan's attention snapped to her mother, who turned towards her with vengeance carved in every etched line upon her face. Morrigan barely dodged the blast from her mother's searing magic, and it scorched a path through her sleeve, burning her arm in a stinging hail.

Self-preservation drove her on instinct. Morrigan turned tail and fled down the stairs. The thunder of booted feet behind her told her that at the very least, the grandmasters had given chase. She rushed through the door at the bottom of the stairs onto the exposed battlements, where a cold wind relentlessly buffeted her. She pushed through ranks of soldiers, risking a glance behind her. The grandmasters gave chase, followed by her unyielding, ice-cold mother.

The Order parted before them like butter.

Morrigan bit out a curse as they advanced. She had a run of wall behind her, and then it ceased in a dead end. Nothing but the crenulations, and beyond that, a deathly fall. Her heart hammered in her chest, her hands shaking with unspent fear and adrenaline coursing through her. There were no options – at least, no good options.

Around her, people shoved others out of the way to escape the wrath of their feared leaders. They choked the sole other escape route, an exposed staircase leading down, hugging that outer wall. She would be picked off in an instant, for that open stair and the blockage of people would leave her entirely at their mercy.

Was the roaring in her ears the dragons, descending at last, or her own fear? Morrigan surged into motion once more. She scrambled onto the nearest embrasure, clinging onto the merlons on either side. She chanced a look down and yanked her neck back in at the stomach-churning fall onto hard stone far below.

The last of the bodies separating them were clearing, hurrying out of the way. Gritting her teeth, Morrigan hauled herself up onto a merlon, the rough stone biting into her hands, scraping her knees through the thick trousers. And then, she ran. *One step, two steps, leap.* Across the embrasure, onto the next merlon. *One step, two steps, leap.*

Behind her, the arrogant laugh of Grandmaster Hadir had her blood roil with fury at the elf's pure arrogance. She would be damned if she died without a fight, if she let them stab her in the back, literally or metaphorically. Fear kept her leaps true, the precipice on her left opening her to assault from the foreign forces below and the gap to her right keeping her vulnerable to attack from her own people.

Far too soon, she ran out of places to climb, or run, or leap. Morrigan turned on the very corner of the last merlon, her dark figure carving a silhouette against the white skies beyond.

Hemmed in by her grandmasters and her mother, the oracle, who now approached at a leisurely pace, knowing they had her entirely at their mercy, Morrigan drew the twin knives on her back and let out a wordless snarl as her challenge to them. Below, the foreign forces advanced. Her masters would waste no time ending her. At least that was some small mercy. She would die quickly so they could return to battle to try to save their worthless, miserable hides.

Something with her railed at that, rebelling, still fighting, even though the end was inevitable with every step they approached.

She was going to die.

Morrigan side-eyed the drop to her rear. Her stomach churned, bile rising.

Should she do it herself? Have the dignity of choosing the end of her own life? Was that better or worse than being murdered by her own masters and mother?

CHAPTER 45

The ground troops were almost in place, tantalisingly close to the battlements, almost in range to attack – and be attacked. Yet Vasili's attention had swung elsewhere. To the confrontation and the blasts of magic emanating from one of the open towers. Three black-cloaked and hooded figures, their frames suggesting males, and two females. Two females that could have been twins but for the age separating them, from the streaming, raven hair, to the pale skin, to the crescent scars upon their cheeks.

His stomach lurched with roiling nausea as he beheld Morrigan and her mother – the oracle – and the grandmasters. Morrigan, cornered by them all. Attack bloomed, focused on her. She still wore his borrowed clothes, he realised, the fabric baggy on her thin frame. Something twinged within him. Something desperate and primal. There was still time. Doubt undermined him. Was there still time?

Without a thought, he broke the carefully organised

formation of Winged Kingsguard that held in the sky, waiting for battle. He would wait no longer. He *could* wait no longer. He could not sit idly by and watch her die, by whoever's hand, and right now, every instinct of him screamed that she was in imminent danger.

Panic drove him, but Icarus, calm beneath him, unperturbed by the rush of emotion in his rider, was a carefully honed weapon. He funnelled his wings and dropped like a stone. The oracle, as if somehow sensing their approach, turned. Vasili saw dark eyes blazing fury for a second as she perceived him. And then a blast of magic barrelling their way. Icarus tumbled away, his only option to snap his wings shut to fall under the attack, but his screeching roar bit into Vasili's very soul as the assault clipped his wing.

Pain bled across their mental bond. Vasili pushed out healing energy to soothe Icarus as the dragon snapped out his wings to break their fall and wheel away to gain altitude once more. One of his wings had a tattered edge where the attack had grazed it. It rained boiling blood on the stone below.

Vasili swore. The pain that crossed their barrier was washed away by a surge of anger from the dragon at the woman that had dared to attack him. Icarus flapped powerfully, gaining height and banking to circle back around.

"What in the damn hell are you doing, rider?" General Elyvia's voice berated, and from the flinch of the dragon below him, he knew she had spoken into both their minds.

Vasili relayed back to her a mental run-through of what he had seen. *"Please, ma'am,"* he begged her. *"Please let me help her."* He could see Morrigan now, barging against the flow of bodies on the battlements, outnumbered and running out of options.

Elyvia paused for so long that he thought she would not acknowledge a reply, and when she spoke, he grimaced, expecting a reprimand for his insubordination. *"Damned be it, Vasili, I do not understand your crusade for her soul's redemption."*

Her next words were cold, calculating – Vasili knew she was considering Morrigan's value as a target to be acquired for the alliance. *"If you retrieve her, get well clear of the battlefield. You have one chance, and then, should you fail, you return to your position immediately. Understood? I will not risk my warriors for the sake of one woman, no matter how valuable her intelligence may be."*

"I won't fail, ma'am."

Vasili did not hesitate, nor Icarus under him. The dragon surged forward again, the powerful thrust of his wingbeats driving them around the stronghold from a distance to approach in full sight of Morrigan, behind the oracle and grandmasters that now had her cornered upon the parapet.

Those below in the stronghold saw him. Rocks and missiles peppered up, pelting the sky and falling back to earth, unable to hit the dragon and rider at such speed and height. Icarus dodged spearing magic attacks easily, the lesser skill of those magic-wielders apparent in their clumsy and weaker attempts.

On his back, Vasili bent lower, closer, streamlining himself for any advantage it would give in reaching her more quickly as Morrigan hopped onto the very last piece of stone before the void and teetered on the edge.

Vasili's howl stuck in his throat as magic bloomed from

the oracle and the grandmasters before her, and he realised that truly, she was in mortal danger.

He had seconds to reach her before she was annihilated by her own people.

Morrigan could not withstand the attack. She knew it. They knew it. Namir, the cocky bastard, had even put down his hood for the sheer pleasure of having an unfettered view of her demise. She saw in his lazy smile, in his glimmering, dark eyes, the smug pleasure he took in having this power over her – power that he had never had before, as she had rejected his advances time and again, and he had had to suffer the shame of it. Males like him were, after all, not accustomed to being told 'no' by a female. Now, he held the power of her end, and damned be him, she knew he would enjoy it.

That thought alone made her want to hurl herself off the parapet and take that choice from his unworthy hands. And still, she hesitated.

Not scared, she told herself. *I'm not scared. Defiant.*

She would take them out if she could, when it mattered. They were a disgrace to the Order and everything it stood for.

Alone, ahead of the grandmasters, Bellatrix stepped forward. Something in the gait of her movement was off. Morrigan's eyes flicked to her mother's. In them, she saw inky blackness.

A chill scraped down her spine.

Something dark and raw was waking in there. No longer

was the woman standing before her Bellatrix. Now, she was the true oracle. Bearer of Valxiron's power. Vessel of their very master himself. Her mother was the living anchor that tethered Valxiron's power to the world of Altarea. One generation after another, the oracle kept the fire burning, the spirit alive, with the strength of their own will and the life force of their own body.

The cold, gusting wind around them fell away, as though the world had stopped with the slow, inexorable beat of the mighty power before her.

Valxiron himself.

Awakened.

"Master," she breathed. "Lord." She would have sunk to her knees had there been room, but she could barely stand upon the merlon, which was a foot deep. If she moved now, that yawning fall awaited.

"I am true to you," she swore. "These cowards and traitors—"

"Stop." The whip crack of a voice echoing from Bellatrix's mouth was not her mother's own. Darker, deeper, ancient, and crueller, she knew now beyond doubt that she conversed, for the first time, with Valxiron himself.

"I see your truth." Every word was like a physical blow, each syllable filled with crackling power and dire promise. "I deem it false."

For a moment, all fell away, and Morrigan felt as though she no longer inhabited her own body. *No...* Everything she had done had been in service to her people, their cause, to *him. Hadn't it?*

The crowing of the grandmasters, like dogs being sent in for the kill, came from a distance. Instants became seconds, which accelerated as she watched them leap into action, surging forward, calling their power to annihilate her in service of their master – and her mother. Her eyes were pure black – their master looked out, not the woman who owned that vessel, but she would not care, not truly, that her daughter would die in but a moment.

I'm going to die.

It crushed the breath from her chest, and she could not react, as though her entire being had accepted the inevitability of it.

I failed.

At everything.

She had held her cause to the end, and it was not enough.

She had burned any bridges she had had with the folk of Pelenor – with Vasili skies above, she could barely think his name without flinching – and it was still not enough.

She had returned to her people to warn them, to arm them, and it had still not been enough.

She had returned to discover they held nothing of the same fervour for their cause, nor love for her – only punishment and accusations of disloyalty and treason.

Worst of all, she had faced her master through the vessel of her mother, and he himself had rejected her utterly. When all was stripped away, she did not follow her mother, or the grandmasters, or the Order, she followed *him*. She followed Valxiron and his promise for a better, purer world. She had shed blood for that – her own and others. She had been willing to kill for that. She had been ready to *die* in the hands of her – Lord Valxiron's – enemies for that.

Had she somehow failed him in her lifetime of fervour,

placed a foot wrong, or misunderstood the doctrine? She had not done it knowingly or willingly, if so. For an instant, she crumbled in the face of her unworthiness, and shame flooded her. What had she done?

No, something fierce within her protested. *You were his to the core.* And that meant...

I have been betrayed on all sides. Had she betrayed them too? She had no idea what to think anymore, her thoughts tumbling over themselves like the churn of a river. She could not breathe with the shock of it. Nausea curdled within her.

All thoughts of leaping to her death, to at least snatch her own demise from their hands, were gone as she watched magic bloom, fiery and terrible, in her mother's hands and the grandmasters' flanking her.

It was beautiful, in a deadly sort of way.

She had mere moments left.

Would it hurt? she wondered, the abstract thought causing no fear as it should have done. She was past that now. She had played all her moves and failed – she would not do herself the injustice of cowering before her inevitable end.

CHAPTER 46

A flash of green blurred past, faster than everything else. *Dragon*, Morrigan's mind suggested, because that seemed the least shocking conclusion in her final moments.

And then a familiar voice carved through the roaring in her ears. "Morrigan!"

Vasili.

Time sped up once more, and now she felt – she felt *everything*. Razor-sharp fear sliced through her once more in the face of the dark maelstrom brewing before her. Panic froze her even as her own magic exploded in terrified response because, no, damned be it, she could not face her own death without fighting at all.

"Trust me! *Jump!*"

At the same moment, the storm before her erupted.

Morrigan had not a second to think. Something deep within her jerked to obey. His voice was not a command to her. It was a message that resonated deeply within her, that called to her to choose *life*.

There was no chance of survival. Her choices were death or death – but she did not want to die. Even if there was no way she could live, she still had to try to find a way out.

Morrigan turned and leapt from the parapet into the void as an inferno blasted the precise point where she had stood. The stone parapet exploded into myriad shards above her, the noise and force of it seeming to catapult her faster down. Her stomach was in her mouth, a scream of terror lost to the wind.

She was going to die!

The impact crushed the breath from her, and Morrigan's eyes squeezed shut on instinct. Yet she was not broken. It did not hurt – not enough to be dead, surely. *Has it happened so quickly? Am I dead? Is that it?* She had thought it would hurt more. She had thought she would simply cease to exist after, but her thoughts remained unbroken, that fear still singing through every nerve.

The wind still rushed by, and as her winded lungs fought to take a gulp of cold, biting, life-giving air, something constricted around her chest like bands of steel.

Morrigan opened her eyes. The world was sideways, and she was far above it. Vomit threatened to bubble up.

Claws.

Claws attached to giant feet big enough to wrap around her were doing just that. Her stomach fell away, and a wash of dizziness overwhelmed her. The green wings outstretched above her gave her no doubt as to what had happened, though she did not believe her own eyes.

Am I dead? Dreaming? For it seemed that an emerald dragon now bore her away from certain doom.

High above the ground they soared, lurching with every gust of wind in a way that threatened the paltry contents of her stomach even more with every jolt. Assaults followed them from the castle below. Magical attacks and physical missiles that fell far short, but Morrigan could feel something larger brewing.

Morrigan craned her neck to the crux of that power. Her mother. Dark power emanated from the oracle, tendrils feeling into the air like blood seeping into water. Morrigan knew it sought *her*.

The crenulation lay in smoking, blasted ruin where Morrigan had stood but moments before. Had she remained, she would have been ash and bones on the wind. The realisation struck her. Had it not been for Vasili, she would be.

He came for me.

That left Morrigan with feelings that were altogether too complicated to add into the weight of relief and terror she already battled.

A wordless cry escaped her, using what little breath she could scrape into her squeezed lungs. It was not enough to warn Vasili or his dragon as an attack speared from her mother up through the sky to meet them.

Fire and death. They were going to die anyway. She had survived, snatched from the jaws of her doom, shown a briefest reprieve of hope, for it to be taken anyway.

No! Morrigan rejected it with every fibre of her being, and her own power blasted out, lashing at her mother's tongue of magic carving through the sky. Knocking it aside. Off course.

Icarus wheeled away, taking evasive action – Morrigan had bought him a moment, but it was enough. A howl of pure, molten, dark fury erupted from the oracle below, deafening them all. A howl of cunning – but one of defeat.

Then, with powerful thrusts of his wings, Icarus rolled and curved through the sky, as fluid as water, disappearing around the bluff with the mountainside to shield them.

And she was *alive*.

Morrigan passed out from the sheer damn relief of it.

CHAPTER 47

*A*midst the throngs of wood elves and Pelenor soldiers, Aedon and Lief advanced with the rest, crunching on the packed snow flattened by the lines marching ahead of them. Around them, the trees thinned, and the very earth cracked and groaned, as though the trees themselves longed to rip free of the frigid earth and join them.

The first ranks far before Aedon and Lief met the walls, breaking like the sea upon a cliff. Too impenetrably high the walls rose for any man or elf to scale. It would be impossible, Aedon reckoned. Despite their age and long abandonment, the stone was still smooth, repelling any attempts to climb it. They had no siege warfare to aid them, nor weeks to build any.

Attacks peppered down from above, and defensive magic flashed as Pelenor sent blasts of magic to those daring to peer out from the crenulations overhead. Aedon and Lief drew to a halt, unable to advance or fall back. Aedon muttered a curse, shifting his weight from foot to foot. It did not help his nerves to have to stand and wait. He wanted to get it over with, damn it, but it would take an age of sniping as each side picked off the other one by one at this rate.

He glanced up. Dragons wheeled in the sky, the gusty winds of their making battering those below and twisting the branches wildly. *Why aren't the dragons attacking yet?*

It felt strange for Aedon to not be amongst them, even now. Once, he and Valyria had held General Elyvia's and her dragon Britte's positions at the forefront of the ranks of riders. Now he was reduced to a faceless foot soldier on the ground amidst the churning dirty snow, a pawn of a strategy he was not privy to or in control of. He could have laughed with mirthless irony at it. The once mighty general, now little better than sword fodder.

Yet their purpose was no less important than the dragons'. Perhaps more so. Song swelled outwards from Queen Solanaceae, taken up by the mouths of all those around Her and imbued with the innate magic only the legendary wood elves of Tir-na-Alathea possessed. The ability to Sing magic into true being and life – precisely as they did now.

Aedon could not help but stop, turn, and stare as at the centre of that focused power, a golden orb wove itself into existence, made of pure magic and light, a thing of such beauty and craft that he had not seen before, though he knew what its purpose would be.

Lief turned, her mouth opening to carry the swell of melody. Her words were foreign to him, but they flowed from her tongue like honey, enriching the very air around her with the energy she charged into it.

Captivated by the beauty of her Singing magic, Aedon stilled and watched her. Far away from the front lines and in the throb of the wood elves' Song, he could no longer hear the crash and din of battle. He could watch her sing forever.

As the wood elves Sang, their craft bloomed. Outwards that orb grew, fine golden threads soon passing around the wood elves, into the sky, deep through the earth, insubstantial and ethereal, yet Aedon knew their power was real. It was a net of sorts, one that would, with the collected strength of their people, form a glamour so huge it would sink under stone and earth and above mountain and cloud to encapsulate the whole fortification, halls above and tunnels below, within a great orb. One that would not permit anyone within to evanesce out.

Before, in the mountains where the Order had nestled their hidden settlement, the Pelenor Winged Kingsguard had been powerless to stop the grandmasters and the oracle fleeing into smoke and wind. This time, it would be different. This time, the grandmasters, guilty of so many crimes against humanity, would be stopped. This time, the oracle would be destroyed so that the ember of power she nurtured within, which fuelled all of Valxiron's lasting imprints upon the world, would be gone forevermore.

At last, the orb grew large enough to rise into the clouds above, passing through and around the dragons in the sky. A blast sounded, puncturing through the sweet notes of the elven Song, and Aedon wheeled around to watch as a lone green dragon far from the rest of its kind evaded being crushed under the weight of exploding masonry as one of the battlements inexplicably exploded.

What in Pelenor's name?

But Aedon did not have time to wonder on it further, for with a mighty roar, the collective throats of every one of the dozens of dragons in the skies uniting as one, the Winged Kingsguard attacked. In formation, a great wedge driving through the air, they dove in a sweeping wave over the citadel.

It was momentarily blinding as a wave of fire unleashed from their collective maws, and Aedon blinked furiously to clear it from his vision as battle ceased for a moment, thousands of others doing the self-same. Above the crackle of the inferno, nothing could be heard for long seconds, until the wave of dragons passed and the eruption eased. And then a different song interwove with the wood elves'. The screaming of the dying, harsh and piercing, agonizing and terror filled.

Regret punctured Aedon. This was the part he hated. When two sides collided, death followed – and hardly ever was it the deaths of those orchestrating affairs. No, instead it was those who took little part in such grand affairs who died for their masters, or their causes, or for the sheer misfortune of being compelled or caught in the middle.

This was the part he had most despised as the general of the Winged Kingsguard – and the part that had riddled him with most guilt. His decisions had meant death for people he had never even met, who would have no say in their own demise. Yet what other choice did they have? If they did not repel the darkness the Order of Valxiron perpetuated, it would spread so much terror, suffering, and death unchecked. Some had to suffer now to save so many later. He loathed it all the same.

With the dragons' attack, the stronghold was aflame, a giant torch burning against the dark stone mountain, spilling more light into the day than the very sun itself. And with it, the deadlock eased in the alliance's favour.

Around the battle, the golden net endured, shimmering, half seen and half unseen against the blaze of light from the fires. Those ethereal golden threads held firm, passing through air, stone, and earth around the citadel and tunnel networks below. Containing any and all who might try to flee their inevitable fate.

Aedon dragged his glance away from the burning keep back to Lief. She was drawn, her warm, tanned skin pale. Her brow had a deep furrow set into it as she continued to Sing with all the vigour she possessed.

He knew the power such a Singing would take out of her – out of all of her kin – yet still they persevered, feeding that glamour with their own power and leeching what little they could from the frigid earth beneath them to draw into it. They had no choice but to continue, not if the alliance were to succeed.

Aedon drew close, lifting Lief's hands in his and pressing a kiss to each set of knuckles. Through their skin-on-skin contact, he lent his own strength, buffering her vitality with his. He felt almost utterly useless, unable to join them in the Singing, unable to fight in the wave of dragons above, useless in the front line's fight to breach the walls, as ash and death rained down upon them all.

Upon the walls, through the haze of the inferno, black-cloaked figures endured. The grandmasters, Aedon reckoned. Of course they had some means to protect themselves against dragonfire, as impossible as that ought to have been. They were well-trained in all manner of arcane sorcery. However, in the next moment, they had vanished.

Aedon blinked, wondering if he had imagined it – and then, through his connection to Lief and her magic, and through that, the collective magic of her people, he felt the impact upon the net. Like little punches, like flies caught twanging in a spider's web, it felt, somewhere low on the rise where the net passed through air into earth. It was a flicker in the power he helped to feed.

An outcry arose on the walls, and he wondered if those left alive there had realised their grandmasters had fled, or attempted to, and that they had been betrayed and abandoned to their fate. For he was certain with each passing moment that was what had happened as a pair of dragons wheeled away from the main ranks and raced in the direction of that disruption in the golden net, as though to check. Aedon saw their targets – two dark figures on the horizon.

Battle broke out a moment later in an isolated pocket far from the main fight. Aedon could not see it from where they were on the ground, but he craned his neck all the same to try to catch a glimpse. They *had* to capture the grandmasters, alive or dead, so they could not perpetuate Valxiron's darkness further. This had been the alliance's collective mistake the last time their forces had clashed, decades before on the battlefield. They had cut the head off the snake – and left the body, not knowing it would simply grow another head.

As he watched, a bolt of pure darkness speared out from the top of the citadel. Like a giant arrow tethered to its source, it drove to where those dragons now scuffled, blasting fire and roaring mightily with foes unseen.

No! Aedon's stomach dropped with raw fear as he watched that darkness surge towards them, not doubting for a second that it was the oracle's, and thus Valxiron's, work and that those riders would not be able to withstand it.

"Traitors!" Magically amplified, a voice that belonged to no mortal man or elf seared across the battlefield, crackling with dark anger.

A second later, the mighty blast shuddered into the golden net, burning a hole right through it. The wood elves' Singing intensified, drawing perilously close to the reaches of their energy as they sought to repair the breach. He could see it now, on the rise just above the treeline, where that net intersected with the snow-covered ground. The two dragons wheeled away above, but where two dark figures had stood moments before, their magic flashing in defiance of the aerial attack, there was nothing but a crater of smoking darkness.

Aedon gazed in fearful wonder at the spot, then back towards the citadel, a chill that had nothing to do with the frigid air raising the hairs across his skin. Valxiron had obliterated his own grandmasters? That was enough to give pause for thought. Furthermore, if the oracle was capable of such destruction, perhaps they did not stand a chance, alliance, grand plans, and all.

As if answering his thought, darkness blasted out from the citadel, swallowing the walls in a plume of ashy black and sending an impact ricocheting through the fabric of the earth, swaying them all on their feet. Aedon braced, Lief's hands still firmly clasped in his. *No...*

From the top of the citadel, that void of utter darkness spread down through the levels. Above soared the dragons, distancing as they disengaged to evaluate the new possible threat. Through the crackle and roar of the fires still blazing in the keep, an eerie silence fell as that void spread, quieting the screams and shredding cries of the dying, muffling the struggles and dissent of the living, until all signs of life faded in mere moments.

He wondered if they had choked upon it, for it looked as noxious as smoke. They could all do nought but watch – watch and Sing in the wood elves' case – as that wall of inky blackness bled down through the air, swallowing the whole citadel in waterfalls of obsidian vapour that then encroached upon the Pelenor forces below who had crossed the no man's land.

Screams of raw pain severed the air from their ranks as they were slowly engulfed, line by line, by that darkness. With the ebbing and flowing winds, it teased them, advancing and retreating – but then Aedon saw.

He saw as the darkness forced its way down the throats of living elves, sending them tumbling to the floor with expressions of fear and agony frozen upon their deathly faces. He watched in growing horror as they twitched upon the ground – twitched as no dead things ought to, their skins paling unnaturally and...

With a flood of pure fear, Aedon realised what was coming to pass. Something he thought never to see again in his waking or sleeping nightmares.

Black, spidering veins that he recognised all too well from the blighted elves of Lune spread beneath their faces, the only exposed parts of their bodies he could see. Their eyes gleamed and dulled to black, and then they moved as one, limp and lifeless, yet animated still with unearthly power. By Valxiron's will.

The dead climbed to their feet, ungainly, and turned away from the walls of the Order of Valxiron's defences to face the alliance's own forces on the ground.

CHAPTER 48

Valxiron's power continued to bleed out, sinking to the ground so it swathed their ankles in black smoke that crept forward across the ground.

Suddenly, it was a scramble to retreat as the powers above realised what Aedon had, and the frigid ground became a treacherous icy slope as all those in the face of Valxiron's deathly powers sought to escape. Any that slipped or tripped and fell into that crawling smoke did not rise again. Not living, in any case.

Valxiron's powers continued to bleed from the oracle who stood rigid, her arms outspread, at the top of the highest tower, indiscriminately claiming any it touched to raise an army of the dead without dissent or cowardice but with single-minded obedience.

The wood elves' Singing continued until Aedon felt the wholeness ripple through the sundering that Valxiron's sorcery had wrought, and then the Singing faltered at last as th creaking and groaning of the earth around them intensified. Cracking and ripping the earth around them, boughs shuddered. The Queen's Song was a call to war now, and she rose the trees with her ancient power, calling the forest from slumber to the defence of the living.

Their glamour complete, with Valxiron's darkness facing them all, in life and fire and Song would be their solace, as the ancient warning had said.

Aedon and Lief were too close to the front lines to remain, and with the cessation of their Song, Lief once more opened her eyes, to behold the deadly terror that had become the battlefield before them.

"We must go!" Aedon urged her, lacing his fingers through hers and half-dragging her away in their haste to retreat. Already, the front lines had reached them – what remained of them, at least, bringing with them the stench of fire and death.

They wove with streams of her kind through the writhing, creaking trees as roots ripped from the frigid earth, causing elves to trip and fall and scramble to their feet, dashing and dodging over and past and under evergreens as the trees advanced, walking upon their roots like feet.

Aedon had not seen such a display in the light of day for decades, but he did not stop to look at the magnificence of nature's wrath, called forth by its Queen to stem the flow of the abomination before them. The *dhiran*, the living forest, became the front lines, forming a chain of impenetrable branches against the line of undead elves that shambled their way, oozing darkness and death as their master bid them from on high to attack.

Dragonfire rained down from above upon those dark ranks, catching unfortunate trees in the attempt. As the wood elves, Aedon and Lief in their midst, made for the rise where Valxiron's crater still smoked, where the two cowardly grandmasters had met their untimely end, stone cracked as the *dhiran* tore literal chunks from the citadel, their roots finding purchase and strength where hands could not, ripping and tearing the stone even as they did the self-same to the ensorcelled dead army, wrenching them limb from limb to end them.

It was terrifyingly beautiful and deadly to watch, and Aedon could do little more than that, what little remained of his magic brimming, ready to protect Lief, no matter the cost to himself, from the ranks of shambling dead that still approached through breaches in the line of trees.

Song rippled through the wood elves' ranks once more, ragged and desperate, the desire for survival fraught in every note. Lief caught the Song too, her amber eyes blazing defiantly in the face of the death that approached them, her hand firmly clasped into Aedon's as they stood together, not sure whether this would be their last stand.

A glorious last stand it would make, if so. The great wave of *dhiran* ripping the dead and the citadel to shreds in a great wave, crunching through the stronghold and tearing through man's, elves', and dwarves' creations as only nature could. The elves Sang and the dragons burned, and all their lives refused to be extinguished – not whilst they still drew breath to fight.

CHAPTER 49

A great silver dragon landed between the wood elves and the citadel, its rider General Elyvia herself. It turned, glaring balefully at the citadel as Elyvia dismounted, her armour smeared with ash.

Queen Solanaceae strode through the foremost ranks of Her people to meet the General, who did not waste time offering any bow or platitude.

"We have not the strength to take him down. He repels our fire like oil to water, curse him! It needs your magic, my Lady." General Elyvia's eyes burned with desperate fervour as she glanced up at the Queen, who drew Herself tall, a regal figure, even in the face of defeat.

"You know our aversion to fire." Solanaceae glanced at the dragon.

"You know it is necessary."

Were it anyone else, any other place or time, Elyvia would have been crushed for her insolence, but the Queen stirred, unhappy but knowing that She had little other choice. She leaned closer, and neither Aedon nor any of the other elves watching with bated breath could discern what was said.

"It shall be done." Elyvia retreated back to Britte and mounted the dragon, grim-faced.

Solanaceae did not return to the fold of Her people but marched away towards the chaos of the front line, where *dhiran* met the dead and where they tore down the citadel stone by stone.

As She walked, the earth shook as, before them all, the highest tower with that darkness atop it collapsed, sinking into itself and crashing into oblivion as the *dhiran*'s work finally destabilised the base. As it fell, it took out a swathe of the impregnable outer wall and crushed several *dhiran* in the process, rending their woody limbs apart until all that was left was their wrecked remains, twisted and ruined amidst piles of stone and clouds of dust.

Dragon and *dhiran* worked in harmony, exterminating the faltering lines of dead that Valxiron's dark spirit had raised, but still, he remained, the head of that snake – and Solanaceae continued Her advance alone.

"What is She doing?" Aedon asked in hushed tones. But Lief did not answer, watching her Queen, grim-faced, and continuing to lend what strength she had in a fresh Singing.

That darkness reared as the last of the lines fell before it, and only Solanaceae stood on the no man's land before the ruined citadel.

The tower had fallen, and any mortal would have perished in the calamitous event, but Aedon did not dare to hope. He was not so foolish. They all watched on as the creeping darkness withdrew into that cloud of settling dust, coalescing into something deeper and darker than anything around it, as though a pure absence of light sucked into a void.

No longer did Valxiron wear a mortal shape. The oracle's body no doubt lay crushed under the keep somewhere. Now, the shape of a man, tall and lithe, wearing a dark, nine-pointed crown, made entirely of shadow, with two glowing coals where eyes ought to have been, emerged from the gloom.

"Valxiron," Solanaceae said coolly, as though She greeted an old acquaintance.

Valxiron did not reply, save to let out a laugh filled with such dark derision that She challenged him.

In a moment, She diminished as he grew before She straightened and raised her chin. At the same instant he attacked, so did She. Light met darkness with an almighty *crack*, and then the two of them were a blur, striking and retreating, attacking and dodging, neither touching the other. Again and again they went, advancing and ceding, circling each other like the wary adversaries they were, powerful sorcery raging around them as dark struck light and life fought death. Until, at last, with a sizzle, Solanaceae's light lashed around Valxiron and dragged him in.

It was a double-edged blade. Close enough, and tethered together, now he too could attack.

With a screech laced in pure pain, as though She had been burned, Solanaceae fell back, and a lash of darkness followed. She reeled and staggered back, blood blooming on Her cheek and then Her arm, ruby red against Her deep skin and scattering off in droplets into the dirtied snow at Her feet.

"In life and fire and Song be solace!" She howled, almost in defiance, Her beauty savage and terrible, passionate and undimmed in the face of his darkness.

He struck Her, a whip of magic sending Her flying into the dirt, and fear struck into the hearts of all those watching as it fell to them to know that perhaps their Queen was not immortal, not invincible.

Solanaceae pulled Herself up onto a knee, Her foot planted in the churned ground to rise as Valxiron advanced, growing in size yet more, as though already savouring his victory. He towered over Her, and still, She did not rise, looking up at him, Her expression hidden from everyone waiting in expectant horror on the hillock far behind Her.

The wood elves' Song faltered, but at the moment their note missed a beat, Her own pure mellow voice joined it, swelling with strength and in turn rallying them. As Valxiron raised his hands, sucking power towards him, growing a darkness big enough to smite Her and taking an extra moment to savour Her demise and his ascension, She struck.

Light burst from Solanaceae, a sword-like shard longer than her arm materialising before Her. She plucked it from the air and, like a spear, drove it up into his torso.

High above, the roar of dragons drowned out the wood elves' Song, and no one could tell if Solanaceae still Sang, for She fell back to the earth under an onslaught of Valxiron's wrath, lost amidst the darkness for a moment.

And then dragonfire rained down.

It obliterated everything.

CHAPTER 50

Silence fell upon the battlefield as the last dragon's fire died, and the inferno fanned by the beat of their wings fell away to nothing upon the scorched earth.

The churned snow was now burned mud, scoured and dried and scorched black. *Dhiran* were twisted skeletons, hulking piles of steaming ash, in a circle around where their Queen had fallen, trying to protect Her until the last. Trying and failing.

The Wood elves' song took on a keening tone as a mournful wail spread amongst Her people, who rushed from that rise, paying no heed as to whether Valxiron had lived or been vanquished, only that their own matriarch had fallen in service of them all.

The last of the flames fell back. Revealing a scorched cocoon of crisscrossing roots rising from the earth. They had been alive to form such an impenetrable shell, but now they were charred to white ash, to crumble at a single touch. And indeed, the wind gusted them as General Elyvia landed first on Britte and ran to the site of the last fight.

At the forefront of the wood elves' surge, Aedon and Lief were soon amongst the throng, forming a silent circle around a scene of devastation. On the ground, black, glittering ash of no material Aedon recognised drifted in an errant breeze.

"Do not touch it," said Elyvia sharply to those who dared to lean close.

Aedon realised what it must be – the last remnants of Valxiron's form. *Is he truly gone?* He did not dare to hope, not when his chest had caved in, unable to conceive of Solanaceae's loss – of her sacrifice.

Elyvia gathered the strange material in a bubble of magic, sealing it into a crystalline orb the size of a head – securing it. The general turned to the crisscrossing orb of roots. The earth, it seemed, had tried to protect its Queen, even to the last. As they watched, the ashy remains began to crumble, littering on a form curled within.

Solanaceae still knelt, that lance of light clutched within Her grasp, head bowed over Herself, a curtain of hair loose where Her braid had ripped free during battle. Dimmed. Small. Unburnt.

As they watched, She swayed and fell.

But of Valxiron, there was no trace.

CHAPTER 51

Venya and Sylvio had opened the portal every hour as commanded by the general of the Winged Kingsguard. Every hour with the ringing of the bell as dawn had turned to day, and day had turned to dusk – and then darkness had fallen.

A small portal, one a messenger could slip through from the other side – a messenger with news of victory or defeat. But no one came.

It was freezing, as a result, in the castle's courtyard, where ranks of soldiers and healers waited for whatever news would come. The High Council waited inside the castle doors, holding an impromptu court in the hallway, by the sounds of it.

As the moon rose and the stars glittered in an uncharacteristically clear night, Venya ached, and still she watched as Sylvio opened a portal, yet again, into the dark land beyond.

This time, light spilled through.

A messenger followed.

It was chaos after as Sylvio made the portal as large as he could. Venya could do little but stand by and watch as rank after rank filed through, or flew in the case of the dragons, who swooped in through the breach and made straight for the dragonhold.

It was endless and brought with it the squelch of booted feet and the stench of smoke mixed with the tang of blood and something inexplicably more fetid she could not place. Venya could not see her brother, so dark was it that all the dragons looked the same to her – big, bulky, misshapen things yawning shadows though the night.

The call that took up the halls of Tournai, however, one of quiet, dogged relief, was one of *victory*.

It was dawn by the time they could close the breach, once the last stragglers returned. Had there been so many left? Or so few? Venya was too tired to wonder. She held out for any sign of her brother, until at last, he arrived through the breach and she sagged to her knees in relief.

CHAPTER 52

Vasili transferred Morrigan onto the paltry nest of straw in Icarus' cave in the dragonhold. Icarus' flanks heaved from the exertion of it all. Morrigan was a dead weight in Vasili's arms, and he rested a palm on her ice-cold forehead, but her chest still rose and fell with breath.

"I'll have to take her to my parents'," he muttered absently, rubbing a hand over his face, though it did nothing to dispel the deep-seated, bone-aching exhaustion within him. "She needs a healer." How would he carry her? He blinked slowly, his eyelids heavy. Icarus was too large to land in the street, and he had no horse. It made his head hurt to think.

When next Vasili awoke, he lay in an unfamiliar bed. Plain white linen, slightly scratchy, the pillow thin and rough against his face. He cracked his eyes open further. An infirmary. *How did I get here?*

"Good morning, sleepyhead," Icarus' voice rumbled into his mind.

"Where am I?"

"Where you need to be. You were very dehydrated, tired, and had some bumps and bruises. You've slept for three days."

"Three days!?" Vasili exploded, sitting up – and groaning at how much it hurt to do so. He quieted as he saw the bed next to him.

Morrigan. Her hair fanned across the pillow, and she wore a simple shift that he knew she would hate, with no weapons or leathers in sight.

"They are treating everyone. The infirmary is full, and many more places besides commandeered."

Vasili did not reply, his attention fixed upon Morrigan. She looked subdued in slumber, the perpetual frown or scowl upon her visage gone, replaced by the wrinkle of consternation instead. He slipped his feet out of bed and padded across the cold stone floor, pulling a stool from the end of the bed close, where he could sit beside her. Her hand lay on the coverlet. He did not dare touch it, even though some part of him longed to, perhaps if only to feel like he was not entirely useless.

It was the first time he had seen Morrigan – properly, at least, and not for an instant in the midst of battle – since their altercation. Since she had stabbed him, left him for dead, and fled. How did he feel about that?

Confused.

He did not hate her, and that confused him even more.

Vasili sat, with the churn of his thoughts, long into the day, waiting for her to wake – both willing her to and scared of what would happen when she did.

CHAPTER 53

It was warm. The first feeling to greet Morrigan. It felt pleasant and yet unsettling, as she was so used to the brittle cold that kept her permanently shivering. Her toes, her fingers, her skin tingled with the luxurious pleasure of it.

Morrigan cracked open her eyes, lifting a hand to rub away the gritty sleep that had formed.

Vasili swam into focus, sideways – after a moment, she realised that she was lying and he sat beside her.

Now she knew she was definitely dead. She had imagined it all – the battle, the dragon, her total annihilation had definitely happened, because it was impossible that her perception, that they were safe, warm, and not dead in some infirmary, was in fact the case.

She stared at him. Taking in the dark hollows underneath his eyes. The growth of stubble grazing his chin. The steadfast patience in his violet eyes – those same eyes that had flashed betrayal and pain at her the last moment they had truly met.

"Morrigan," he said softly, breaking the silence.

She swallowed. She could not bear to speak his name. Not after what she had done. Guilt gnawed at her, and shame burned her cheeks hot. How was he alive? She had not taken the easy killing blow, but still, he would have suffered. It had been her doing.

She knew now he had extended a hand of hope to her. He had shown her kindness and trust, and she had betrayed it all, even though she had thought she was doing the right thing. To return to her people. They had betrayed her in the same way she had betrayed Vasili.

"Morrigan?" His voice held a caring edge to the questioning inflection.

She squeezed her eyes shut. Damned be it, something inside her wanted to tear itself out, and rage, and cry, and scream – yet she did not even have the energy to sit or stand.

"What happened?" Her voice was little better than a hoarse whisper, shredded from screaming.

Vasili shifted beside her. Uncomfortable. Her attention sharpened upon him.

"Tell me," she demanded.

"The Order of Valxiron is no more," he said, meeting her eyes before his gaze flicked away, as though he did not have the courage.

"What?" she breathed.

"After you leapt and Icarus caught you, the dragons attacked. The tower collapsed, breaching the walls."

No! No, no, no.

"The oracle. Something happened to her. She was the

dark one. She killed the grandmasters when they tried to flee the attack."

Morrigan stared up at the whitewashed vaulted ceiling, though in her mind's eye she relived the final moments she had seen her mother. A cold- and darkness-filled husk bearing her master's essence. Condemning her to death. It squashed the spike of satisfaction she would have otherwise felt at learning of the grandmasters' deaths.

"A dark smoke poured out of her, and she – *he* – killed everyone in the castle, and plenty in the Pelenor army, before raising them from the dead." Vasili shuddered, revulsion oozing from his hunched body, his lip curled and his eyes glazed over as he relived it.

Horror chilled her at his bleak description of such ghastly sorcery. She had not known her master practised that, and now, that added to the weight of the confusion swirling within her.

"The Queen of the wood elves raised the forest in defence of the living. It was magnificent," he murmured, almost in afterthought, "though terrifying. They faced the army of the dead, and the Queen faced the Dark One. She defeated him, and survived – just."

He fell to silence, and she could see that he was miles away in memory.

"You saved me."

"I did." He glanced at her, his face impassive.

"Did anyone else survive?"

"No. Well, they were searching the tunnels when we left," he amended, "but it appears that the Dark One killed all of the Order before raising them from the dead to serve. They were all completely obliterated when the dragons and living forest attacked."

"The whole Order is *gone*?" There were pockets of followers everywhere, but the grandmasters and the oracle had been there. The upper echelons. The masterminds. The shepherds. Without them, anyone else was a speck of dust floating in the wind, lost and adrift.

"Yes."

Silence yawned as Morrigan tried to grapple with that truth.

"Please tell me I am dead," she croaked past that hateful lump that squeezed her throat shut.

"You're not dead," came the soft reply, and sadness coloured it. "Do you want to be?"

She nodded, and those treacherous tears slipped out from the corners of her eyes, dashing down into the hairline by her ears at either side.

"You don't mean that." His words were some kind of plea – but what did he know?

"My entire life is a lie."

Vasili sighed. His hand lightly rested atop hers. She flinched and pulled away. He did not follow. She heard the slight drag of his hand on the fabric of her bedspread as he withdrew.

"It will be all right. I promise."

"You don't know that." Every word bit past her teeth gritted against the torrent of pain raging inside her. Her own *mother* had seen fit to exterminate her like vermin. The grandmasters that ought to have revered her as their future oracle had only ever seen her as a tool for their own selfish ends. And her master...he had seen the sliver of doubt in her heart and dismissed a lifetime of loyalty and servitude without second thought. "I have nothing, and no one."

Her throat hurt too much to speak further, clogged with a lump, and hot tears pricked at her eyes. That betrayal stung more than anything. She still felt utterly nauseated by it. None had betrayed her more deeply than her own master. She had given *everything* to Valxiron. Devoted her entire existence to his mission. What was she supposed to believe now? The Order and Valxiron were no more. Everything she had worked for had been obliterated. Her life's calling, her whole future, and the roots of her identity were in tatters. What was left, save for an empty, spent husk?

A pause. And then, "You have me."

She did not reply. That was too hard to think about – what that even meant. Sworn enemies, somehow between them had grown the wary tendril of – of what? They were not friends, nor more. Perhaps equals, but who knew? Not her. Could they be anything after what had passed between them? She had done nothing but hate and mistreat him, and she knew too much of people and men to hope that he would extend any kindness towards her again.

"There is a way forward, Morrigan. I will help you, if you will let me."

"I don't know where to go from here," she dared to admit in a hoarse whisper. Practicalities aside, for she had nothing to provision a life with, emotionally, it was too yawningly vast to contemplate.

"You do not need to know the answers – just trust that you can find them."

Morrigan squeezed her eyes tighter shut, trying to keep inside the cascade of tears that wanted to fall. He was *wrong*.

They both were. She had always been so arrogantly sure of herself. How could she trust herself when she had been so wrong about *everything*?

"If you don't trust yourself, you can trust me, you know. How about that?"

A flicker of hope uncurled within her – a tiny anchor in that raging sea of hopeless anguish.

Could I do that?

He had given her no reason to distrust him so far. Throughout all, he had stayed true, even though she had pushed and tested him more than was kind or fair or right.

Could he be the bridge back to figuring out who she was supposed to be now her entire world was gone, and if she would move past any of it?

"One day at a time. That's all this is. One hour at a time if that's what it needs to be. I'm not going anywhere. You can take as long as you need." She heard the determination in his voice.

Foolish young man that he was, she had hated that quality of his so much, and now it was a lifeline. She could have kicked herself with the irony of how she longed to cling to that for any certainty.

CHAPTER 54

Aedon and Lief had collapsed together upon that ruined battlefield, a tangle of limbs and breath and relief. Relief that they had survived. Relief that an end to the horror was in hand. Relief that finally, at long last, they had won their *peace*.

Aedon simply did not have enough room in him for the love, gratefulness, and happiness that thought brought – he would not have to worry about losing Lief again. They could be together at last, whatever that looked like.

They returned to Tournai with the rest of the wood elves, who were greatly subdued at the state of their Queen. A jubilant army it ought to have been, but they had prevailed at great cost, and the horrors of the battlefield haunted each of their steps. There would be much to sift through in the aftermath.

The old warning had proved true – that life and fire and Song would prevail against that ancient darkness, but their doom had approached so near that it was still scarce able to be believed that the two of them had lived. So many had not.

Queen Solanaceae had survived by a thread and had been carried back through the gateway in a perilously weak state. It seemed only the song of Her people and the living roots that had given themselves to Her had managed to save Her from falling into the inferno and darkness to Her ultimate demise.

The *dhiran* and dragons had decimated Valxiron's violated monstrosities wrought of sorcery and death, and none had remained. No power of his had either. General Elyvia had safely contained the fine, black, diamond-like dust that had remained and returned with it to Tournai so that it could be determined how to be destroyed or made safe so that no essence of Valxiron remained.

Nothing else of the Order of Valxiron remained, for the grandmasters and oracle had perished too – the one living soul who had returned with them was the oracle's daughter, Lady Morrigan, in the care of Lord Dimitrius' son. Aedon did not know what to make of the compulsion of the boy to rescue his mortal foe. In him, Aedon saw such a trace of his mother, Lady Harper, and her determined compassion. Aedon would have gone to the ends of the world for Lief – perhaps the young man felt the same of his lady.

The one treasure to be recovered was not made of gold or jewels, but a simple casket, older than them all, from the bowels of the tunnels. Erendriel's relics. It had already been declared that they would be laid to rest in a safe place under starry skies, their location forgotten forever more so she could rest in peace, without desecration.

Perhaps, Aedon thought, as he held Lief close, not caring that she stank of sweat and dirt and smoke, they could all now find some peace. He craved it more than anything. The chance to live a simple life and choose the joys of each day.

CHAPTER 55

*V*asili strode behind Elyvia through the halls of the Athenaeum – his sister Venya's territory. She waited for him at her First Librarian's study and flicked him a small smile, filled with tired relief. His mirrored it. Briefly, they clasped hands before following the general into the room, where Nieve awaited.

"Thank you, General." On the desk before her, one grimoire lay, quiescent. *Sylvestri di Niani Verdiatris*, the Book of Gateways.

"Sylvio here has agreed to assist your cause. He will help you search for the remnants of any anchors laid down by the Dark One and create gateways to and from them on your travels so that they may be safely neutralised to remove any future threat of the Dark One's ascension."

Elyvia bowed deeply. "I thank you. I know what trust you place in me by allowing one of your precious tomes to leave the Athenaeum."

"Quite." Nieve smiled faintly. "I think Sylvio is up for the adventure and will behave?" She raised an eyebrow, glancing at the grimoire.

He rustled his pages in reply but stayed quiet. As pliant as he would ever get for a tome of such acerbic humour.

"It appears that he will stay in the family, in any case." The First Librarian's warm gaze passed to Vasili.

Elyvia chuckled. "Yes, I suppose so. I have accepted young Vasili here into a new post. He will help on this vital task."

It would be weeks yet, though, and Vasili was grateful for it. He needed some kind of reprieve, not just for Morrigan's sake, but for his own. His life had been horror filled for several moons now, thanks to the Order, and the nightmares still plagued him, waking and sleeping, after what had passed.

He slipped outside, dismissed with Venya, as the two older elves discussed their business in private.

Venya embraced him tightly. It was the first time they had had chance to speak. "It's so good to see you."

"And you." Relief was palpable in his tone.

"I was so worried."

"I can take care of myself, sister."

"And still, I shall worry! Don't think I will stop with you sent even further afield on thrilling missions – I shall no doubt treble my concerns."

He chuckled and drew back. "And I am grateful for them. What of you? This is hardly normal for your job, is it?" Hardly as stuffy as he had imagined.

Venya grimaced. "Most definitely not, but I am grateful for it, for it has brought new opportunities. I am still to train here, but Nieve has placed me upon an accelerated programme to reach full librarian status, with personal tutelage in sorcery and grimoires. She says that there is no use in all this knowledge languishing here if it is never used, rather that we ought to be practising far more of it, sharing it too. There could be so much knowledge that the world needs locked up in these vaults."

Vasili warmed at the uncharacteristic tinge of pride in Venya's tone. "I'm pleased for you, sister – and proud."

She flushed. "Look after Sylvio, promise me? I'm quite attached to the old rascal."

Vasili smirked. *She never could take a compliment.* "Of course."

Elyvia slipped out of Nieve's office with Sylvio wedged under her arm and gestured for Vasili to follow her.

"See you later, sister."

Her voice followed down the hall, warning ringing in it. "Dinner tonight at Mother and Father's. Don't be late!"

Vasili would be. He always was. Especially now he had somewhere more pressing to be.

CHAPTER 56

It was another two bells before Vasili made it back to the infirmary. He had been released, relatively unscathed, but Morrigan had remained for an extra night and day under observation. He had been back as often as he could, though mostly they had sat in silence. He found her sitting up in bed, reading a copy of a book the healer had lent her – an old, battered copy of fairy tales. There appeared to be something different about her.

For a moment, he simply watched her as she read. Morrigan seemed to be somewhere else, her face slack and free of cares and a cascade of raven hair tumbling over one shoulder, shielding her from the view of the rest of the ward.

"I'm sorry I took so long," he said as he approached.

She glanced up, blinking. Her features hardened as she returned to the real world.

"How are you feeling?"

"Fine. I wish they'd let me go already," she said irritably. "I don't like being around this many people."

Vasili could appreciate that. "Well, I think they're planning to let you out tonight." Back into his family's custody for now, until all matters were smoothed out. She had stabbed him and caused grievous injuries to others in her escape, after all. There would be consequences – though he did not want to think about what they might be. "You're welcome to stay at our family home – we're to have dinner tonight. Would you like to join us?" His tone was light but inside, nerves roiled. Would she accept or decline?

She nodded. "No people, though?" she added in a sharp tone, glancing at him suspiciously.

"Not if you don't want."

"I don't."

Vasili suppressed a smirk. She was still as forthright as ever, even when her world had fallen apart. "Then so be it. We can dine separately from the others – or you can eat in your room alone, if you wish?"

"That's fine." She did not say which.

He did not press her further.

The book lay closed, clasped in her hands, her thumb running over the woven grain of the fabric-lined hardcover, worn and stained with age, the gold embossed lettering long faded.

"I am to be stationed in Tournai from now on," he said as he took the stool next to the bed and clasped his hands before him. He might fly far on missions, but it was to there he would return – and perhaps to her, if she allowed it. A new idea had sparked – one he would not present to her. Not yet. Not unless she decided to place her faith in rebuilding a life outside the Order of Valxiron.

After all, in his new venture, he would find relics of Valxiron – and supporters. There would be those others, scattered to the four winds and now leaderless, who followed Valxiron's teachings. They would not listen to an outsider, but perhaps one of their own, say, an oracle's heir, might be able to persuade them that there was a better way in life.

He just needed *her* to give it a chance first.

Will she?

She looked at him and said nothing, her expression unreadable.

CHAPTER 57

Inside, emotions still whirled, faster than Morrigan could catch them and larger than she wanted them to be.

Vasili continued, "So you are welcome to return to my home – to stay in the same room as before. I shall be opposite. I won't be returning to duty for some weeks yet. Not until, well – there is much still to sort after...everything," he finished lamely, as though that one small word could encapsulate the gravity of what had passed.

Hurt still burned, raw and deep and savage inside her.

"Would you like that?"

Where else did she have to go? He must have thought much the same. She nodded jerkily.

Vasili released a small, pent-up breath. "Good. That's settled, then. Look, I meant what I said yesterday." He met her gaze. "I cannot imagine what you're going through, but I am here to help you try to make sense of it, one step at a time. If you wish?"

Damn it, the reading had merely distracted – taken the edge off the cavernous grief that threatened to suck her in and never let her go. Now, with some simple words, he had scratched it raw once more. Somehow, he did that – softened all her jagged edges and cut her to the core with mere words. She clenched her jaw.

She felt so small against the enormity of her grief. So very hopelessly tiny.

Her head bowed over the book in her lap, and her eyes clenched shut. What did she want? She had no idea. The terrifying unknown of her future was so much larger than her that she wanted to give up and stop fighting. What was the point when all she had fought for had rejected her so utterly and was now gone?

And yet that same tiny, glowing ember remained within her. The one that had made her hesitate upon the precipice instead of leaping to take her own life or letting her masters destroy her. The one that had trusted Vasili's hurried plea to take that quite literal leap of faith into the void and trust to him, and to survival, and to the promise of life.

"Morrigan?"

She still wanted that. No matter how small her flame had diminished, she still wanted *something*, even if she did not know what it was. A wall of hurt, grief, rage, fear, and darkness stood in the way. Morrigan knew the direction of the first step, deep down, if she truly wanted it.

The only way was onwards.

The only way was *through*.

The only way was to take his offer – and discover what was beyond all she had known, even though it terrified her more than she would ever voice to herself in the dark shadows of the night.

Morrigan nodded.

CHAPTER 58

"I cannot believe you are choosing to return to Tir-na-Alathea again, my friend." Harper chuckled, embracing Aedon fondly.

"I would be nowhere else, these days," he said lightly, fully aware of the irony of those words compared to his past self that had loathed, feared, and avoided the legendary forest.

"You are welcome to stay? I know the repairs to your apartment might take a while, but you may remain here as a guest," Harper offered.

Aedon shared a glance and a secret smile with Lief. "I thank you for it, but this is no longer my home. Not as it once was." And it was true.

He had thought, returning to his old abode, that it would feel as though he slipped on a long-worn and familiar shoe. Not a stranger's garment that did not fit and felt as though it never had. It had cemented what he had already known, deep inside. Home was not a place so much as it was a feeling. And for him, home was wherever *she* was. Lief na Arboreali.

Harper's knowing glance flitted between the two of them. "I understand. You must visit though, promise me? I shall be furious if you leave it for so long before we meet again."

Aedon laughed. "Only if you return the favour."

"Done." Harper's eyes glittered with the promise of it. "I would love to see the realm that has so enchanted you."

It would be possible now, for even in her weakened state, Queen Solanaceae had declared that the borders of Tir-na-Alathea be opened to allies, encouraging travel and free trade as never before between Her realm and others, Pelenor first and foremost.

"And now you may. You would be welcome, I'm sure." He cocked an eyebrow at Lief.

"Of course," Lief murmured, laying a hand on his arm.

"We should not delay. El'hari waits for us." The commander of Emuir had agreed to accompany them on the return leg as she made her way home to prepare for the injured Queen's homecoming, and, no doubt, a Singing of such magnitude to restore her health.

El'hari had also granted another boon for which Aedon would be eternally grateful – Lief's freedom. With Lune destroyed, El'hari had released Lief from the Queen's service – with the promise of a post always remaining open for her, should she wish to take it, in El'hari's own command.

With that, it meant both Aedon and Lief had the thing they had sought most, aside from each other. Freedom.

"It's been good to see you. Truly." Harper's embrace was long and tight – to both of them. "Take care of him," she said thickly to Lief.

"Thank you," Aedon said to Harper – and she knew what he meant. For so much more than lodgings and food. They had enjoyed a last dinner the night before, with Harper and Dimitri's children and the strange Lady Morrigan, who had been an elusive guest, and it had warmed Aedon's heart even more to know one of his oldest friends had found happiness. Happiness that he now dared to believe he might enjoy too.

They stepped outside into the cold of another winter's day – soon to be the warmth of the eternal summer forest as they returned to Tir-na-Alathea. Aedon found that he had missed it, humidity and all, strange as though it felt to admit that as he strolled down the cobbled street, arm in arm with Lief.

Aedon offered his arm to Lief and waggled an eyebrow, his grin filled with mischief. "Where to, m'lady?"

"To meet my parents," she said dryly, shooting him a coy glance. "And my brothers. I warn you. They're overprotective."

Aedon's smile wavered. "Remind me, how many brothers do you have?"

"Five."

"*Five*. Right. Well, then," he said faintly. "I thought I had earned my peace and quiet, Lief na Arboreali. You did not warn me there would be trials ahead."

"Oh," she replied airily and planted a light kiss upon his cheek. "I have no doubt you will rise to the challenge, thief."

He stopped and pulled her against him, the cold plumes of their breath mingling. "With a fearsome wood elf such as yourself by my side, how can I fail?"

And as he stole a kiss from her willing lips, he thought he might die with the happiness of it and know no regrets now he had such light and hope burning within him, thanks to her. Wherever she was, he would follow, as long as she wished it. Wherever she was would be his home. Wherever they went, it would be together.

THE END

AUTHOR'S NOTE

Dear readers,

Hello, my friends, and a warm welcome to the very end of this series (though, if you want a tiny bit more, please do check out the exclusive bonus epilogue available on my website at www.megcowley.com).

For those of you who have been with me from the very beginning of the *Chronicles of Pelenor* series, and who were so passionate about Aedon receiving his own follow-up tale, this series is entirely thanks to you. It would not have happened without your enthusiasm and support. (His ego is very stoked, and I am humbled.) So from myself, and Aedon – thank you! (If you haven't read the *Chronicles of Pelenor* quartet, I recommend that you do. It gives so much depth to what happens in this series!)

It has been a pure joy to tell this saga – to be able to delve into the tangle of who Aedon has become after such a long journey since the first pages of *Heart of Dragons* (*Chronicles of Pelenor, Book One*), when he sprung into mind fully formed as

AUTHOR'S NOTE

an endearingly charming rogue, and give him the happy ending I have longed to craft for him since the very beginning.

Lief has been a wonderful character to bring into this world. Fiery and competent, yet with an inner strength waiting to grow into. She gave Aedon the belonging, sanctuary, and hope he desperately needed...he gave her the courage to overcome her demons and strike out on a path of her own.

I wanted too, to revisit Harper and Dimitri in some way, for they are so dear to my heart from the *Chronicles of Pelenor*, and I received so much love for them from you, and questions too, wanting to know what happened to them next. I hope you will be satisfied seeing a little slice of their 'happily ever after'.

Vasili and Venya were natural products of that. Venya contains a lot of myself as a younger woman. Bookish (I too spent most of my school years hiding in the school library with books as my solace), shy, and fearful of anything outside her comfort zone – but forced to grow, before realising that she is indeed, braver than she thinks. And, wouldn't we all like a Nyx? I would. Oh, the fun (mischief) we would have!

Meanwhile, Vasili's growing was of a different sort – initially, I wondered if he would seek redemption from the shadow of his tainted family name. It became clear that more than that, he was on a quest for *truth* – a more coming of age journey to understand, investigate, and question the premise of his life, perhaps selfishly fixating on Morrigan's redemption without yet realising his own deep-seated needs for validation of his life purpose too.

AUTHOR'S NOTE

Morrigan was an entirely unexpected heroine (anti-heroine or villainess perhaps!) of Vasili's storyline. One who walked onto the scene and refused to leave until I told her tangled story. I rather think she stole the show in this final instalment, don't you? Her story arc was hard to tell, both in the brutality of her life and extremism with which she was raised, and the painfully slow turning of her spirit towards the hint of light.

I hope you will be happy with where she ended this tale too. For her, there was never going to be a happily ever after in such a short span of time...but her ending was the light and hope inviting her that something *better* was out there, if only she dared to believe it, and take that leap of faith to discover what is beyond the darkness.

One day, a long way in her future, I hope she will get there. That is the same for us, too. No matter how dark, there is always light. Sometimes, things are so hard that we can only go one day, sometimes even one hour or one minute at a time, but our strength remains in the fact we choose to keep going at all. That is beautiful and powerful.

That seems especially poignant perhaps, since this series was birthed in the midst of a pandemic which continues to devastate so many lives globally. I don't think I know a single person who has been immune to its effects. I write this with hope that one day – sooner rather than later – it will be over, and we may live free from its shadow.

This series has certainly helped me cope and weather the challenges of the last year and a half. I hope in reading it, it has brought you some escape, solace, relief, or entertainment too. That has been the underlying theme I think I always end up gravitating to – no matter how dark, challeng-

AUTHOR'S NOTE

ing, and scary, there is always happiness, hope, and light, and that we can weather this and come out stronger together, my friends.

With all my love and thanks,

Meg Cowley
September 2021

ACKNOWLEDGMENTS

With thanks to so many people for helping make this book and series happen. Thank you to my husband first and foremost. My biggest supporter and inspiration. I am truly grateful for the way you encourage me to shine, grow, and love. You give me the space to become the best woman I can be, and in turn that helps me write the best stories I can. I'm still a work in progress, as are my books, but isn't that the journey for us all? I wouldn't want to be walking through life beside anyone else. I choose you every day.

To my Noble Turtles, I am honoured to be able to share in your journeys and I thank you for your part in mine. I look up to you all hugely and I am so grateful I get to learn with and from you every day. Together, we shall conquer the world with 'kissy stabby books' (and a mutual appreciation for one certain H)!

Thank you to my weekly sprinting group. Dan, Sam, Pan, Renee, Faye – you helped me drag this book out one painful word at a time when I was mired in the boggy middle of such a disagreeable manuscript. I appreciate you cheering me along every step of the way – and keeping me sane!

Thank you to my editor Laura. I don't know what I would do without you. You are a *Goddess*. I send you stories so roughly uncut and you turn them into brilliant diamonds. *Thank you* from the bottom of my heart for always helping me tell the story as it was meant to be. (And I promise I will continue to work on my terrible writing habits!)

Thank you to my favourite deviant Sacha. The Universe sent you at precisely the right moment in this project. Thank you for reminding me to save the cat, and for helping me wrangle side characters who were too big for their boots back into line. You got me through the midpoint impasse, and I am so thankful for your good friendship in that moment especially.

Thank you to the lovely Clare for your outstandingly beautiful formatting! You helped me create every bookworm's dream – a gorgeous book.

Lastly and certainly not least, thank you to my readers, each and every one of you. Without you, none of these stories would have happened. Thank you for the best fellowship I could ever ask for. Across the world, our love of stories unites us, and I am so grateful for our community. I dedicate this book to all of you.

READER DEDICATION

For all the readers who have followed me from the beginning, or joined the path more recently, this book I dedicate to you. Without you, none of these stories would exist. I am eternally grateful for and humbled by your support, encouragement, and love for my characters and stories.

I dedicate this book to;
Gayreth Walden, Anne Langkilde, Mandie Sagen, Elda, Jay Phillips, Lana Turner, Michael Murphy, Sara Lawson, Caroline Atkins, Debbie Harris, Rocco Casucci Jr, Runar Skjegstad, Maria Arcara, Fiona Andrew, Gale Osborne, Jackie T, Jan Drake, Kanyon, Kimberly Grube, Mary Elizabeth Koch, Michael Eitniear, Russ Bailey, Scott Engel, Sheila Wood, Stuart McClements, JuliAnne Raypholtz, Nerys Moakes, Montague Watkins Sr, Brittany Timmins, Lisa Miller, Cory Cravens, Sherri Stone, Kim M Simcox, Karen

Hernandez, Andrea, Joanne Rimmer, Keri Hunter, Donald Knappenberger, Janice Dupuis, Kevin McKeon, Renee Novak, Sandra Bray Linebaugh, Davena House, Arissa Marquard, Warner Gros, Beverly Coleman, Carline Samedy, Elaine Robbins, Juliana McMullin, Hima Li, David Mengore, Douglas Shimek, Christopher Paul Barrett, Rebecca K Williams, Bev Christensen, Crystal Stewart, Glenda Dykstra, Marita Lawler, Anaru Hiku, Michelle Radford, Sue DeNicola, Deb Drabble, Michelle Reeve, Amanda Hill, Philip M Reilly, Jennie, Stephen Rives, Reena, Allan Gillard, Diana Lynne, Dennis Morris, Tara Leigh, Bev Kittle, Donna Swenson, Sara Wertheimer, Michael Kivlen, Sheila Richards, Barbara McGahey, Michelle Carew, Roberta Partridge, Lynda Hagen, Debbie L Smith, Katelyn Wadland, Samuel Robbins, Hattie Weatherford, Kim Simcox, Danielle Henderson, Renee Nichols, Mary P., Rhonda Broman, Richard Callanan, Danita Matney, Liza van der Pluym, Debra Reeves, Dave Groncki, Juliana, Catherine B., Alice Weems, Ali Goff, Jens D. Racherbäumer, DeAnsin Webb, Fiona Harrison, Rohayna, Marla, Katie Stahle, Joe M, Jeanne Lyons, Mark Farrow, Rick, Denise C. Allen, Cassandra Manning, Sherry Otis, Amanda Meeks, Jezzyca Callista, Zeljka Bajic, Deborah, Rachel Cass, Victor Yu Fen, Crystal Rymer, Gerrie Adkins, Larissa Faulkner, Ruth, Sherry Emrith-Mahabir, Deb LeBlanc, Carol Ardeeser, Brent Weber.

≫ ≪

Thank you to every reader, whether you are listed above or not. See you for the next adventure!

ABOUT THE AUTHOR

Meg is a *USA Today* bestselling fantasy author from the windswept moors of Yorkshire, England, where she lives with her husband, young son, and two mischievous cats. Her favourite past times are reading, walking, cooking, and travel.

Meg writes sweeping epic fantasies filled with betrayal, intrigue, romance, adventure, high stakes, and twisting plots. She enjoys exploring the complex nature of humanity, and her books are widely praised for having gripping, compelling, multi-layered characters. Meg works best when fuelled by margherita pizza, earl grey tea, and characters who won't do what they're told.

Meg credits her parents for her vivid imagination, as they fed her early reading and drawing addiction. She spent years in the school library and in bed with a torch, unable to stop devouring books. At home, Meg had a 'making table', where her mum and dad contained the arty mess she created with various drawing and craft projects. At school, if Meg wasn't reading a book under the desk, she was getting told off for drawing dragons in all her classwork books.

Visit www.megcowley.com to find out more, discover Meg's books, and join her reader group newsletter.

Printed in Great Britain
by Amazon